PRAISE FOR
Hidden Places

Bobbi Graffunder tackles a tough, emotional, multi-faceted social issue with grace, compassion, and level-headedness. Sometimes a story speaks more clearly than a lecture; this is one of those times.

—Kim Vogel Sawyer
Award-winning author of *The Librarian of Boone's Hollow*

Bobbi Graffunder bravely and honestly presents the intensely conflicted but brightly redemptive faith journey of a young woman facing the choices of an unplanned pregnancy. It is a story of God's grace and the uneven but eventually beautiful reception of God's shame-breaking love.

—John Lynch
International speaker, co-author of *The Cure*,
and founder of John Lynch Speaks

Bobbi Graffunder's new novel tackles a dilemma which doesn't get discussed above a whisper in some churches. With grace, she shares the story of one young woman's path from initial shame to God's glorious forgiveness. Sharing real-world options to counter unexpected consequences, she illustrates God's great love amid the hard choices. It's an unfortunately familiar problem in this day and age, yet the outcome is underscored by hope. God is the only One who can bring good out of situations that seem bad.

—T. Elizabeth Renich
Author of the Shadowcreek Chronicles

HIDDEN
Places

a novel

HIDDEN Places

a novel

Bobbi L Graffunder

ISBN 13: 978-1-64645-253-8 (Paperbook)
         978-1-64645-254-5 (ePub)
         978-1-64645-255-2 (Mobi)

LCCN   2022907932

To my parents, who taught me
that people *make* mistakes,
but no one *is* a mistake.
When we all get to Heaven,
what a day of rejoicing that will be.

To my husband, who believed in me.
To my family, who inspired me.
To my friends, who prayed for me.
To my Savior, who redeemed me.

Author's Note

*E*very year, thousands of young women are faced with choosing between abortion, adoption, or parenting. Before you think this is not a reality within our churches, think again. We can thoughtlessly judge choices, carelessly dismiss statistics, and easily forget . . . each statistic comes with a story.

This is a story about one of these young women and the options she faced. Her story is a compilation of real stories, the kinds of stories many women carry in hidden places—maybe someone in your family or your best friend or the girl in the third pew. She could even be you.

CHAPTER 1

May 23
The McPherson Residence
Traverse City, MI

Meghan stood at the bottom of the stairs, feet glued to the floor. Her eyes followed a soft, yellow glow leading to a thick oak door. The beam swept across opaque gray tiles and illuminated a path her feet rarely followed. When was the last time that door had opened to her?

Her feet felt like bricks as she stepped into the light, but her soft-soled flats cloaked her nearness to the office. Her mind re-created the all-too-familiar scene on the opposite side of the barrier: her father, Peter, seated at his workstation sandwiched between two large monitors peppered with the codes used by technical engineers. Other than the name of his employer, Great Lakes Applied Design—GLAD— Meghan had no idea what her father did for his job. She knew almost as little about his life as he knew about hers. In the five years since her mom had left them, Meghan and her father had slowly lost their ability to connect. There was no one to help them learn again. No incentive or motivation to even try. After all the misunderstandings and miscommunications, why expect anything else?

In addition to his job, Dad was predictable in other ways. Every workday he wore a signature three-button, black polo shirt paired with gray dress pants. On the right sleeve of every black shirt was the GLAD logo stitched in silver thread. And the uniform wouldn't be complete without a black leather belt and black Oxford shoes. On the weekends, if he wasn't working in Chicago, Dad donned a pair of jeans and, maybe, an Ohio State T-shirt. Special occasions were few and far between, but Meghan knew he was going somewhere out of the ordinary when his pleated khakis were folded on top of the dryer. Though much had changed over the last few years, Dad's wardrobe had stayed the same.

Something was different tonight. Something behind the door was missing. Normally the TV shouted the latest news or replayed college football games. The broadcasts served as a distraction, a noise to fill the void in their life. For her part, Meghan had tried to fill the emptiness with good grades, good behavior, and good deeds. No matter how hard she tried, though, nothing closed the distance between them. Tonight she needed reassurance she was loved. Tangible proof she mattered. Maybe she could find the strength to try once more.

Her hand closed around the doorknob at the same moment her ears identified muted tapping. Her fingers froze in place, and the handle remained rotated halfway, as if not sure which way to turn. Clockwise, the door would open. Counterclockwise, the latch would reengage. Meghan longed to burst through the door and run into her father's arms as she had when she was younger. Back then, tears over a scraped knee or broken toy were easily wiped away by her father's capable hands. Her little-girl eyes had seen a daddy who could fix anything. Her little-girl heart had known she could always run home to her father.

But Meghan knew better. Those days were a lifetime ago. His arms no longer welcomed her, and he certainly couldn't fix what was broken. She was no longer that little girl.

Little girls didn't do what she'd done with Zac tonight.

A shiver rippled down Meghan's spine. She suddenly felt like an intruder about to get caught. With deliberate caution, she used her other hand to steady the fist clenched around the knob. Too anxious to breathe, she poured her concentration into releasing the handle.

Success. The latch hadn't made a sound. She wiped her sweaty palm on her jeans and tiptoed backward until her hand brushed the edge of a thick wooden post. Meghan gripped the railing and slipped off her shoes before climbing the dark stairway. She closed her eyes and exhaled a wave of relief. No light was needed. With a brush of her fingertips, she let the sturdy, unchanging boundary of the walls guide the way.

As she opened her bedroom door, the hinges groaned. She paused, wondering if her dad had noticed. *Did he not hear me, or is he ignoring me?* She closed the door, flipped the light switch, grabbed the puffy quilt off her bed, and crossed the room to the window seat. She dropped her shoes by the edge of the bench and realized her room was just as quiet as the rest of the house. The only sound she heard was the pounding of her heart.

The cushioned bench was long enough to stretch out on, but Meghan curled up and pulled her favorite pillow to her chest. Zac's grandmother, Abuela Maria, had made it for her eighteenth birthday last September. The same birthday Zac had given her a thin silver band holding a small sapphire stone. When he'd slid it on her finger, he'd promised to one day replace her birthstone with an engagement diamond. Through joyful tears, Meghan had promised not to take it off until that day arrived. And she hadn't.

Now, an unwelcome blanket of heaviness settled over her as she twisted the eternal circle.

A pulsating hum interrupted her thoughts. *Zac!* She launched onto the bed, grabbed her phone off the nightstand, and flipped it over. *Oh.*

"Hey, Andi. What's up?" Meghan tried to hide her disappointment.

"I can't find the packing list you sent me," a frantic voice replied. "Can you send it again?"

"Sure," Meghan answered. "Wait. Are you seriously packing right now? As in the night before we leave?"

"I know . . . I know," Andi admitted. "I should've started earlier. Can I help it if I hate packing?"

When it came to planning and organizing, Meghan and her best friend, Andi, lived on opposite ends of the spectrum. Somehow, the teeter-totter of differences between them balanced their lifelong friendship.

"Sending the list now. I would come help but—"

"—but I can't bear to tear myself away from Zac," Andi teased. "No worries, Megs. I wouldn't ask you to. This is your last time seeing him for months. You two behave now, you hear? Don't do anything I wouldn't do."

Andi laughed, but Meghan wasn't amused. She mumbled something about needing to go and ended the call. Meghan tossed the phone on the bed and mechanically shuffled back to her seat by the window. This time, the reflection in the glass startled her. Untamed curls stuck out like tangled vines and mocked the hour spent perfecting auburn ringlets. The dim mirror distorted the guilt swimming in her sea-green eyes. Andi's words echoed as questions. Last time seeing Zac? Behave? Don't do anything Andi wouldn't do? The questions morphed into doubts and then regrets. Too late.

All through high school, Meghan and Zac had only kissed. Then, as graduation approached, he began hinting, even outright suggesting, they take things further. He was so respectful of Meghan's apprehension, she'd actually felt bad for pushing him away. What if her hesitation disappointed him and he found someone who wouldn't resist? It would be her own fault for letting him down. He wouldn't ask her to do anything that was seriously wrong, right?

She was probably overthinking it, making something out of nothing. She couldn't, wouldn't, risk losing Zac. Especially not over something that didn't seem like the big deal everyone made it out to be. If that was what met his needs and reaffirmed his love for her, then her choice purchased security and significance. It made sense. It didn't have to be complicated.

So why did she feel bad?

Meghan couldn't relax. The seat cushion bunched up as she wiggled her feet free of the quilt. She'd already packed, repacked, and re-repacked. Desperately, she scanned the room, looking for something to do. Nothing was out of order or needed cleaning. Every item was exactly where it should be and would be when she returned at the end of August.

Still, she no longer wanted to be here alone in the deafening silence that filled her house. She tossed back the quilt and shoved her feet into her shoes. Then she threw open the door and let it bang against the wall as she stomped loudly down the stairs. At the bottom of the stairwell, she paused and looked toward her father's office. A shadow broke the beam of light and her eyes locked onto the doorknob as it turned slightly to the left. Meghan curled her fingers around the banister as a spark of hope flared in her heart. She nearly cried out when a sudden explosion of noise from the TV doused the spark and made her jump. Booming voices again argued the latest headlines. Dad wouldn't open the door. He didn't want her to come in. *Fine. If that's the way you want it.* Just for good measure, she slammed the front door on her way out. Andi would be happy to see her. The walk would do her good, and Andi's house, unlike hers, would be anything but quiet. She always felt welcome there.

Flickering streetlights illuminated the sidewalks all the way to Andi's, but it was faster to cut through the neighborhood's shadowed alleyways. The few minutes it took to jog across the three blocks was enough to help Meghan think clearly again. Clearly enough to remember she hadn't done anything to fix her messy hair. It would be a telltale sign something out of the ordinary had happened.

Meghan slowly opened the back door and was relieved to see an empty, dimly lit kitchen. Surround sound blasted up the open staircase from the basement. Friday night was always movie night. As Meghan tiptoed over the creaky floor, she saw evidence of a party. Balloons and streamers hung from doorways and light fixtures. Crumbs and cupcake wrappers littered the counters, and a large poster covered the front of the refrigerator: "Con'grad'ulations, Andi!" The words were surrounded by stick-figure horses and a garden of colorful flowers. She had been invited to the family celebration but chose to go to Zac's instead. Now she wondered if she made the right choice.

Meghan passed through the kitchen to the front entryway. Before she climbed the stairs to Andi's room, she snuck into the bathroom and borrowed a wide headband. She wished she had a hat instead.

"Hey!" Andi, seated on her bedroom floor, looked up as Meghan stepped inside. "What are you doing here?"

"Obviously, I can't trust you to pack for yourself." Meghan swept aside a pile of clothes with her shoe, clearing a space to sit on the carpeted floor, then pointed to the overflowing suitcase hanging precariously over the side of Andi's bed.

"Hand over that thing. It's a mess."

"Bossy firstborns," Andi replied, but she plopped the luggage down next to Meghan with a grin.

Meghan didn't feel like playing the game. Tonight the words stung. "Technically true, but since I'm an only child, that also makes me the middle child and the baby." She rearranged and refolded Andi's summer wardrobe while assessing smaller piles strewn about the room. "I don't see rain boots. Go get 'em."

"Yes, Mother." With a shake of her bobbed blond head, Andi obeyed the directive. In a household of seven, even a simple task could take a while.

By the time Andi returned, Meghan had repacked the clothes and made room for more. "If you roll each item, you create twice the space."

"If you roll them, it's twice as boring," Andi countered. "Changing the subject . . . why are you here folding my laundry instead of on a hot date with Zac? Did something happen?"

Something. Definitely something. Meghan felt a lump in her throat push hot tears from her eyes. Head down, she grabbed an empty duffel bag and reached for Andi's boots and flip-flops.

Andi plopped onto the bed and let out a gasp. "Oh no. You didn't, did you?"

Meghan's head snapped up so fast, a searing pain shot across the back of her neck. Her green eyes opened wide, and the lump in her throat caused her to cough.

"What did you say?"

Andi tilted her head to the side and narrowed her blue eyes. Meghan panicked as she considered the possibility Andi somehow knew.

Andi laughed. "You should see your face. Chillax. What do you think I'm talking about? Sex?" She laughed again.

What was Andi talking about if not—that?

The air in the room grew stifling. Panic threatened to unravel a secret Meghan wasn't ready to reveal. Avoiding eye contact, she zipped the bag and rose from the floor.

"I . . . You can finish—"

With that, she bolted from the room.

Determined to get away, she barely heard Andi's plea, "What'd I say? I only meant did you get in a fight?"

Halfway down the tree-lined block, her phone rang. The last thing Meghan wanted to do was talk, but if she ignored the call, Andi would end up following her home. She stopped to text an excuse, gulping for breath and grasping for words.

> I'm fine. Hard leaving Zac. Just tired. See you in the morning.

Andi bought it.

> Sorry. I should have been more sensitive instead of teasing you. Sleep well. We've been waiting a long time for this.

Back home, Meghan once again tucked herself into the shelter of her window seat. Thoughts and feelings spun, creating a tangled mess of confusion and loneliness. For as long as she could remember, her parents had said sex before marriage was wrong, but no one had ever explained why. It was thrown in there with, "Don't lie. Don't steal. Don't be selfish. Oh, and don't have sex before marriage." Sermons and Bible lectures had sent the same message, but that was another lifetime ago. A life when they all went to church. A life before her parents had separated. Lots of things changed after that. Lots of things that once seemed important didn't matter anymore.

And who were her parents to act like they knew better? She was twelve years old when she figured out they'd celebrated their one-year anniversary only six months after her birth. It took a couple years longer to figure out her birth weight of eight pounds, two ounces likely disqualified her as a preemie. Her parents got married because they were pregnant, and they lied about it. She definitely couldn't trust them when it came to this subject. Or most others.

And if God really thought it was wrong, why would it be so hard to obey? If He was so against it, why would He make His rules so easy to break?

As her fingers numbly traced the colorful embroidery on the pillow, Meghan whispered the words sewn with love for her. Just a few of the many Spanish words she had learned from spending time with Abuela Maria. "*Padre nuestro que estás en los cielos.* Our Father who art in Heaven." Overcome with a mixture of guilt and blame, she flung the pillow across the room. Heaven was far away. God was far away.

"Where are you? Why did You leave us?" Meghan scolded God. "You were supposed to love me. You were supposed to help me. Instead, You make rules that are impossible to follow and then leave. Just like Mom. Just like Dad."

CHAPTER 2

Meghan's hands shook as she placed her breakfast dishes into the sink. It was almost time. Zac would be waiting when she dashed out the front door to greet him. He would look at her with those brown-sugar eyes and tell her he wanted her—no, *needed* her—to stay. He would tell her that last night had renewed his commitment to her and he was sorry he had been distant. She would assure him they would be together soon and nothing could come between them.

Meghan pulled back the edge of the curtain and saw Zac's little blue truck coming down the street. She willed herself to rise above the nervous flutter in her stomach. *You can do this. Don't say anything stupid. Last night was just . . . weird for both of us. He's going to say he loves you. He's going to ask me to marry him for sure now. I mean—*

She glanced into the mirror on the wall. Minimal makeup, messy-bun. Zac's favorite look for her. She exhaled deeply and pasted a bright smile on her face. On cue, she opened the door just as Zac stepped onto the front walk.

The smile faded as she realized Zac wasn't playing his part. They met halfway between the porch and his truck. Each stopped at opposing edges of the paved walkway, three feet apart. It felt like a mile. Zac's head was down, his hands stuffed into his pockets. And then, instead of proclaiming his undying love, he glanced down the street and said, "Looks like Andi's late again, huh? Well, I hope you two have a fun summer on the island."

Meghan's heart dropped. "Thanks." If his hands weren't in his pockets, she would have reached out to him.

Silence stretched between them until, finally, Zac cleared his throat. "Okay, so, I guess I should be going. The guys are waiting at the field."

He kissed Meghan on the cheek.

No gazing into her eyes. No reassuring smiles. No tears. No lingering embrace. The reunion, all one minute of it, was empty and awkward. Neither mentioned what had happened last night.

Zac turned away, and sadness washed over Meghan. Even worse, a sense of shame filled the growing space between them. He didn't turn around, not even once, as he walked back to the street and climbed into his truck.

She was leaving for the whole summer, and he had walked away from her as easily as if he would see her tomorrow. Obviously, she had been a disappointment.

She could see only the back of Zac's head now. He wore his favorite baseball cap backward, just like always. For once, the green-and-white *G* embroidered on the bright-gold Packers cap didn't represent his favorite football team. Instead, the word echoing loudly inside Meghan's head was *Goodbye*.

Nothing about this goodbye was good. She didn't want to go away like this but didn't know how to fix it. Zac pulled his truck into the street and slowly drove away.

Her phone alarm made her jump. Andi wasn't late after all. It was the sound of horses' hooves galloping. Pounding. Thundering.

Meghan wanted to chase after Zac, but something held her feet in place.

From the other direction, a red hatchback sped toward her, horn honking and radio blasting. Meghan saw Zac's tanned arm reach out and wave as the two vehicles passed. The car stopped at the end of her driveway. Andi rolled down the window and shouted, "Freedom! Look out, Mackinac Island, here we come!"

The last grain of sand dropped from the hourglass. It was too late to do anything about Zac. Andi pulled up to the garage and hopped out. She grabbed the luggage Meghan had neatly stacked on the porch and carried it to the car. Silently, Meghan added her bags to Andi's in the narrow back seat while her friend continued to chatter.

"Netta texted and said the apartment is ready. It's Hanson's Carriage House. Hey, that sounds perfect for a history nerd like you."

Meghan interjected. "We nerds prefer the term 'historophile.' Thank you very much."

"Oh sure," Andi huffed as she rearranged some items to clear the view out the back window. "That sounds way less nerdy. Do you want to hear the rest or not?"

Meghan pinched her thumb and forefinger together and slid them across her pursed lips. Andi rolled her eyes and continued.

"She also said it's on the downhill side of town. Two bedrooms and completely furnished. It's not ground floor, but there's a place to keep our bikes inside when it rains. Bonus, right?"

Andi's enthusiasm was infectious, and Meghan's mood began to lighten. She gave one final shove to Andi's duffel bag and leaned against the car. *Done.* It was time to focus on the future. She and Zac just needed a little space. They were entering a new phase of life and needed time to adjust. Last night was a one-time mistake, a momentary weakness. They had transitioned from being high school sweethearts to an adult relationship. Come September, they would have a new beginning and move forward as if last night had never happened.

With that glimmer of hope, Meghan turned for one last look at the two-story brick house. Her heart raced when she saw the curtain flutter.

Dad? Are you coming out to say goodbye?

Just as fast, the last ember of expectation faded and vanished. He wasn't home. He wasn't coming to say goodbye. Their last interaction had been yesterday morning when he'd handed her an envelope of cash and a debit card. Their last words had been short and to the point.

"What's this for?"

"Your summer expenses."

"I'll have a job. Two actually."

"Do whatever you want with it."

Meghan longed to hear "I'll miss you," or "It won't be the same without you," or "Keep in touch." But the last words she'd heard were nothing of the sort.

"I need to pack. I have to go to Chicago tomorrow."

Fighting tears, Meghan pulled down her sunglasses and climbed into the passenger's seat. "Well, what are we waiting for? Let's get outta here."

Andi bounced over the edge of the curb as she backed out of the driveway and began the drive from Traverse City to the Upper Peninsula. The crystal clean windshield framed a masterpiece. The brightening sky peeked through puffy purple clouds. Orange and yellow streaks shimmered like fire across the surface of Lake Michigan. Meghan kept her eyes on the sky as her fingers decrypted the items in her purse.

"Glad we're driving north. I hate staring into the sun." Andi said.

"Uh-huh."

"By the time we stop in Petoskey, the cloud bank should pass."

"Yep." With her eyes now glued to her phone, Meghan no longer admired the vast brushstrokes of creation.

"Oh!" Andi gasped. "That reminds me. Open the glove box."

With her other hand, Meghan pushed a button, and the contents sprang out like a jack-in-the-box. "How did you fit so much junk in here, and what am I supposed to be looking for?"

"Dig around and you'll know. Your clue is the word 'pass.'"

Meghan rummaged through the jumble of receipts, napkins, and collection of sunglasses. She held up an unopened envelope. "Pas . . . t due notice?"

Eyes on the road, Andi shook her head.

Meghan held up a slender tube. "Pas . . . tel lip gloss?" Again, no.

Finding a small, red leather booklet, she chuckled at the title: Official Travel Document. She waved it for Andi to see. "Really? My passport?"

"You know it. Uncle Ray would be hurt if we didn't bring them. Lucky for you, I happened to find yours in the trash bag after our last trip. Nice try."

Meghan rolled her eyes. "Aren't we a little old for a Yooper passport? We aren't ten anymore."

"Well, I wouldn't bring that up to Uncle Ray. You know he would remind us we were thirteen before we figured out you don't need a Michigan passport to travel between the mainland and Upper Peninsula."

Meghan opened the booklet and grimaced. "I don't want to hurt his feelings, but can we at least update our photos? I have braces and frizzy bangs in this one."

"You think that's bad? At least you had braces. I didn't have mine yet. And what about my glasses? It doesn't get worse than that."

"Not our finest days," Meghan agreed. "Maybe Uncle Ray will forget."

"Not a chance. He considers it his official duty to, in his words, 'protect and defend Yooper patriotism.'"

"I don't know why people from the UP think it's so funny being Yoopers. Don't they know people make fun of them?"

The melody on the radio caught Andi's attention. She reached over to turn up the volume. "My favorite song!"

Andi was singing her second favorite song as they reached the northern limits of Traverse City. Meghan stared nervously at the shrinking sight of home. Would it look the same when she returned in three months?

Andi glanced sideways and caught Meghan's moody expression. "C'mon, Megs, eyes forward. Shake off the past. Car dance party. Go."

Meghan didn't feel like dancing. "It's going to be a long day, Andi. Better ration that energy."

"Are you crazy? We've been waiting our whole lives for this. Our first chance to be on our own. No parents. No school. No boring summer chores or PK duties. Best of all, no VBS. In fact, you are witness to my first adult decision." Andi held up right hand. "I, Andrea Elizabeth Thomson, do hereby and forever swear to never, *never*, ever go to, help at, or otherwise be involved with vacation Bible school for the rest of my life. So help me God."

"Oh sure. We'll just be working and paying rent and cooking and buying our own groceries. That's way better than VBS." Meghan nudged Andi's hand back toward the steering wheel. "I'm not sure 'adulting' is what you think it is."

"Don't spoil my fun. You don't have to be so serious all the time. This summer is going to be the best ever. Enjoy it. Stop thinking so hard." Andi reached for the radio again. "You know what I always say. You think so hard—"

"—you make *my* head hurt," Meghan finished Andi's classic line, and they both burst out laughing.

Meghan watched Andi sing and dance and wished she could be so playful and free. She was much too worried about being embarrassed or being laughed at to take such personal risks. She had long ago stopped being playful. She had grown up too soon.

Sweet, innocent, easygoing Andi had spent her adolescence in a model Christian family. Perfect dad devoted to his church and family. Perfect mom who homeschooled perfect children. Andi never seemed to have a care or worry.

Meghan had spent her adolescence taking care of herself and her dad. At first it was like playing house. Making shopping lists and clipping coupons. Mom had trained her well in the basics, and father and daughter worked as a team to survive her absence. But, as time went on, it seemed to Meghan her dad had decided having a career was easier than having a daughter. So Meghan had learned how to manage her time and responsibilities, both at school and at home, on her own. And when she couldn't figure something out, Andi's family was always there to help.

Being a preacher's kid might have its downside, but at least Andi had a mom instead of having to fill the role of being a mom. She also had a dad who actually spent time with her, and she had siblings too.

Meghan leaned her head against the window as fields of cherry trees passed in a blur—white blossoms, only beautiful and fragrant for a short time. Each delicate flower held the potential to become a mature fruit. If you didn't stop to enjoy them, they'd be lost. A strong wind or pounding rain would tear the petals from the trees.

Meghan sighed. Her life was also a blur of something beautiful for a short time, it seemed. As a child, she had never felt unsafe or unsure. From good-morning hugs until bedtime prayers, life had been carefree and filled with joy. Until one day, it all changed. A storm came and left a devastated landscape. What had blossomed as a picture-perfect childhood hadn't become the fruit it was meant to be. When Mom left, Meghan had lost more than a parent. She had lost her home, her family, her security. And now would she lose Zac too? No. She wouldn't let that happen. The storm was her past. Zac was her future.

College. Marriage. Careers. Family. That was the plan. Yet, like the orchards of white, the unknowns of her life stretched out as far as she could see. Maybe Andi was right. There would be plenty of time for adulting later. For now, she'd focus on the present. Enjoy the beauty of the blossoms.

Andi reached over to lower the volume. Concern etched her face. "Are you okay? Considering we've waited eight years for this day, I thought you'd be more excited."

"Sorry," Meghan replied. "Just tired, I guess." Partly true.

"Did Zac hassle you about leaving for the summer?"

"Don't I wish." Meghan immediately regretted her hasty response.

Andi shot her a sideways glance but didn't press. "Do you remember the day we made our promise?"

"How could I forget? We've been planning this summer since we were ten years old."

Andi slowed to let a pair of spotted fawns cross the road to their mother.

"I wish we still had the contract we made our parents sign."

"Contract? I don't remember a contract."

"Meghan Lea McPherson!" Andi sounded hurt. "I can't believe you don't remember the contract. Our own Declaration of Independence."

"Well, it was eight years ago. Give me a break." Meghan was surprised by her prickly defensiveness and hurried to soothe Andi's bruised feelings. "Refresh my memory, please."

"We were nine the first summer we went to Mackinac. Remember how we walked around holding our noses?"

Meghan nodded. Sometimes she still did that. With as many as six hundred horses on the small island, the abundance of manure was unavoidable.

Andi continued. "The next summer we saw Anne's Tablet on the map and begged our parents to take us there."

Meghan's brain retrieved a vivid scene. "I do remember that! It was during our *Anne of Green Gables* phase. We were convinced Lucy Maud Montgomery wrote the books there."

"'Anne with an *E*' we told our parents. That was our brilliant ten-year-old logic." Andi laughed.

"I think the real reason they didn't want to take us was the flight of stairs on Crow's Nest Trail. Now that I'm older, I don't want to climb all those steps either."

Andi slowed again as the road crossed Pine River Bridge in Charlevoix and turned inland.

"That would explain why they let us go up there by ourselves. If they'd have known how steep the ledge was, they probably wouldn't have."

"Well, my parents, anyway," Meghan interjected. Andi's parents had been less cautious.

"In any case, we stayed up there a good long time before coming down."

"And we didn't let our parents see how disappointed we were. I still don't remember a contract though."

"We didn't write the contract there, but we did make a pact. We promised we would one day come back to the island by ourselves. Later, when we asked our parents how old we had to be, they said eighteen."

More details emerged as, together, they recounted the scenario. "Oh, we were staying at the resort that year, right? We wrote the contract so our parents couldn't change their minds and say no once we were eighteen."

"Exactly! Another stellar example of our logic, but somehow it paid off, because here we are."

"Here we are, indeed." Meghan grinned as Andi turned into the parking lot of their favorite donut shop. "Petoskey, right on cue."

CHAPTER 3

Meghan stared at the dark screen. *Please, Zac. Text me.* An hour and a half had passed since they'd left Traverse City. Zac was probably still at the field, but couldn't he at least have sent something? Maybe he was waiting for her to go first.

The morning sun had yet to dry the dewy table on the terrace of Petoskey Patisserie. Meghan barely noticed the dampness soak through her denim shorts as her last thread of hope frayed into a whispered prayer. She typed a desperate message, but before her index finger could hit Send, another hand reached in and grabbed the phone.

"Nope. Give him a chance to miss you." Andi placed a waxy white bag in Meghan's now empty hands. "Besides, we haven't dunked yet."

Meghan had bigger concerns than a donut-dunking contest. She should be mad at Andi for interfering. She should have gone after Zac. She should have said something while she had the chance. She should have called him last night.

She should have—but she hadn't.

Andi cut the rainbow-sprinkled halo exactly in half, while

Meghan removed the lid on the steaming cup of creamy hot chocolate. Andi then stepped onto the wooden bench, held the two halves toward the sun, and delivered the official proclamation with overdramatic flair.

"May the donut rise up to meet you.
May the cocoa not burn your tongue.
May the gulls not steal your breakfast, the sprinkles fall
soft upon your lap, and until we stop for lunch,
may the carbohydrates satisfy your hunger."

Meghan rotated away from the big glass windows. "Well, that was as embarrassing as always."

"I believe we composed that during our Irish-dance phase."

"Thankfully, one of our shorter phases." Meghan held out two napkins to receive the ceremonial halves.

"You had the right hair but the wrong feet. I had the right feet but the wrong hair." Andi laughed as she jumped down, bowed to the customers inside the café, and joined Meghan on the tacky bench. "Like my mom says, 'Sometimes things are only for a season, and seasons change.'"

Meghan scraped away frosting with a napkin. "Speaking of change. My taste buds have changed. To be honest, I don't even like these anymore."

Undeterred by her friend's confession, Andi positioned the cup between them. "Too bad. It's tradition. Ready? three . . . two . . . one . . . dunk."

Meghan dipped her donut into the hot chocolate.

One . . . two . . . three . . . lift." Andi's half resurfaced soggy and broken. "Snap! I went in too deep. Looks like you win the advantage for the next challenge."

Like a child with a favorite teddy bear, Andi clung to traditions and showed no signs of letting them go. It was easier to surrender than fight. Truth be told, Meghan found a measure of comfort in the familiarity. Even before her parents' divorce, being an only child of only children hadn't offered much in the way of family traditions. Andi, second of five children, relied on rituals as a matter of strategy. They provided opportunities to wrestle control from, in her words, her "bossy older brother and spoiled younger siblings."

"You aren't going to make your customers at the island coffee shop do this, are you?" Meghan passed her uneaten portion to Andi.

"I might." With her finger, Andi smeared frosting onto a bare spot. "All the middle children vacationing on Mackinac Island need someone looking out for their best interest."

With Petoskey Traditions Part 1 complete and mochas in hand, Andi drove to the shore of Lake Michigan. Petoskey Traditions Part 2 involved a treasure hunt for the infamous Petoskey stone. The advantage of winning the donut challenge was a sixty-second head start on the breakwater beach. With Andi's family, at the sound of the bell, a mad rush of both children and adults joined the hunt. The kids usually ended up in the cold water because the tiny hexagon designs were easier to distinguish if wet, or so they claimed. The first person to find Michigan's iconic fossilized coral earned the right to choose the location for lunch.

Meghan had won once and regretted the victory. With such a large group, pleasing everyone was impossible. She didn't want to be the cause of someone's disappointment. After that, even if she saw a potential Petoskey stone, she passed it by.

Maybe today, since it was just the two of them, she would try again. She stood alone on the shore as Andi's voice called from the edge of the grass. "Are you ready? Your sixty-second head start begins . . . *now*!"

Meghan's gaze darted back and forth over the rocks. A likely candidate, just two yards away, caught her eye. Andi would be disappointed if the hunt ended so quickly. Instead of picking it up, she jogged over to the shoreline.

"Ten more seconds!" Andi called.

While gulls circled above and waves gently rolled toward her sandaled feet, Meghan scanned the rocky lake bed.

Andi ran past. "Game on!"

An unfamiliar desire to compete bubbled up inside Meghan. She wanted to win. She wanted to choose the restaurant. Her eyes zeroed in on a perfect candidate—dark gray, smooth surface covered in small boxes separated by white borders. The frigid water hurt her feet as she stepped toward it. But before she could reach in for the rock, Andi's voice rippled down the shoreline.

"Petoskey stone! I win!"

Meghan stepped out of the water and waited for Andi to bring her treasure for inspection. "That was fast."

Andi defied her skepticism. "You know spring is the best time to find these. The melting ice churns up the rocks and pushes them to shore."

Meghan didn't know that. She dipped the stone into the water then pulled down her sunglasses to critique the specimen. "Hmmm. Radiating sunburst pattern. Appears to be fossilized coral skeletons. Rounded in shape. I would say you have a perfect Petoskey stone, except for one thing."

"What? Are you crazy? This *is* a perfect Petoskey stone."

Meghan stepped back to the grass and shook off her wet sandals. "Sorry. Petoskey stones are gray, and this one definitely has a pinkish hue."

"A pinkish hue? What's that supposed to mean?"

"It means it's not limestone. Sorry."

Andi refused defeat. "Let's ask the all-knowing internet." She pulled out her phone. "Ha! You are so wrong. Not only did I find a winner, but I found a rare variety. It's pink because iron leaked into the coral as it was hardening. I win fair and square."

Meghan surrendered the stone and the challenge. "Fair and square . . . this time. You take your Petoskey stones very seriously."

"When the stakes are high, you bet I do."

"Let me guess. The Harborview Café?"

"Um, yeah," Andi replied as they climbed the slope back to the car. "I certainly wasn't going to pick *your* favorite restaurant. Besides, if we eat on the patio, we can scope out the guys coming off the ferries." She raised her eyebrows and rubbed her hands together. "There should be a good selection, considering all the summer workers arriving. You have Zac. We need to find a guy for me."

You have Zac. The words echoed loud in Meghan's ears, and she turned for one last look at Lake Michigan. Bigger waves splashed the shore as a fishing boat crossed to deeper waters. As each wave broke the shoreline, the undercurrent created by the next one pulled it back out, into the lake. The mesmerizing, soothing rhythm calmed her fears and eased her doubts. Even if Zac had pulled away from her, he would come back. He had to.

"Hello? Earth to Meghan. What do you think?"

"About what?"

"About driving the rest of the way."

"Yeah, sure, no problem." Andi feared open water, and the five-mile suspension bridge over the Straits of Mackinac was a galaxy away from her comfort zone.

Meghan moved to the driver's seat, and they continued north on Highway 31 toward Mackinaw City. Forty-five minutes later, as they drove onto the bridge, a text dinged. Meghan recognized the alert tone. *Zac.* Andi's eyes were closed, and they'd stay that way the whole way across the bridge. Could she sneak a peek? The problem would be getting the phone out of her purse. As she reached to grab it, Andi's outburst startled her.

"Meghan! Do you have both hands on the wheel? Don't make

me open my eyes to check."

Meghan glanced over and saw Andi's knuckles turning white above clenched fists. With eyes on the road and hands on the wheel, she assured her friend. "No worries. I've got this. It's not even windy today, so it should be a smooth drive across to St. Ignace. In five minutes, you'll be handing your passport to Uncle Ray."

Andi spoke around clenched teeth. "This steel grating is grating my nerves."

Meghan rolled down the window, paid the toll, and proceeded to follow the route to the ferry dock. "You did great."

"I'm just glad it's over and I won't have to do it again for ninety-seven days." Andi rolled down her window and inhaled. "But who's counting?"

"Apparently you are." Meghan pulled into the main lot and spotted a familiar figure. "Better get those passports. Here comes the Upper Peninsula border guard."

Andi stared straight ahead and held the documents out the window. Her uncle then walked around the car, tapped on the roof, and inspected the windshield wipers. While doing so, he eyed the car suspiciously then stopped at Meghan's window and bent down to peer inside.

"Did we pass, Uncle Ray?" Andi reached over to retrieve the booklets.

"You've passed inspection. Welcome to the UP." With that, he saluted and waved the car through to baggage drop-off, where another familiar face waited to greet them.

As the dock porters carted away a summer's worth of luggage, Andi crawled into the back seat. "Thanks for finding us a summer parking spot, Aunt Jenna."

Ray's wife, Jenna, navigated the car to the parking space she'd arranged for them. Autos weren't allowed on Mackinac Island, so the car would be staying here. All that was left to do was board the ferry.

Andi and Jenna walked arm in arm back to the dock. Meghan lagged behind and took advantage of the opportunity to read Zac's text.

> I'm sorry for what happened.
> I hope you have a great summer on Mackinac.

Not exactly reassuring, but better than nothing. She tried not to overthink it before she responded.

> Thanks.
> I miss you.
> See you in August.

Meghan tucked her phone into her purse, then jogged to catch up with Andi and Jenna. The ball was now in Zac's court. The next move would have to be his.

With little time to spare, Meghan and Andi said goodbye and joined the passenger line. They boarded within minutes, and the boat glided away from the mainland and picked up speed.

Meghan zipped her thin cotton hoodie. The warm breath she blew into her hands fogged her sunglasses. Even with the sun shining, the temperature on the open-air deck was chilly. She wouldn't last the eighteen-minute ferry ride from St. Ignace to Mackinac Island.

She descended the steps and entered the warmth of the interior cabin. A quick head count tallied sixteen other passengers. She slid across the blue plastic bench where Andi already sat and huddled close to her.

"Back so soon?" Andi didn't even look up from her phone.

Meghan defended her retreat. "It's freezing up there. Too early in the season, I suppose."

The hazy silhouette of the island soon gave way to recognizable details. Andi concentrated on solving another sudoku puzzle, while

Meghan pointed out familiar structures and landmarks. Her eyes welcomed the sight of Victorian mansions perched high on limestone bluffs. One after another, the trail of 1880s summer "cabins" led downhill to the iconic white-columned Grand Hotel.

"Pop quiz," Meghan challenged. "Six hundred sixty feet."

Andi still didn't look up. "What is the front porch of the Grand Hotel."

Even as a young child, Andi hadn't liked looking out the windows of the ferry. "Pop quiz" became a substitute for "I spy." Over the years, it had become the way Meghan communicated the location of the ferry as they crossed Lake Huron.

As the world's longest front porch passed in the distance, Meghan squinted. She envisioned herself sitting in the row of wooden rocking chairs with Zac beside her. Their white chairs would glide in rhythm as they held hands and dreamed of their future on the other side of the lake. The picture faded as she thought of the tension between them. Would he still come in July? Would he keep his promises? So much had changed in just twenty-four hours. How much more would change before his visit in two months?

The ferry passed Round Island Lighthouse and entered the rocky breakwaters channeling the harbor. Netta Schmidt and her husband, Steve, stood at the end of the pier and waved as the ferry docked. Once the bikes were unloaded, the passengers disembarked.

Netta embraced both of them at once, then, between bits of news and greetings, rotated between them with more hugs. Meghan relished the affection, yet fought another wave of disappointment. The warm welcome was the complete opposite of Zac's cool goodbye.

"First things first," Netta directed as the troupe walked up the wooden dock. "Steven, why don't you and Meghan collect the girls' things, while Andi and I get a table for lunch at—" She turned to look at Andi. "Whose choice?"

Andi laughed. "Me."

With a grin, Netta turned back to Steve. "Harborview Café."

Andi rolled her eyes. "Am I really that predictable?"

Three voices harmonized one word. "Yes."

Over lunch on a lakeside patio, Netta and Steve outlined work schedules and job descriptions. Andi would work downtown with Netta at the Somewhere in Thyme coffee shop, while Meghan would assist Steve at the Marquette Inn closer to the edge of town. To help fill her evenings, Meghan had also picked up a part-time position at an ice cream shop.

"We've been so looking forward to your arrival." Netta beamed. "Do you need a couple of days to settle in?"

"No," Meghan answered. "I'll be ready to report for work first thing tomorrow morning."

"Me too," Andi said. "Unlike my roomie, I will unpack as I go."

Steve choked on his fish taco, which started a coughing fit. "That reminds me. Andi, your dad said to let him know when you arrived." He paused for a long drink of water. "He also said he sent a couple of books for me. Does your system of unpacking mean I shouldn't be in a hurry to get them?"

Meghan missed Andi's comeback. She was distracted by the glaring reminder her dad rarely checked in on her well-being. Should she text and let him know she'd arrived safely? For all he cared, she could be lying in a ditch somewhere or halfway to the Florida Keys.

She shook off the unpleasant emotions. What did it matter? From now until the end of August, the island was her home, and these people were her family.

CHAPTER 4

Meghan laid an ice pack over the plum-colored welt spreading around Andi's ankle. "Two weeks on the island and this is your third injury. I didn't know pickleball was a contact sport."

Andi winced. "It's usually not. But did you see how cute the EMT was?"

"Really? That's what's important here?"

"Well, not entirely. At least we're still undefeated. My injury resulted in the winning point."

Meghan tucked a soft throw pillow under Andi's legs. "Or maybe the winning point resulted in your injury."

"I'll be fine, Mother Meghan. It was an epic drop shot."

"And you've got an epic bruise to show for it. At least you don't need crutches. Eww, can you imagine?"

Andi laughed. "That would be so gross—all the horse manure on this island."

"Yeah. Even if you stayed on the sidewalks, you'd still have to cross the road at some point."

Meghan turned her attention to the growing stack of items by the door. From the pickleball racket on top to a pair of polka-dotted shorty rain boots at the bottom, it was proof of Andi's hectic schedule, and it had been bothering Meghan all week. Andi's clutter was getting out of control. Everything needed to be put where it belonged, but if Andi hadn't done it before, she sure wasn't going to do it now. Meghan sighed and began sorting the items.

Andi shook her head. "Why do you work so much instead of having fun? Your dad puts money in your account every month. It's not like you need it."

Meghan's two jobs consumed time she could have spent socializing. Though her workdays were long, she felt more freedom on the island than at home. Everything here was predictable and consistent. Here, she was only responsible for and accountable to herself. She didn't have to watch doors close or suffer through awkward interactions with her dad. She didn't have to fold his laundry or wash his dishes. She didn't have to eat meals alone. Andi wouldn't understand, but that monthly deposit into her checking account equated to a regular reminder of her dependency on someone who didn't want her around.

She grabbed Andi's backpack and hung it on a coat hook. "I'm saving for a car." That was language Andi could relate to. Being from a large family, the necessity to work and save made sense. "I'll need it for college."

"Uh-huh." Andi didn't sound convinced.

Meghan avoided eye contact and pulled a sweatshirt over her head.

"Guess I'll have to ride solo tonight. Will you be okay for an hour if I zip around the island?"

"As long as you bring me my daily fudge fix," Andi stipulated. "Go on. Get outta here."

Biking around the island had led to a new Mackinac tradition. At the end of each complete loop, they visited one of Main Street's fudge shops. Samples were free, and there were dozens of flavors to choose from. Meghan hoped to try every flavor before the end of summer.

Riding her bike usually cleared Meghan's mind, but it wasn't working tonight. Until recently, she hadn't realized how much her life revolved around only two people: Zac and Andi. She wondered if she even needed to carry her phone anymore.

Since leaving Traverse City, communication with Zac was almost nonexistent. Only sparsely scattered texts and short, awkward calls. The distance between them was more than physical geography. The chasm grew wider every day, and Meghan didn't know how to bridge it. Wasn't sex supposed to bring you closer? Make your relationship stronger?

The fresh air and exercise didn't lead to answers, but it did feel good to stretch her legs and warm her muscles. State Highway 185 circled the entire eight-mile perimeter of the island. She'd made quick work of the first four miles, and British Landing was just ahead. She parked her bike near the historical marker and purchased an order of fried pickles from the concession stand. Not only were they Andi's favorite snack but appropriate compensation after a pickleball injury.

Meghan sat on top of a wooden picnic table and waited to hear her number called. Across the road, a dozen or so people enjoyed the lakeshore. Two teen girls took selfies by the cannon, something Meghan and Andi had done many times. A man scooped up a toddler making a run for the water. A woman threw a stick for a golden retriever. A tandem bike pulled off the road in front of her, catching her attention. A preteen girl dismounted first, followed by a woman who looked like an older version of the girl. They had to be mother and daughter.

Meghan remembered people calling her "the spitting image" of her mom. When she was little, she'd loved hearing that. But in junior high, she'd bristled every time someone made the comparison. That was another good thing about having moved to Traverse City. No one knew what her mom looked like. No one knew about her mom at all.

Something hard smacked against her shoulder. She jumped off the table before she realized it hadn't hurt so much as surprised her. A quick look under the table revealed the source. She scanned the grassy area and found the instigator.

"Is this yours?" She stooped to pick up a squishy yellow football.

A boy, probably about eight years old, ran toward her. His big blue eyes told Meghan he was scared.

"Sorry. It got away from me."

"No worries." Meghan lifted the ball. "Do you want to go out for a pass?"

The boy answered with a gap-toothed smile.

Meghan lined up her fingers for a spiral throw. A bold letter *G*, set in a green circle, appeared on the top of the ball. The kid was probably from Wisconsin. Other than Zac and Andi's little brother, Meghan didn't know anyone who flaunted the green and gold in Michigan.

Zac. He was never far from her thoughts. What was he doing tonight? Was he thinking about her, or had he forgotten her altogether?

A crackle traveled through the airwaves, followed by "Order 513." The muted words were loud enough to interrupt the moment. Saved by the bell. Or by the megaphone in this case. With a smooth motion, Meghan launched the ball from her hand and thoughts of Zac from her mind.

Tucking the insulated container into the bike basket, she began the second four-mile ride of the evening. Because of a stiff breeze, the trip home took longer than expected, and the pickles arrived tepid and soggy. Over Andi's objections, Meghan crisped them in the air fryer.

In the meantime, Andi was distracted by other things. "What flavor are we trying today?"

"We?" Meghan questioned. "*We* didn't ride eight miles. *I* did."

"That's just mean. Haven't I suffered enough?" Andi pouted. "Besides, you don't want to break our tradition, do you?"

"Okay, okay. The tradition continues. Get out your list. Tonight we can cross off rocky road fudge."

"What say you?" Andi asked, after savoring her morsel. "A contender for your top spot?"

Meghan shook her head. "Three out of five. You?"

"One out of five because of the nuts. Cookies and cream still holds my number one."

Ouch. Another reminder of Zac. Last summer she had asked him about his favorite flavor of fudge.

"Cookies and cream." Then he'd kissed her and added, "But nothing could be as sweet as you. You're my favorite everything."

And she'd believed him—then.

CHAPTER 5

*A*ndi's ankle improved, but Meghan's energy declined. The evening bike rides drained her more each time. Tonight she couldn't keep up with Andi at all. Just past Mission Point, she slowed her pace, not sure she had the energy to ride another seven and a half miles.

Andi circled around and pulled up behind Meghan. "Let's stop at Arch Rock and sit by the lake for a bit."

Meghan gave a thumbs-up as Andi passed on the left and pedaled out of sight.

Half a mile up the road, Andi waited, shoes off, feet dangling in the cool water. Meghan chose an adjoining boulder and tossed her sandals to the rocky shore.

The gentle waves soothed her mind and sore feet as gulls and coastal birds swam nearby. She never got tired of the bright turquoise waters surrounding Mackinac Island. "If I didn't know we were in Michigan," she sighed, "I would think this was the Caribbean instead of Lake Huron."

"If I didn't know we were sitting on rocks instead of soft sand and if the water was actually warm, I might believe you," Andi teased. Then in the next breath she blurted, "I'm worried about you. You don't seem yourself lately. Are you okay?"

Meghan hesitated. In quiet moments like this, guilt over what happened between her and Zac caged her mind and imprisoned her words. Like the rock she sat on, her heart felt hard and heavy. Too ashamed to disappoint her friend, she retreated from the truth. "I'm okay. Just tired. Probably working too much."

"And worrying about Zac too much?" Andi ventured. "I notice you two haven't been doing much texting or talking."

"Just busy, I guess."

"Busy avoiding each other?"

"Honestly, I don't know. Something's changed between us, and I don't know how to fix it."

Andi turned to sit eye to eye with Meghan. "Remember my friend Keira? The one from camp?"

Meghan recalled the first night of summer camp last year. "The Keira who sang on the worship team?"

Andi nodded. "She texted today and said Zac was at the Van Andel on Saturday."

Meghan turned her gaze back to the lake. "So?" She shrugged. "I know he was in Grand Rapids. He gave me concert tickets for Christmas, but when I got the job here, I told him to go without me. He took Brayden instead."

"Snap." Andi gritted the word under her breath. "That makes this even harder to tell you."

What did Andi know that Meghan didn't? Her head felt dizzy as she waited to find out.

"Keira asked me what happened between you and Zac."

What happened between her and Zac? Who'd told Keira? Maybe Zac told Brayden and Brayden told Keira? And worse, who else knew?

Anxiety slid toward full-blown panic. Meghan stood so quickly, she banged her foot on a sharp rock. The pain barely registered.

"What do you mean, what happened? Why would she ask that? It's none of her business."

Andi raised an eyebrow. "Umm . . . maybe because she saw Zac kissing someone who wasn't you."

The momentary relief of understanding her secret was safe quickly gave way to the meaning of Andi's words.

"What? Not possible." *No way.* "Maybe Keira just saw someone who looked like Zac."

"I said the same thing. That's what Keira thought too, at first." Andi held out her phone. "Pictures don't lie."

With one look, Meghan's world shattered. As soon as she spotted Zac's hat, the one she'd given him, there was no doubt. The air sucked out of her lungs, and the empty space filled with a pressing heaviness. And who was that girl hanging all over him? The look on his face said he was enjoying it.

"I can't . . . He wouldn't . . ."

Without another word, Meghan tossed the phone back to Andi and stumbled to the bikes. Fueled by anger, her bare feet pressed hard on the pedals. She had a few questions for Zac, but no one on the island would have answers. That didn't keep her from voicing them.

"How could you? How could you do this to me? After what we did! I thought—Didn't it mean anything to you?"

A whiff of fudge filled her nostrils as she rounded the corner into town, but before she could appreciate it, the pungent odor wafting from a cart of horse manure left her squeamish. When she reached the apartment, she dumped her bike on the lawn, raced up the stairs, and went straight to the bathroom.

Minutes later, she came out, wiping drips of mouthwash from her chin. Andi wasn't back yet. Still angry, she slammed her bedroom door so hard that the picture of Zac toppled off the dresser and into the trash.

"Perfect! Saves me the trouble."

CHAPTER 6

The aroma of coffee and fresh-baked pumpkin muffins drew Meghan from the shelter of her room the next morning. Pumpkin was her year-round favorite, and Andi knew it. Careful not to look at the picture in the trash can as she opened her door, she stopped to listen. The quiet in the apartment assured her that Andi must have already left for her day off in St. Ignace. With a sigh of relief, Meghan headed toward the kitchen. She wasn't ready to talk about last night. And maybe, if she timed it just right, she could be in bed by the time Andi got back.

She turned the corner in the living room and found Andi sitting at the kitchen table. Two place settings showcased golden muffins dripping with cream cheese glaze. Meghan crossed the room and leaned against the counter.

"I thought today was your day off."

"It is." Andi reached for the coffeepot sitting on a thick braided hot pad. "Listen, Megs, I feel just awful about last night. Do you hate me?"

So much for not having to talk about it.

"No. I hate Zac. It's not your fault he's a cheat and a liar. I can't believe he did that to me after—" Meghan stopped short of confessing her sin.

"After . . . after what?"

"Nothing." Anger toward Zac flamed.

"Not nothing. Did something happen?"

Yes. Something had definitely happened. "It doesn't matter anymore." Shame also burned.

"What doesn't matter anymore?"

Why are you being so pushy?

"Nothing. None of it matters anymore."

"Meghan, what aren't you telling me? What happened between you and Zac?"

"Andi! Let it go. Nothing happened. When did I say anything happened?"

Andi's eyes widened. Meghan knew she wasn't trying to get on her nerves, but the hurt and anger pushed against the cracks in her heart and threatened to burst through. "I have to leave for work soon. Are you going to let me eat one of those muffins, or did you make them to torment me even more?" Even as the words spilled out, she knew she was being unkind.

Andi looked like she was about to cry. This was on Meghan to fix. She crossed to the table and sat down.

"I'm sorry. I'm angry with Zac and taking it out on you.

"I get it, Megs, I do . . . I think. I'm sorry he hurt you. I wish I hadn't shown you the picture, though."

"You did the right thing. I needed to know the truth. I just wish it weren't the truth."

"What are you going to do about it?"

"Not sure yet." Meghan looked at the clock. "Yikes. I better get going."

Andi handed her a brown lunch bag. "I get to be Mother Andi

this time." She grinned. "Usually that's your role."

"Thanks, Mom."

Andi stood on the small wooden balcony, in her bathrobe and slippers, waving. "Have a good day, honey. Don't give in to peer pressure. Pull over to the curb if you get hungry. Call me when you get there."

Meghan was halfway down the block and could still hear Andi's voice. Thankfully, there weren't too many people out yet. Meghan could smell the pumpkin muffins, and her gnawing stomach loudly reminded her she hadn't eaten breakfast. It would be messy but worth it. She reached into the bag and pulled out a gooey muffin.

At the same time cream cheese frosting was coating her fingers, her phone pinged a string of texts. It would just have to wait. She needed to wash up before starting her shift or she'd end up with a sticky keyboard.

By the time she clocked in and was seated behind the front desk, eleven text messages had piled up. All from Andi. Eight were more of the same banter.

> Are you there yet?
> Did you get run over by a horse?
> Why aren't you replying?

And the picture of Zac with,

> I think you know what you need to do.

Another muffin and one hour later, bent over the toilet, Meghan faced the fact she needed to confront Zac. First, the stress over Zac had exhausted her. Now, the worry and anger made her sick. As soon as she felt strong enough, she texted Andi.

> Noon. Zac. Truth.

She spent the rest of the morning perfecting her strategy.

Lunchtime arrived, but Meghan had no appetite. Alone in the breakroom, she texted Zac.

> You never told me about the concert Saturday night.
> Did you and Brayden have fun?

Zac must have been on his lunch break too.

> It was awesome!!
> They have the best live shows.

Meghan didn't hesitate or overthink her reply.

> I figured you had a good time.
> It sure looked like it in the picture.

Pause for effect, followed by,

> Care to explain?

Zac's quick reply:

> Huh?

Meghan forwarded the picture.
Three simple words bounced back.

> We'll talk later.

Talk about what? Why not now? How much later? Why did it always seem he controlled their relationship? Somehow Meghan needed to get through the next four hours. "Don't cry. Don't cry. Don't cry." No matter how much she wanted to obey those words, she pushed aside her uneaten lunch, laid her head down in her arms, and sobbed until she had no more tears. How was she supposed to be friendly and fun for guests when all she wanted to do was curl up and die? Her heart hurt. It had been a long time since she'd felt this kind of ache. A long time, but a familiar pain. Was it the feeling a person got when someone they loved rejected them? Abandoned them? Because it was the same hurt Meghan had felt when her mom left.

The rest of the day passed in a blur. Thankfully, the afternoon was busy with new guests. One check-in after another provided enough distraction that 4:30 came quickly. Meghan hurried home, thankful for an empty apartment. Andi's note said she was taking the ferry to St. Ignace and would be home in time for Bible study.

Meghan opened a can of soda just as her phone rang. Zac's familiar tone no longer brought her joy. She answered but didn't say hello because Zac was already talking.

"Listen, Meghan, I was going to tell you. I swear. I'm sorry you had to find out this way."

Meghan's throat muscles tightened as questions tumbled like a landslide. "Find out what exactly? When were you planning to tell me? Who is she? How long have you been cheating on me?"

A loud exhale preceded the final blow. "Do you really think any of that matters now?"

"It matters to me!" Meghan shot back. "How could you do this to me after what happened between us? What about your promises? You're such a jerk!"

"Fine!" Zac exploded. "You want to know? Here it is. We met on Facebook awhile back. I didn't go looking for it, but it happened. I wanted to tell you, but it didn't seem right since you were leaving for the summer."

"*Now* you're concerned about right and wrong? *Telling me* seemed wrong but *sleeping with me* seemed right?"

"Face it, Meghan. With you going to college in Grand Rapids and me going to Ann Arbor, there's no way we'd stay together anyway."

Meghan couldn't breathe. Looking down, she caught sight of the ring on her finger. She twisted it viciously. And then, for the first time in almost a year, she pulled it all the way off. The sight of it infuriated her, and she threw it across the room.

"If you felt that way, Zac, why did you keep pushing me? Why did you let things go so far? We can't undo—"

"You think I don't know that? I can't say anything that will make this easier."

"I hate you, Zac! Stay out of my life!" Meghan hung up.

The phone rang. She ignored it. Over and over until she threw the phone across the room too.

"How do you like being on the receiving end for a change?" The walls closed in. Meghan needed air. And space.

Andi heard a ringing phone as soon as she opened the door. She followed the sound and reached behind a chair just as it stopped. The screen reported ten missed calls from Zac. When the phone rang again, she answered.

"Don't be a brat, Meghan—"

"Zac. This is Andi," she interrupted. "Where's Meghan? What's going on with you two?"

"Nothing anymore. It's over. Tell Meghan I said we're done."

Before Andi could respond, Zac hung up.

Andi put away the groceries and decided to skip Bible study to search for Meghan. She knew her friend and knew the island. Since Meghan's bike was still chained to the rack, she would likely be in one of two places—Anne's Tablet or the porch at the Grand Hotel. Anne's Tablet was closer.

Andi jogged across Marquette Park, questions swirling in her mind. She pushed them aside to concentrate on finding Meghan. Sure enough, even before she got to the hidden stairway, she saw Meghan's silhouette at the top of the ridge.

Breathless after the climb, Andi entered a grove of evergreens. The tangy aroma of cedar and the soft blanket of moss filled her senses.

Meghan's shoes poked out from behind their special tree. Over the years, they'd confessed their deepest dreams and fears sitting back-to-back against its sturdy trunk. Offering up a plea for wisdom, Andi joined the chorus of flitting chickadees and broke the silence.

"Your talk with Zac didn't go well?"

"That would be a colossal understatement." Meghan's nasally voice replied.

"Do you want to tell me about it?"

Meghan looked up, eyes puffy and red. "I'm just so stupid."

"You aren't stupid. You're human. And humans can't be perfect all the time."

"Well, I certainly proved that," Meghan concluded. "If I tell you, you have to promise never to tell anyone. No one can ever know what we did."

Andi sat on the opposite side of the tree as Meghan recounted her conversation with Zac and what had happened between them that last night in Traverse City.

"You must think I'm a terrible person," Meghan said. "Every day I ask God to forgive me, but I don't think He ever will." Her eyes filled with fresh tears. "Why should He? I knew better but did it anyway. And if my dad ever found out, he would disown me for good. Probably change his mind about helping with college too."

"Don't be so hard on yourself, Megs. I've never had a boyfriend, so I won't pretend I totally understand. Honestly, I've always been kind of jealous of you and Zac. But that's not the point." She scooted around the tree to sit next to Meghan. "We all make mistakes. Everyone does. You sinned. You repented. It's over. You know what my dad always says—'There's nothing that can separate us from God's love and forgiveness.'"

Meghan found no consolation in that promise. "Your dad has to say stuff like that. It's his job."

"No. You're wrong. He might be a pastor, but he hasn't always trusted God's love."

"That's great for him. He hasn't done anything as bad as me."

Andi stood up and held out her hands. "Come on. Let's head back to town and stop at all the fudge shops on the way home. Chocolate always helps."

CHAPTER 7

*M*eghan glanced at a text from Andi.

> Rats! That time of the month. Forgot to buy supplies.
> Hope you don't mind I opened a box of yours.

The ice cream parlor burst with customers. With no time to reply, she slid the phone into her back pocket and scanned the shelves lining the walk-in freezer. Two weeks ago, Meghan had alphabetized the inventory and been amply rewarded with praise from the manager. Now, running a gloved finger along the shelves, she quickly proceeded from *A* to *S*: Black licorice, Chocolate Chip, Island Fudge, Raspberry Cheesecake, Strawberry . . .

As soon as she stepped out of the freezer, a coworker grabbed the white bucket. "Vanilla, please. Make it two. We just had a big shake order."

One bucket tucked in each arm, Meghan glanced at the office clock as she passed by. 7:27 p.m. The last rush of tourists was cooling off with a final treat before catching the eight o'clock ferry.

At 8:45, she hung up her apron and set off for a slow walk home. The sun had set, leaving the sky painted deep shades of purple. The withering blossoms of abundant lilac bushes adorning the street displayed complementary hues. Meghan broke off a branch and allowed the distinctive fragrance to calm her mind. An uneasy feeling surfaced, followed by an alarming realization.

She pulled out her phone and opened the wellness app. Her eyes searched the screen, not wanting to see but needing to know. She was late. Her last cycle had started on May 2. Seven weeks ago. Not only had she skipped May, she hadn't had any of the usual symptoms in June. In fact, she'd been so preoccupied with the stress of what happened with Zac and the busyness of work, it had never entered her mind.

Like a clap of thunder, an intense panic startled her. Missing her period wasn't the only change. What about the persistent fatigue and nausea? She'd attributed it to heartache over Zac and the aroma of horses, but now? After the realization she'd skipped her period?

Legs trembling, Meghan sank onto a bench. Her fingers shook as they tapped an internet search: *am I pregnant.* The first result was a simple quiz.

What kind of contraception did you use? NONE

How long since your last period? 49 DAYS

Are you feeling unusually sick lately? YES

The results exposed an inconceivable probability: "According to your answers, there is a good chance you may be pregnant." Not wanting to read more, Meghan powered off her phone and went home.

After work the next day, Meghan took the ferry to Mackinaw City to shop at Dollars and Discounts, the close-out store. She tried to be discreet as she walked the aisles, terrified she would see a familiar face. When her turn came, she concealed her fear and embarrassment by avoiding eye contact with the cashier. One by one, the pile of unnecessary products uncovered the single item she came for.

The grandmotherly associate made no comment as she scanned the pregnancy test. She wrapped it in a separate bag and sandwiched it in the middle of the other items.

Aboard the ferry, Meghan knotted the plastic handles tight and clutched the bag tighter. Thankful she'd ridden her bike, Meghan hurried back to the apartment and straight into the bathroom. Andi was playing a pickleball double-header but, if the games went quick, she could walk through the door any minute.

Meghan followed the instructions included in the box and waited. Time crawled as she stared at the white plastic stick in her hands. One thin blue line became two.

Not possible. This could not be happening. Something must have been defective with the test. Probably expired or something. That would explain why it was so cheap. Her hand shook as she pulled up the shopping app on her phone. This time she chose a brand with both the highest reviews and a claim of 99 percent accuracy. How reliable was the medical diagnosis of a generic test kit anyway? She ordered two and paid extra for next-day shipping . . . only to end up with the same results.

Following the suggestions from the test kit, Meghan scheduled a doctor's appointment. There was no way she would visit the tiny hospital on the island. Everyone who worked there knew everyone else's business despite privacy laws, and she wanted the added protection of anonymity. Three days later, she was back in Mackinaw City.

The young doctor seemed so matter of fact when she confirmed the results. "Your due date is February 7. That places the fetus at eight weeks. Still plenty early to decide between a medication or surgical abortion."

Stunned, Meghan barely heard anything after that. Eight weeks? *Abortion*? Who said anything about that? She had the feeling this was something assumed, not discussed. At the end of the appointment, the doctor handed her brochures, a follow-up appointment sheet, and a blister pack of mifepristone and misoprostol. The combination of these two medications would swiftly and quietly cause an end to the pregnancy. The doctor also stressed the importance of acting quickly, because in two weeks the option wouldn't be available.

According to the chart on the exam room wall, the medication was simply a hormone blocker. A steroid safer than acetaminophen. Take the first tablet. Wait up to twenty-four hours for it to take effect. Take the pack of four pills. Wait for the symptoms to pass. Then go back to work.

Meghan drove Andi's car back across the Mackinac Bridge to St. Ignace and boarded the outgoing hydro-jet ferry. Every boat coming in and out was jam-packed with noisy passengers, but Meghan was numb to the commotion. The ride to the island passed in a haze. Even the open-air deck smothered her. Thoughts swirled in her mind, and the swaying of the boat added to the queasiness surging in the pit of her stomach. She needed somewhere quiet, preferably dark and quiet, to sort it all out.

Meghan cautiously entered the apartment, expecting to see Andi watching TV or experimenting in the kitchen. But all was quiet. She erased her fake smile, secured the door behind her, and locked herself in the bathroom. It was the safest place to spread out the items from the clinic.

According to the brochure titled "Your First Trimester," the fertilized egg had already developed from two cells to the size of a dried bean. Six weeks from conception, the tiny embryo had a beating heart as well as internal organs and external facial features.

All of that had happened before she'd even known she was pregnant?

The next brochure explained Michigan law and possibilities for women facing unexpected pregnancies. It included a hotline number and link to scan. Meghan didn't want to talk to anyone, so she opened the website on her phone. It was obviously an abortion clinic.

Meghan sighed. Until today, abortion had been an unthinkable sin. An unforgivable sin. Her hands gripped the rim of the sink as she stared into the mirror. She searched the face returning her gaze. Who was the person looking back? What did she believe?

Until this moment, she'd claimed to be pro-life, without question. It was what her parents believed (or at least used to). What her church believed. It was a common value embraced by almost everyone she knew. It sounded good. It seemed reasonable. Straightforward and simple. Until now.

This time she needed to make the decision. Nothing was simple anymore. *What is wrong with me?* she wondered. *Am I really considering this?*

A loud knock on the door startled her. "Meghan? You okay?"

Oh no! How would she get out of the bathroom without Andi seeing anything?

"Uh . . . I'm fine. Just girl stuff." She quickly shoved everything to the back of the cupboard under the sink. After Andi went to bed, she would retrieve it and stash it in her room.

It was hard to act normal during dinner. It was hard to talk about work and friends and social media when such a huge decision loomed over her head. She would have to make the decision soon—either go ahead with the first pill or ask for help. So many questions raced through her mind.

Should I tell Andi?

> *What about Zac? Does he have a right to know after he cheated on me?*
>> *What about my parents? What would they say?*
>>> *What about God?*
>>>> *What about college in the fall?*
>>>>> *What about my career goals? My plans?*

She almost laughed out loud when she pictured herself at college. "Michigan Christian University" in bold letters, stretched across her baby bump. Her dad said it was a mistake to enroll there. He must be a prophet. She should have declined the scholarship and chosen Ann Arbor with Zac. *Zac.*

He had begged her to join him there. Maybe if she had, they would still be together. There were too many reasons for terminating the pregnancy. Why should one mistake affect so many lives? Change so many things? The baby wasn't actually a complete baby anyway, not yet. It was mostly a lump of underdeveloped tissue that had the potential to grow into a baby. It wasn't like she would be taking something away from a real person. No one would ever know, and life would go on as if this were only a bad dream.

After dinner, Meghan settled in front of the TV and waited for the opportunity to sneak the items to her room. The next thing she knew, the clock on her phone read 4:00 a.m., with battery power drained to 7 percent. This day was not off to a good start.

She tiptoed into the bathroom. Careful not to knock anything over, she emptied the cabinet's contents onto the floor. There was no sign of the white bag. The black and white tiles felt cold underneath her thin leggings. Surrounded by cleaning supplies, towels, and styling irons, Meghan suddenly had the feeling she wasn't alone.

"Looking for these?"

Meghan froze. Andi's voice was quiet and calm. Perhaps the calm before the storm. "Be sure your sin will find you out" had been reinforced after every childhood transgression. God's disgust delivered through those more qualified, more righteous, more worthy. Meghan deserved Andi's loathing and would gladly bear whatever punishment would atone for her sin. Though there wasn't a hint of condemnation or accusation in Andi's voice, it took everything Meghan could muster to turn around and face her friend.

Andi stood in the doorway with such a look of sorrow, Meghan's defenses were disarmed. Andi dropped to the floor and wrapped Meghan in a soothing embrace.

"Why didn't you tell me? Why are you going through this alone?"

Meghan's tears soaked into Andi's soft robe. "I am so sorry. I didn't know what else to do."

Meghan accepted Andi's help up then followed her to the living room. As they settled onto opposite ends of the couch, Meghan let a wall go up between them. "I know what you're thinking, and I would think the same thing if I were you."

Andi made no reply.

"There was just so much I didn't understand before. It's not as bad as it sounds. Really, no one will get hurt."

Meghan repeated what the doctor had said, but Andi didn't seem convinced. And, as she heard herself say the words, neither was she.

After an hour, Andi stood up and handed Meghan the bag of pills. "I need to get ready for work. You know what I believe, but do you know what *you* believe?"

Now alone, Meghan held the package in her hands. Her decision about those tiny pills carried the immense power of life or death. The choice was hers alone. She had no doubt about Andi's beliefs, but unlike her, Andi would never face this situation. It was easy to see something clearly when you were on the outside looking in.

Meghan was young, single, and in no position to support a baby. What kind of life could she provide with a high school diploma? Zac was already out of the picture. The thought of crawling back to him and begging for support appalled her. She didn't have a family who would help raise a baby or even a real home to go back to. Her dad compensated for his absence by paying her living expenses and adding a nice monthly allowance on the side. She couldn't expect him to fund her mistakes too.

If Zac could move on with his life, it was only fair she could too. Meghan opened the box and pulled out the contents. Five tiny white pills and this would all be over. She reached for her phone and texted her boss:

> Steve, I'm sick and won't be coming to work today. Sorry.

CHAPTER 8

*A*ndi rushed home after her shift, expecting to find Meghan in the stages of a self-induced abortion. As her hand lingered on the doorknob, she prayed.

God, I don't know how to respond when I walk through this door. Part of me is furious with Meghan, and part of me is sad. At least that little baby is with You now. Nothing will ever bring it back. How can I show Your love to Meghan? How do we go forward from here?

Turning the latch, Andi eased the door open. The scent of chocolate chip cookies didn't compute. Meghan was bent over the oven, pulling out a pan of fresh-baked goodness. She looked up and smiled. "I didn't take the pills."

Relief flooded Andi's heart. Knees weak, she sank into the overstuffed chair and went limp.

Meghan set a plate of warm cookies between two small glasses of milk. "Come join me and I'll explain everything."

Andi wasn't sure her stomach could handle anything but pulled out the chair opposite Meghan and waited for her to continue.

"I was planning to do it. Then, all of a sudden, I remembered that lady from the pregnancy center. You know? Maddy's mom?"

Andi thought for a moment. "Carol? She spoke at youth group last summer."

"Yep, that's her." Meghan paused. "She said having an abortion isn't the solution to a problem, because the problem isn't the baby. The problem is the sin in our own hearts. At the time I didn't understand, but now I do. That's when I knew I couldn't go through with it myself. I couldn't be directly responsible for an abortion."

Andi reached over and clasped Meghan's hands. "I am so sorry you had to go through that. But you made the right decision."

"I definitely feel better about everything."

Andi took the first bite of her cookie. "So? When is the baby due?"

"Due?" Meghan looked confused. "Well, February, but why does that matter?"

Now Andi was confused. "Why does it matter? It matters for lots of reasons."

"Andi, I decided not to take the pills. That doesn't mean I'm not going to have an abortion—I'm just not going to be the one to do it. I made an appointment at the women's clinic on the fourteenth, but I won't be able to drive afterward. Will you take me to Grand Rapids?"

Andi couldn't believe what she was hearing. Never in her wildest dreams could she have prepared for this moment. "I—you—" Thoughts whirled, but words wouldn't come.

Meghan wanted her help getting an abortion? What kind of friend would ask that?

"I—I don't have an answer. I need to think about it." And pray about it.

Now it was Andi's turn to climb Crow's Nest Trail. Alone under the cedars, Andi poured out her heart to God. *Father, I'm so confused. First Meghan gets pregnant, and now she's planning to abort the baby. Where are You in this? Where am I supposed to be? I don't know what to think. I don't understand what I feel. What I can do. She wants me to take her to the clinic, but, God, I don't agree with Meghan's choice. I don't want her to do this. If I drive her, won't I be supporting her decision? Won't I be partly to blame?*

Andi remained on the overlook as the evening breeze cooled. Eyes closed, she leaned her head against a tree, wishing she could close out the world. The pungent sweetness of the cedar trees became the incense that carried her prayers to Heaven. The chickadees chirped their songs overhead. Sounds from the city below were muted but discernible. Metal horseshoes clinked on the paved streets. A ferry horn signaled the next harbor departure. Children laughed in the park. Among these sounds, Andi listened for God's Spirit to speak to her heart. Silence. She needed something to go on. She reached for her phone and texted her dad.

CALL ME ASAP. IT'S URGENT.

Within five minutes, her phone rang. As soon as she answered, she burst into tears. Her dad patiently waited as Andi gathered her emotions. His reassuring voice reminded her to slow down and focus.

"Remember the breathing prayer? Let's try it together."

Andi recalled the calming prayer exercise her parents had taught her when she was little and prone to tantrums. She closed her eyes and followed her dad's lead.

"Focus on your breathing. In through your nose. Out through your mouth." After only a few tries, her heart rate slowed.

"Now, as you breathe in, think, 'Jesus.' Exhale and think, 'I am Yours.' Good. Let's do it again."

The breathing prayer helped clear her mind. "Dad, I don't know what to do. I need you to tell me."

"What's going on? We'll figure it out together."

Andi didn't use names as she explained about a girl on the island planning to have an abortion. "She asked me to drive her to the clinic. How could she? How dare she drag me into this? Why would she think I would even consider helping her do that?"

Andi's dad was quiet, so quiet she was afraid the call had dropped. As she was about to hang up and redial, he spoke.

"Yes, Andi, we do believe it's wrong, but God loves your friend just as much as He loves her baby. Your friend is scared, and right now this seems like the only solution to what she sees as an insurmountable problem. She can't see her baby isn't a problem. She can't see God's love and grace, because she is focused on a mountain of fear and unknowns. If she could trust God hasn't turned His back on her, maybe she would see abortion isn't the way to the freedom she's searching for."

"But what do I say to her? How can I make her see that?"

"You can't. We can't *make* anyone believe anything. God gives each of us free will and never forces us to love or obey Him. Even Jesus said, 'Your will, not Mine.' You can speak truth in love. You can pray. You can trust nothing is ever wasted when it's given to God. Everything is redeemable through His grace. There is nothing, including abortion, that can separate us from God's love."

"I wish you could say that to my friend."

"I'm not there, but you are. Watch and pray. Watch for God's leading and pray for His strength to follow."

"Would you pray now, Dad?"

And he did.

Andi felt peace. Choosing to trust God was hard. Waiting for God to work was even harder. But armed with her dad's wisdom, she determined to speak in love whenever Meghan was ready to listen.

CHAPTER 9

*E*ach morning, Meghan found a new sticky note on the bathroom mirror. She appreciated what Andi was trying to do. She believed the Bible was true . . . and it was. For people like Andi.

Thursday: *"For I know the plans I have for you," declares the Lord, "plans to prosper you and not to harm you, plans to give you a hope and a future" (Jeremiah 29:11).*

Friday: *Therefore, there is now no condemnation for those who are in Christ Jesus, because through Christ Jesus the law of the Spirit who gives life has set you free from the law of sin and death (Romans 8:1–2).*

Saturday: *If we confess our sins, he is faithful and just and will forgive us our sins and purify us from all unrighteousness (1 John 1:9).*

Sunday: *Who shall separate us from the love of Christ? Shall trouble or hardship or persecution or famine or nakedness or danger or sword? . . . No, in all these things we are more than conquerors through him who loved us (Romans 8:35, 37).*

Monday was a quiet afternoon at the inn. Meghan sat behind the front desk and stared out the window. The steeple of Sainte Anne's church stood perfectly framed within the antique glass. Somehow, she'd never noticed. Until today.

A weathered white cross, glaring down, casting judgment. The sight reminded her there was only one way to God, and she'd blown it. Contrary to Andi's messages, the words playing in Meghan's head weren't about God's love or forgiveness. No, the voices inside were busy reminding her of all the reasons she wasn't worthy.

They taunted her. *You sinned against God and your own body. You messed up.* Condemned her. *Just wait till they find out. Everyone's going to be so disappointed in you.* Accused her. *Look at the "good girl" now. You never were good. You're a fake.* Labeled her. *You're junk. Damaged merchandise. Nobody's gonna want you now.* Questioned her. *What kind of role model would you make for a kid anyway?*

Meghan couldn't stop the words, but she could change the view. She retrieved a potted sago palm from the veranda and placed it on the far end of the high counter. Returning to her chair, she adjusted her position to block the steeple from her field of view. She was so involved in rearranging, she barely noticed when two people entered the side door.

"Oh, umm, I'm so sorry. I didn't see you come in." Meghan did a double take. The couple looked familiar. Where had she seen them before?

"No problem," the thirty-something woman assured. "We wondered if we might check in a little early."

Meghan tried not to stare as she switched to business mode and began her usual monologue. "Welcome to the Marquette Inn. We're so glad you've chosen to stay with us during your visit to Mackinac. Is this your first time on the island?"

"It certainly is." The man answered this time. "My wife has been nagging—I mean persistently requesting—for years. We're not even done unpacking from the move and she drags me across the lake."

The wife delivered a playful poke to his ribs.

"What my husband means to say is, yes, this is our first visit to the island, and we are so happy to be here."

The husband added a ploy for sympathy. "That's what you heard me say, right?"

Meghan enjoyed their banter. These were the kind of people who made her job fun. "Well, something like that. I know better than to get in the middle." She refreshed the computer screen. "Now, let's see if your room is ready. What name is on your reservation?"

"Carson. Dante and Ava Carson."

The name didn't sound familiar, and this was their first time to the island. No luck there. She scanned the reservation file for more information.

"Found it. Mr. and Mrs. Carson. It looks like you're staying in the Lilac Suite for six nights." As Meghan scanned the reservation, her pulse spiked. Someone had messed up. The most expensive room at the inn showed a charge of only $100 per night. This was the kind of mistake that could cost someone their job.

Mr. Carson noticed the hesitation. "Is everything in order? Do you need more information?"

"Nooooo . . ." Meghan drew out the word as a stall tactic. As the couple exchanged a questioning glance, she intercepted their suspicions. "Does the Lilac Suite sound correct?"

The tactic worked.

"It sounds perfectly wonderful." Mrs. Carson closed her eyes as a smile spread across her face. "But"—she opened her eyes and smiled wide—"please call us Dante and Ava."

"It would be my pleasure. Ava." Meghan felt drawn to this woman's gentle spirit and welcoming gaze. If only she could place the familiarity. "My name is Meghan, and you will find me here in the lobby every day between eight o'clock and four-thirty. I would be happy to help you plan your days, choose a restaurant, or suggest specific activities. I can also help with any needs that arise while you're here." She paused for feedback. "Any questions?"

Simultaneous headshakes signaled "No."

"Now, before we get you to your room, let me show you around." She snapped a screenshot of the confirmation and sent it to her phone. After the Carsons settled in, she would show Steve and let him figure out who was responsible for the expensive blunder.

Meghan stepped through the French doors separating the lobby from the sunny atrium. "Here is where our deluxe continental breakfast is served from eight to ten each morning."

Dante pointed toward the back of the room, and Meghan answered his silent question. "I see you've spotted the afternoon refreshments."

Dante ducked beneath hanging baskets of flowers to make a beeline for the treats.

"For the sake of other guests"—a smile spread across Ava's face—"you may need to ration your inventory. I'm not much of a cook, and when Dante has a chance for sweets, he sometimes forgets to share."

Dante, cookie in each hand, laughed but didn't deny his wife's statement.

Meghan pointed to a dark walnut buffet table as she and Ava followed the main pathway through the room. "Well, he has definitely come to the right place. Each afternoon, you will find fresh coffee, cool lemonade, and an assortment of the inn's famous home-baked goodies." Guests and employees alike benefited from Netta's culinary skills.

Today's treat drew quite a reaction from Ava when she reached the table. "Look, Dante, snickerdoodles!" As she nibbled on a crispy edge, she added, "Your favorite. Almost as though they knew you were coming."

"Mmm, maybe." Dante looked at Meghan and winked.

Now, why would they think the cookies were made specifically for Dante? Maybe Ava wasn't kidding about his sweet tooth. Meghan gave a mental shrug and pointed toward the door leading to the back porch. "If you're interested in biking, we supply rentals for an affordable hourly or daily rate. We stock a variety of sizes as well as tandems, and I highly suggest at least one trip all the way around the island."

"It's at the top of our list," Dante announced. Then, out of the blue, he grabbed Ava's hands and broke into song. "It won't be a stylish marriage. I can't afford a carriage. But you'll look sweet upon the seat of a bicycle built for two." Taken aback, Meghan looked to Ava for explanation as Dante twirled her around. The hanging baskets swayed behind them as they waltzed toward the exit.

As Dante bowed, Ava said, "Don't be alarmed, dear. My husband is an occupational therapist at a nursing home. Welcome to my world."

"So you're saying that's a real song?"

For some reason, Ava and Dante Carson thought that was hilarious. Their smiles and the way they looked at each other once again triggered the sense she had seen them somewhere before.

Meghan led the couple back through the lobby and checked the entryway for luggage. "The dock porters haven't delivered your bags yet. It shouldn't be much longer. Would you like to see your room? It's on the second floor."

The Carsons said they were impressed with the intricate details carved on the original staircase and the colorful mosaics of stained-glass windows bordering it. Meghan never tired of experiencing Mackinac through the eyes of first-time guests. Their admiration and excitement boosted her spirit and reminded her why she loved her job.

Ava couldn't contain her delight as she entered the Lilac Suite. She walked straight to the window and unwound her Ankara headwrap. Long black box braids spilled over her shoulders. The look in her husband's eyes revealed complete adoration, and a heavy longing pressed on Meghan's heart. Would Zac ever look at her like that again?

"Dante, see the harbor? That's where we arrived on the ferry. And look! A picture-perfect view of Round Island Lighthouse."

Dante joined his wife at the balcony window and placed a maroon rectangular box in her hands. Then he turned to Meghan. "Mackinac Island fudge, I presume?"

"It sure is," Meghan confirmed. "A little taste of the island to kick off your stay."

Dante stepped away from the window and invited Meghan to be seated in the matching floral wingback chairs. "Speaking of infamous Mackinac fudge, how do you decide which kind to buy when there are so many flavors to choose from?"

"You're not wasting any time, are you, Mr. Carson?"

"Dante, please."

"Dante," Meghan corrected herself. "I have an easy answer to your question, but it will take real commitment on your part. Do you think you're up for the challenge?"

Dante's dark, dancing eyes revealed a boyish playfulness. "I sure hope so. I didn't know it was going to require special skill."

"There's only one way to make the right choice." Meghan leaned in, as if to share a classified secret. "You simply must commit to sampling *all* the flavors."

Ava turned around and raised her eyebrows at her husband. "There'll be no living with him now. He'll be the proverbial kid in a candy store."

"Goodbye low-carb diet." Dante grinned.

"No worries," Meghan said. "Why do you think we ride bikes so much?" She rose to leave and recited the tour finale. "Your luggage will be delivered as soon as it arrives. Feel free to explore the island or enjoy some quiet time. Think of the Marquette Inn as your home away from home. Please don't hesitate to let us know how we can help make good memories here on Mackinac Island."

With that, she quietly closed the door.

Two flights down, Meghan found Steve working in his office.

"Meghan, perfect timing. There's something I need to talk to you about."

Whatever it was, Meghan had something more important. "We have a big problem. A huge problem. And by 'we,' I mean you because this is way above my pay grade."

"Uh oh. Sounds serious." Steve closed his laptop and took off his reading glasses. "What'd you do now?"

Meghan was in no mood for jokes. "It wasn't me. Someone else messed up big-time—the kind of mistake that costs a lot of money."

Now Steve looked appropriately concerned.

But before Meghan could explain, a voice spoke from directly behind her. "Steve-o! Long time, no see."

Meghan turned around to find Dante Carson standing in the doorway, holding two cups of coffee.

"DC! Fancy meeting you here." Steve jumped up and pulled out another chair.

"I was just about to tell Meghan we'd be welcoming special guests today. If I had known you were arriving early, I would have ordered the royal treatment." He turned to Meghan and added, "I apologize if my poor communication caused you any problems."

"Well, Steve-o," Dante chimed in. "If she hasn't already given us the royal treatment, I don't know what else there is. You have a fantastic employee here."

While she appreciated the compliment, she was still confused. Steve-o? DC? These two obviously had a history, which might explain the price discrepancy. "I take it you're old friends," she ventured.

Steve slapped Dante on the back. "One of us is old anyway." Before Dante could retaliate, he continued. "Back in the day, we were college teammates. Been best buds ever since. We played ball and met the wives at U of M Duluth. The Minnesota winters were cold, so we did our best to keep the girls warm. Right, DC?"

"No comment," replied Dante. "I think they only used us when they couldn't get somewhere through the underground tunnels."

The depth of their friendship was not lost on Meghan. "Mr. Carson"—she pointed to the ceramic mugs in his hands—"speaking of wives, I suggest you get that coffee up to yours before it gets cold."

"See?" Dante remarked as he headed for the stairs. "I told you she's good."

Meghan realized suddenly why the Carsons looked familiar. She moved around to the other side of Steve's desk and lifted two framed photos. One held a team photo, captioned with the words *Duluth Dogs*. The other, larger picture was from Netta and Steve's wedding day. Beside the bride and groom stood Ava and Dante.

"How long ago were these taken?" Meghan turned the pictures around for reference.

Steve scrunched his face as he searched for the answer. "Let's see, we're thirty-one now, which makes the girls twenty-nine"—he retracted with an exaggerated headshake—"Oh, don't tell them I let that cat out of the bag."

"And . . ." Meghan waved the photos and drew Steve back to the original question.

"And so, if my math is correct, the football picture was nine years ago and the wedding picture five years ago."

Mystery solved. Meghan studied the images of the two couples and wondered what the picture of her life would look like in five years. Until recently, she'd imagined standing next to Zac on her wedding day. She would wear a long white dress and Andi would stand next to her in coral pink, or maybe dark purple. She would carry a bouquet of calla lilies, and it would be the best day of her life.

Would have been. Another dream that would never come true.

CHAPTER 10

Two mornings later, Meghan pushed her chair back and raced around the desk to the nearest restroom. This was the second time since she'd arrived at work. Too bad she hadn't thought to grab her purse. She wished she had a hairbrush or a scrunchie. Why didn't she at least grab her phone? Anything to help hide the reason she'd stayed in the bathroom so long. And a piece of gum. Ugh.

Meghan pushed damp curls away from her clammy cheeks, unlocked the stall door, and took a deep breath before she pushed it open. She immediately stood face-to-face with Ava Carson.

"Ummm, good morning, Mrs. Carson. Ava." Meghan hoped her voice sounded less shaky than it felt. She didn't wait for a reply and made a ninety-degree turn toward the sink. The only noise came from the water faucet. Meghan gave full attention to her sudsy hands and didn't look up when Ava spoke.

"Are you all right, dear? You don't look well."

Meghan reduced the water flow to a trickle but soaped up again. She hoped Ava would either leave the room or step into the stall. "Must be my lactose sensitivity." That was a lie. The pang of guilt did nothing to help her churning stomach, but it was the only thing she could think to say.

"Do you need me to find Steve? Maybe you should go home."

"No need. I'm fine now. Thank you." Another lie. "Have a nice day." Meghan reached for an extra paper towel and took it back to her desk. She hoped her words were enough to convince both Ava and herself.

Meghan spent most of the morning hidden behind the high counter as guests checked out of their rooms. On the advice of her doctor, she kept a supply of natural remedies in a desk drawer. A cup of peppermint tea followed by a few ginger candies soothed her digestive system. By lunchtime, she was able to eat a banana, yogurt, and a few wheat crackers.

Just before her break ended, Steve poked his head in the oversized pantry. "It's your lucky day. Henri just dropped off a big delivery."

Meghan's smile lit up her eyes as she followed Steve back to her desk. "New items for the gift shop?" For her, this was better than Christmas morning.

Meghan sat on the floor of the lobby and sorted a collection of ceramic coffee cups. Surrounded by sheets of bubble wrap and a growing pile of cardboard, she didn't notice when the Carsons returned from their afternoon bike ride.

A quiet, yet unexpected noise came from behind. "You look like you're feeling better."

Ava. Meghan jumped up as Dante strode into the atrium, no doubt looking for a snack. She burrowed her head close to a display shelf to hide her embarrassment. "Yes, ma'am, much better. Thank you."

Ava reached out and placed her hand on Meghan's shoulder. "If you're free tonight, could I treat you to dinner?"

Meghan flinched at the touch, her cheeks burning. "I work at Island Ice tonight."

Ava persisted. "Tomorrow perhaps?"

Meghan couldn't bring herself to turn around. "Tomorrow works. Maybe Netta and Andi could join us?"

Ava and Netta were waiting when Meghan and Andi arrived at the restaurant. Over a simple meal of soups and salads, the duos of best friends exchanged stories. There were many similarities between them.

Netta and Andi had both grown up in two-parent, God-centered homes; Ava and Meghan had both experienced less-than-ideal circumstances. Netta and Andi were funny, easygoing extroverts; Ava and Meghan were deep thinking, quiet introverts. This surprised Meghan.

"Ava, you don't seem introverted to me. You and Dante are so playful, and you seem so outgoing."

"That has come over time. I used to be a lot more stubborn and arrogant." Ava exchanged a knowing look with Netta before she continued. "After my mom was incarcerated, I floated between relatives and foster homes for much of my childhood. I couldn't afford to let my guard down or exhibit vulnerability."

Wide-eyed at the disclosure, Meghan and Andi set down their forks and waited for Ava to continue.

"By the time I started high school, I had seen and done things I wish I could say I hadn't. I acted out because I didn't know what else to do. Then I started running away and skipping school until I got a big wake-up call. Social Services gave me one more chance and placed me with a loving, godly, foster family. I believe they saved my life."

Ava continued the chronology of her story after the check had been paid and the table had been cleared. Finally, she pushed back her chair and announced, "Well, ladies, I believe the waitress would like her table for another set of customers."

With a smile, Netta suggested, "I'm not ready to go back yet. How about if we pop across the street for ice cream and then walk you home?"

"That's not fair," Ava answered. "Meghan can't have ice cream."

Netta and Andi looked at Meghan then turned back to Ava for an explanation. "Lactose?" Ava explained. "She's allergic?"

"Since when?" Andi questioned.

Meghan's mind raced as she tried to remember what she had told Ava to make her think she couldn't have ice cream. *The bathroom yesterday.* "Uhhh . . ." *Think fast, Meghan.* "It's a sensitivity, not an allergy."

Andi tilted her head and opened her mouth. Just as quickly, she closed it again and offered another suggestion. "How about the candy store?"

After everyone chose a flavored chocolate truffle, Meghan walked with the others toward the park. The fresh air off the water cooled her skin, and her pulse returned to normal. She was able to push the lactose incident out of her mind. For now. Hopefully, Andi wouldn't bring it up later.

They crossed the street in front of the fort and followed the sidewalk that sloped toward the harbor. Seagulls scattered as they approached.

"I have a question, Ava," Leading the pack, Andi turned and stopped. "How did the foster family save your life?"

Ava exchanged a look with Netta before she answered. "They would be the first to give credit to God, but it was God living through them that changed me. For the first time, I saw people who lived their lives as if God loved them and really lived within them. They didn't just talk about God and then turn around and do the same terrible things everyone else did. And they treated me different too. It took a long time to trust *anyone* could truly love me, let alone the God of the universe."

A lump formed in Meghan's throat. "You didn't—" The words seemed stuck. She swallowed. "Why did you think God couldn't love you?"

"Before the Renicks took me in, I had never been loved just for being me. I'm not even sure I had ever been loved at all. I certainly had never been told God loved me the way I was instead of the way I should be. After everything I had done, I thought I was too dirty, too corrupt, to ever clean up enough for a perfect God."

Ava's words raced through Meghan's mind and settled in her soul. Ava had provided the perfect description for the wrestling match happening inside of her. Andi must have read her mind because she voiced the question Meghan couldn't.

"What changed? What made you trust His love?"

Tears trembled on Ava's long, dark lashes as she crossed her hands over her heart. "Grace, girls. I anchored my soul to grace."

The latest episode of a favorite show was filling the living room with sound, but Meghan couldn't concentrate. She couldn't get Ava's story out of her head. She grabbed the remote and paused the playback. They could finish watching later.

"Andi? Did you understand what Ava meant about grace?"

It took Andi a moment to shift her mindset from reality TV to the reality of the moment. Finally, she shook her head. "Not exactly," she admitted. "My dad preaches about grace sometimes, but it's always kind of confused me. I remember him saying something like, 'Grace is a covering of love God wraps around our brokenness.' Maybe that's what Ava meant about Him loving us as we are and not as we should be?"

"Wait," Meghan replied, eyes wide with surprise. "I always thought sin made God angry." Meghan tried to picture her sins being wrapped in love. It didn't feel right. Why would God cover them up? To hide them? To hide her?

Silence stretched between them. The ceiling fan hummed in the background as it pulled a cool breeze through the windows. After a minute, Andi rose from the couch and moved toward Meghan's armchair. Meghan moved her feet to the edge of the cushioned ottoman, and Andi sat down.

"Megs, we haven't talked about the baby. How are you feeling?"

"Still having some morning sickness, but otherwise not too bad." Meghan paused. "Have you thought about my question?"

"I can't think of anything else, but I don't have an answer yet. When do you need to know?"

"Tomorrow. I need time to find someone else if you say no."

Andi looked down at her lap. The silence returned.

Finally, Meghan stood up. "Okay. No pressure. I just need to know either way." She pushed Play and handed Andi the remote. "I'm going to bed. See you in the morning."

The show resumed. Andi's eyes followed the movement on the screen, but her mind focused elsewhere.

No pressure? Are you kidding me? The pressure is crushing me. If I say yes, I help my best friend abort her baby. If I say no, I risk losing her and she has the abortion anyway. If that isn't pressure, what is?

Andi knew she would carry the weight of this decision the rest of her life. She had never prayed so much in her life but God didn't seem to be listening. If He wasn't going to provide an answer, she needed to look somewhere else. She pulled out her phone and sent a group text to the people she hoped could help her.

> Please pray for someone here who plans to have an abortion next week. She asked me to drive her, and I don't know what to do. Please pray she will change her mind. I don't want to have to make this decision.

Everyone replied before the show was over. Every reply revealed a different point of view. Instead of putting her mind at ease, Andi felt even more confused.

> Dad: Praying for you both. Trust God to guide you. Trust His Romans 8:28 promise. "And we know that in all things God works for the good of those who love him, who have been called according to his purpose."

> Mom: If you take her, will you feel responsible for her decision? This is very hard for someone your age. Maybe an adult should be involved? Praying she will change her mind and spare all of you from the effects of this terrible situation. Pray for discernment. I love you. I am so sorry.

> Keira: You can't take her. Abortion is wrong! If you take her, you'll be supporting ending a baby's life!!!!!!!!

> Dad: The verse doesn't say God will work good circumstances. It says He can work ALL THINGS (including bad things) together for THE good (even after bad things). His plan prevails but sometimes we don't understand His plan.

> Brayden: Wow. IDK. Maybe we don't have the right to judge and just need to love.

And in all the confusion, more questions crowded her mind: Where was Zac in all this? Did he even know? Did he have a right to know?

She had twenty-four hours to find the answers, but before she knew it, the clock ran out. It was time.

Meghan stood in the doorway of Andi's bedroom. "What did you decide? Are you going to drive me to Grand Rapids, or should I find someone else?"

Andi wanted to run, but Meghan was blocking her only escape. *God, I'm trying to trust You, but this seems very wrong. Please stop me if I am making a big mistake.* She took a deep breath.

"I'll take you."

Meghan's look of shock quickly changed to relief as she stepped into the room and embraced her friend.

"You're the best, Andi. This is the right thing. You'll see."

Andi couldn't return the embrace. Everything inside wanted to push back. No, this was most certainly not the right thing. Nothing about this situation was right. She wanted to take back her words, yell at Meghan, insist she call Zac. She wanted to turn back time and find a way to stop them from getting into this situation to begin with. *God, there's nothing I can do, is there? It's completely out of my control. Did I make the wrong choice?*

CHAPTER 11

Golden batter bubbled on the griddle, while crispy bacon sizzled in a small frying pan. Meghan closed her eyes, inhaling the swirling, salty-sweet aroma. With a start, she realized, for the first time in weeks, morning food odors didn't upset her stomach. Maybe this was the calm after the storm. The so-called peace that passes understanding. It had to be. Why else would she feel so good?

On the walk to work, Meghan greeted everyone she passed. She even offered to take pictures for an older couple strolling through Marquette Park. She suggested some fun poses and snapped a few photos to send to their children and grandchildren.

Andi's decision had changed everything. For the first time since leaving Traverse City, Meghan felt a welcome sense of hope, relief, and joy. She saw a light at the end of a dark tunnel—a way out of her nightmare.

During the quiet afternoon, Ava approached the front desk with a small plate of assorted macarons. "Would you please help me with these? I couldn't decide which to try and was hoping someone would share them with me."

"Gladly," Meghan said. "Netta's macarons are to die for."

While Meghan retrieved another chair and two cups of coffee, Ava used a butter knife to cut each cookie in half. "I feel like a judge for the Great Michigan Bake-Off. Where should we start?"

Meghan played along with her best impression of a French culinary expert. "On the dish before you is a sampling of classic French macarons. These delicate, meringue-based rounds are made primarily with egg whites, almond flour, and sugar. Buttercream, jam, and ganache are popular fillings sandwiched between the crisp shells." Rolling her r's with dramatic exaggeration, she continued. "The process for making macarons is quite laborious, hence the cost to the consumer. But who can put a price on such perfection?"

Ava laughed. "Your Irish accent is terrible, but do carry on, Chef Meghan."

"It's French." Meghan took that as a cue to play it up even more. "Much akin to the confusion over the pronunciation of 'Mackinac,' in novice circles, you will find many who mistakenly refer to the macaron as 'macaroon.' Try to be patient and gently explain a macaroon is but a simple coconut cookie, while a macaron is a culinary masterpiece."

By this point, Ava was wiping tears from her eyes as coffee dripped down her hand. "Stop. You're making me spill my coffee."

Meghan handed her a napkin. "But you asked . . ."

"That I did. Now I am more curious than ever. Maybe we should get to the sampling while I still have coffee left to drink."

Meghan slid the plate between them and pointed to a shiny, cream-colored confection. "The choices before you, moving clockwise, are vanilla bean, caramel chocolate crème, and a Netta original, lilac lemon."

Ava's eyes opened wide as she picked up the purple and yellow sandwich cookie. "You mean they taste like lilacs? As in the flowers?"

Meghan leaned in close. "It'll be our secret. I happen to know this batch is flavored with lavender, but, yes, lilacs are edible. The filling is Netta's own recipe for lemon-honey buttercream. The light-purple shells are garnished with preserved lilac blossoms, so technically they still are lilac-lemon macarons."

"It's delicious as well as a brilliant marketing angle. Sounds like Steve may have had a hand in this."

Now it was Meghan's turn to be surprised. "Absolutely. You really do know them well."

"After all our years of friendship, I should hope so." Ava brushed delicate crumbs into her hand then onto the plate. "During your impressive macaron speech, you mentioned something I've been wondering about. What's the deal with *Mackinac,* spelled with a *c* for the island, and *Mackinaw,* spelled with a *w* for the city? I never know whether to say 'Mack-i-nack' or 'Mack-i-naw.'"

"It's a common mistake," Meghan began. "Originally this area was named *Michilimackinac*, the French term for the Native American word meaning 'Great Turtle.'"

"Wait. Go back," Ava interrupted. "Mishel-what?"

"MISH-il-ah-MACK-in-aw." Meghan pronounced the word slowly. "The original name came from the island's shape—like a turtle in the water. When the French arrived, they recorded the word the way they heard it pronounced in the Ojibway language. That explains why the *c* is silent. In colonial times, the British changed the *c* to a *w*. But the *w* never really stuck."

"You sure know your history. But I still don't understand why there are two spellings today."

"In order to avoid confusion, Mackinac Island retained the original French spelling and Mackinaw City adopted the phonetic English spelling. When in doubt, just remember no matter how it's spelled, the *c* is always silent."

"That sounds easy enough," Ava agreed. "Thank you for the

fascinating history and culinary lesson. Have you ever considered teaching?"

Meghan beamed at the compliment. "Not exactly. My dream is to be a historical interpreter at Colonial Williamsburg. I love the Revolutionary Era."

"I've never been there, but when you start work, let me know. And speaking of work, I better let you get back to your job."

"It was my pleasure, Ava. Anytime."

"Unfortunately, our time here is running out."

Ava stood and slid her chair under the desk. Before she rounded the corner of the high-top counter, she turned back and took hold of Meghan's hands. Her soft brown eyes looked sad. "If you aren't busy tomorrow, would you like to visit Butterfly World with me? I thought of you when I was there the other day."

"I would love to. I work at the ice cream shop, but not until noon."

"Perfect. Meet here at nine?"

The inn was so close to Butterfly World, they were the first visitors of the day. Meghan knew that would soon change and wanted to take advantage of her time alone with Ava. As they sat among the flowers and free-flying insects, Meghan felt bold enough to ask a hard question. "The other night, when you talked about grace, what did you mean?"

Ava reached over to gently stroke the tiny pink-and-orange lantana blossoms. "Remember what I shared about my past? Not only did I feel unworthy of love, but I was also buried in shame. I didn't only feel bad for the things I had done. I felt bad just because I was me, for being alive. I believed it was more than simply doing wrong, that somehow I was the mistake. Does that make sense?"

"Maybe" was all Meghan could say. "Maybe a little."

Ava continued. "All my life I longed to be good, to be loved, to be wanted. When the Renicks accepted me, I thought I could finally change enough to prove I was worth loving. But then I took the biggest fall of my life."

Meghan was so engrossed in Ava's story she barely noticed a blue morpho butterfly land on her shoulder. It wasn't frightened away when she whispered, "What happened?"

"When I was seventeen, I got pregnant. I was so scared of losing the Renicks' love or, even worse, of messing up another life, that I had an abortion. I didn't tell anyone for years. I carried that shame on top of the rest and channeled all my energy and focus into trying to be perfect. I desperately tried to earn acceptance from everyone in my life. I tried to hide the truth behind a disguise of hard work and good intentions."

Meghan gazed intently at the cascading waterfall as she tried to absorb Ava's transparency. "You seem to have turned out okay. Is that because you worked so hard to make up for your mistakes?"

"Not at all. See, the problem is, when we strive for perfection, we live out of a false, unattainable identity. My motto for life was 'Do more, give more, serve more, be more.' But that only led to a greater sense of failure when I couldn't measure up. The truth is, we can never do enough, give enough, or serve enough to ever be enough. And that's what grace taught me. That's how grace set me free."

Meghan shook her head. "I'm sorry. I just don't understand."

Ava closed her eyes and placed her hands, palms up, on her lap. She looked as though she might be praying.

"It took me years to understand it myself. And sometimes it's still hard to trust, to believe it for me." As if on cue, the blue butterfly fluttered off Meghan's shoulder and onto Ava's open hand. The gentle movement caused Ava's eyes to open, though she kept her body still.

"It's like this butterfly, I suppose. You know every butterfly begins life as a caterpillar, but did you know the DNA of the caterpillar doesn't change when it becomes a butterfly? It's there all along, just not switched on yet. Being inside the cocoon doesn't make it an entirely different creature. Sure, it looks different on the outside, but it doesn't change at the genetic level. The goal isn't for the caterpillar to become something else. The goal is for the caterpillar to show on the outside what it already is on the inside."

Ava lifted her hand, and the delicate creature took wing.

"That's what happens to us when we become Christians. God created each of us to uniquely reflect portions of His completeness. His goal isn't to make us like someone else; it's to help us fully become who He made us to be. To turn on the eternal DNA of Christ in us. That's our identity in Christ."

Meghan began to understand, then remembered her own transgressions and the door to freedom slammed shut. Ava hadn't known better, but Meghan should have.

"What is it, dear one? What is this battle you're facing? I'll stand with you, if you'll let me."

Before she could stop the words, Meghan blurted, "I'm pregnant." People standing nearby turned their heads, and Ava quietly led Meghan to a back corner. Huddled together on a cold stone bench, Meghan poured out the story and her plan to have an abortion on Tuesday.

Ava's words were few. "I'm going to say one more thing, and then I'll let it go. More than anything else, I wish I had understood that people *make* mistakes, but no one *is* a mistake. No person, born or unborn, was created apart from God's design. Every single human is created as a reflection of who God is. God loves you. God loves Zac. God loves your baby. And He has a plan for each of you. A plan for your good and His glory."

Andi was at Ray and Jenna's, so Meghan biked alone to the docks. Dante and Ava were leaving the island on the six o'clock ferry to begin their trip back to Wisconsin. They were already in line when Meghan walked onto the pier. Ava was wearing the same outfit she'd worn the day they arrived and stood on her toes to scan the crowd. When Meghan waved, Ava pushed her bag into Dante's arms and hurried to meet her.

"I wish we could stay longer, but Dante has to be back to work tomorrow evening. Please stay connected with me—anytime, day or night. Please also think about talking to another adult." She glanced over her shoulder as a ferry horn signaled the call to board the boat. "Maybe Netta and Steve? They care about you very much." She took both Meghan's hands in her own. "There's one more person I hope you'll consider. My brother is the summer cleric at Sainte Anne's. He would love to talk with you. Remember my story? He'll understand."

Meghan nodded but couldn't make a promise.

CHAPTER 12

As Meghan waited for her latte, she stared at the barista's baby bump. The woman's hands cradled and caressed the bulge. Instinctively, Meghan's hand dropped to her own abdomen, but nothing seemed different. Nothing felt alive inside her. Today was the last day she would be pregnant. Outwardly nothing would change. Nothing anyone else could see.

Throughout the day, similar thoughts and reminders created a roller coaster of emotions ranging from utter fear to fragile peace. The clinic had sent a confirmation email that detailed her appointment. She knew she needed to arrive ninety minutes before the procedure. She knew the actual abortion would only take five to ten minutes. She knew she would miss a couple days of work to fully recover. She knew she would forever be included with the one-in-five pregnancies that end with abortion.

But she didn't know an army of prayer warriors was fighting for her and her baby.

That afternoon, Meghan stopped at Butterfly World after work, hoping the gift shop would have a postcard she could send to Ava. Mission accomplished, she stopped at the corner of Huron and Church Streets and waited for bicycle traffic to pass. The buzz of an airplane grew loud. She glanced up and saw the steeple cross looming overhead. Then she remembered Ava's parting words.

The steep steps of Sainte Anne's main entrance led to the back of the sanctuary. Meghan stopped just inside the doorway and looked around. No one else was there, and she was sorry she had come. She spun around but, at that exact moment, a robed man turned the corner. The two nearly collided, and Meghan blurted, "I . . . I . . . I'm not Catholic." Strike one. Embarrassed, she focused her eyes on her shoes. She waited to receive a reprimand for breaking some Catholic rule about Protestants trespassing.

Instead, the man chuckled. "That's okay. Neither was Jesus. He was of Jewish lineage, after all."

Meghan looked up into sparkling blue eyes. "You can't be Ava's brother." Strike two.

"Because I'm white?" The man laughed. "Haven't you heard the saying, 'brotha from anotha motha'?"

He was obviously teasing, though Meghan didn't find it funny. "I'm just going to leave now before I completely strike out." Her mind told her to go, but her feet stayed planted.

The man's kind eyes and disarming smile somehow comforted her. "How about if we start over?" he asked. "My name is Father Joshua, and yes, Ava is my sister. My *adopted* sister."

"Oh!" It all made sense now. "You're Joshua Renick? Sorry. Am I supposed to call you Father even if I'm not Catholic?" Strike three.

"Totally up to you. Ava thinks it's funny to call me 'Father Brother,' but she's called me a lot worse over the years."

"I believe you," Meghan said. "She's one of a kind. Oh, I'm Meghan, by the way."

Father Joshua extended a hand. "It's nice to meet you, Meghan. Since you're not Catholic, how about I show you around Sainte Anne's?"

For the next fifteen minutes, Father Joshua led a brief tour of the sanctuary, pointing out unfamiliar objects and explaining their purpose in the Catholic faith. As they stood in front of the roped-off altar, Meghan motioned to the mural on the ceiling. "What does that painting signify?"

Father Joshua followed her gaze. "The mural was painted during a renovation in the nineties—the 1990s. Considering the original structure was built in 1873, the mural is a modern addition. The woman standing is Sainte Anne. She is holding Baby Jesus, and Mary is kneeling beside them."

Meghan pushed away the strange feeling the sight of the smiling infant triggered inside her. "I love that color blue," she said. "Combined with all the white in here, it's stunning."

"If you look closely," Father Joshua continued, "you'll see a distant view of the island behind them."

Meghan could pick it out if she squinted. "So that's the Sainte Anne of Sainte Anne's Church?"

"Lucky guess," Father Joshua teased. "Yes, the one and only. According to Catholic belief, Sainte Anne was Mary's mother. Jesus' grandmother. She is also the patron saint of mothers and pregnant women . . ."

Meghan's heartbeat pulsed heavy in her ears, and she didn't hear what Father Joshua said next. The room closed in as the light faded. Her legs wobbled, and she reached out for something to hold.

Jolted by the grasp on his arm, Father Joshua steadied Meghan and led her to a pew. He didn't ask any questions but sat down in the row behind her. "Do you want to talk about it? I've been told I'm a good listener."

Ava's words at the dock now echoed in the sanctuary of the church. *Remember my story? He'll understand.* Meghan stood at a crossroads. The choice was hers—she could open up in trust or run away in shame.

CHAPTER 13

Meghan moved from her window seat to Andi's cubby near the ferry's exit door. There were very few passengers on Tuesday's first departure from the island to St. Ignace. "Are you okay?"

Andi continued to stare at her phone. It was her usual distraction from the reality of being trapped inside, as she put it, "a floating metal can," but today, Meghan couldn't get her to look up at all.

"No." Another one-syllable contribution to the trickle of words she'd spoken this morning.

They picked up the car, then Meghan tried again as she paid the toll and drove onto the Mackinac Bridge. "Are you mad at me?"

"No."

The silence remained when they traded places in Mackinaw City and began the quietest three hours in the history of their friendship.

A repeating string of thoughts wove through Meghan's mind as she watched the mile markers pass by out her window. *This is the end . . . Erase the mistakes . . . No one will ever know . . . Start over.* The knot in her chest wound tighter as competing voices entered the loop.

She closed her eyes and tried to silence the internal struggle. *Erase the mistakes . . . People make mistakes . . . But no one is a mistake . . . No one will ever know . . . For I know the plans I have for you, says the Lord. Plans to give you and your baby a future and a hope . . . My baby? . . . A future? . . . A hope? . . . Start over . . . The old is gone, the new has come.*

The voices finally faded as she dozed off. The last words she heard were *start over*. She planned to. Soon it would all be over.

"Meghan, wake up. We're almost there."

Meghan stretched and rubbed her eyes. As she blinked away the blur, she saw clusters of people and a jagged row of signs. Closer to the clinic, the words became clear. Some proclaimed guilt. *Murderers go to Hell; Repent before its to late; Death Factory Ahead.* Some begged for mercy. *We Will Adopt Your Baby; God Loves You and Your Baby; There Is Another Choice.*

Overwhelmed, Meghan squeezed her eyes shut and covered her ears. "My judge and jury, and they can't even spell," she muttered. "Drive faster, Andi. Hurry."

Andi turned into the walled entrance, and the security gate closed behind them. A steel blockade ensured there was no turning back. Gently, she tapped Meghan on the shoulder. "We're here. Are you sure this is what you want to do?"

Through the open window, Meghan signaled to someone, then turned her back on her friend.

"No, Andi. This isn't what I *want* to do. It's what I *have* to do."

With that, she jumped out of the car and ducked beneath a big black umbrella.

Andi watched Meghan till she was out of sight. Numb, she didn't know what to do next. Was she supposed to go in? Wait in the parking lot? The more she thought about it, the angrier she became. When the frustration reached a tipping point, she slammed her fist on the steering wheel and shouted, "FINE! If all I'm good for is a ride, then figure it out yourself!" She revved the engine, shifted into Reverse, and spun the car around toward the exit. The security gate shuddered and began to open slowly. Funny how it had seemed to slam shut behind them when she drove in. She waited only long enough for there to be room to squeeze through. Then, with no thought of oncoming traffic, she pulled into the street and drove back the way she had just come. Angry tears blurred her vision as she yelled out to God.

"Why didn't You stop this? Why didn't You stop me? Why didn't You stop her? Is this what You want?"

From somewhere deep inside, a quiet voice whispered, *Go back. I am making all things new.*

"Go back? No way am I going back there! What for?"

Go back. Your ways are not My ways.

"There's no point. I tried the love-the-sinner thing, and it didn't work."

Andi, go back. I am grace and truth. Trust Me.

Too exhausted to argue, Andi surrendered. "Fine! I'll go back. But this time Meghan is going to hear exactly what I think."

She made a U-turn at the next traffic light and retraced the path back to the clinic. "Same dumb signs. Same pointless protesters. What good are they doing?"

She slowed in front of the clinic and locked eyes with a brown-haired woman. Instead of turning into the parking lot, Andi drove to the next block and parked along the side street. As she walked to the clinic's front gate, the brown-haired woman moved toward her. Close behind, an older man matched her hurried pace. Andi decided to let them speak first.

The woman extended her hand. "Hi. My name is Laura, and this is my friend, Tony. May we ask your name?"

Skeptical, Andi hesitated, but something soft and pleading in the man's eyes comforted her. "Andrea."

"It's a pleasure to meet you, Andrea. I noticed you brought someone here today. A friend?"

"Yes . . ." They seemed nice enough, but then again Andi had heard horror stories about these people, these protesters.

"Would it be okay if we prayed for your friend?" Tony spoke this time.

This was not at all what Andi expected. A lecture, yes. Condemnation for her role, yes. Prayer, no. Still uncertain but willing to take a chance, Andi nodded in agreement.

As the warmth of Laura's gentle grip encircled Andi's hands, she realized her own fingers were icy cold. Yet she stood outside an abortion clinic with two complete strangers and felt nothing but love as Tony prayed.

"Father God, we humbly come before You on behalf of Andrea, her friend, and her friend's baby. We believe every child is a gift and every life matters. We believe You are the One knitting that little baby together in its mother's womb. That little baby is being fearfully and wonderfully made and is not hidden from You. Your eyes see its unformed body and every day of its life is known from first to last. We believe You are at work right now. We believe that, even at this moment, You are reaching out to Andrea's friend. Please help her hear Your voice; help her trust Your promise to give her a future and a hope. Help her hear You asking her to choose life today. In the name of the Father, the Son, and the Holy Spirit."

Andi almost said "Amen," but Laura began to pray. "Jesus, though we long for this baby to be carried to term, we know that's not always how the story ends. If this baby will soon be with You, we thank You for welcoming him or her home. We thank You for Your redeeming love that will reach out to Andrea's friend in the days and weeks to come. Help her realize no one is ever too far gone to be disqualified from grace. And, Lord, I pray for Andrea too. Help her carry the burden of this day and help—"

Someone called her name. Andi opened her eyes.

Meghan!

"ANDI! WHERE ARE YOU? DON'T LEAVE ME HERE!"

"That's Meghan!" Andi cried. "Help me find her!"

The trio ran for the front gate as Andi called out, "I'm here, Meghan! Come to the gate!"

Tony reached it first. Andi and Laura breathlessly arrived a few seconds after.

"Let her out!" Andi yelled to the guard.

The guard held up his hand. "Please calm down. Just hold on while I call someone."

Andi joined Tony at the window of the gatehouse. "Excuse me, sir." Though winded, he spoke with gentle authority. "You cannot keep that young woman here if she is asking to leave."

The commotion attracted attention, and a crowd quickly swarmed. Tony stepped over to the group and spoke with a few who came forward. The entire mass of people backed away, gathered into small groups, and began to pray quietly. Mingled with the murmurs of their voices were Meghan's sobs and Laura's gentle voice responding to her. Andi joined them at the fence. Meghan stood inside and Laura outside, their hands clasped together through the iron bars.

Andi took her first good look at Meghan and tried to hide her shock. Meghan's leggings were on inside out, her sweatshirt askew. She was barefoot, and her beautiful auburn hair fell limp on her shoulders. In that moment, Andi felt nothing but compassion for her friend. She focused her eyes on the cement-block building behind the fence. What had happened in there?

A woman dressed in a dark-gray business suit walked from the guardhouse to where Meghan stood, still holding Laura's hands.

Ignoring everyone along the perimeter, she tried to squeeze in front of Meghan. Her bright-yellow chiffon scarf fluttered through the fence like a tethered canary trying to free itself from a cage.

"Meghan, it's perfectly normal to feel scared. Never mind what these people are doing out here. They confused you for a moment, but it's okay now. Let's go back inside and talk."

Meghan didn't move.

The woman tried to turn Meghan away from the fence and shot Laura an icy glare. "Let go of her, Laura. Back away, or I will call the police."

Undeterred by the threat, Laura calmly replied, "Good idea, Pamela. In fact, I'll make the call myself." Laura pulled her phone from her cross-body bag. "Meghan has asked to leave, and the police will be interested to know you're keeping her here against her will."

Instead of arguing, Pamela gave Meghan's shoulders a shake. "Don't bother asking for a refund."

Meghan turned and ran toward the gate.

The guard held the door open for her. His eyes glistened with tears as he whispered, "Run, girl. Run away and never look back."

Andi heard him as Meghan ran straight into her arms.

CHAPTER 14

Under a nearby tree, Meghan clung to Laura as Tony walked Andi back to her car and rode with her to the corner.

"Here's some information." He held out a colorful gift bag, which seemed out of place after such a dark ordeal. "Today Meghan chose life, but that doesn't mean this is over. We can't tell a woman not to have an abortion and then abandon her. She will need a lot of support, and there are many ways she can find help. Starting right now."

"What do you mean, now?" Andi asked.

"In the bag, you'll information about Safe Haven Pregnancy Support Center. Please encourage Meghan to contact them. Or just stop in. Sooner is better than later."

"That would be great." Andi peeked in the bag and saw tissues, lotion, and a small water bottle tucked among some papers. "We have to get back to Mackinac tonight. Do you think they could see her today?"

Tony got out of the car and walked around to the open window on the driver's side. "I'll make a call. But first, you should get Meghan away from here."

Meghan collapsed into her seat. As soon as the seatbelt clicked, Andi drove away from the clinic. At Laura's invitation, they pulled into a nearby church parking lot and waited. Andi hadn't said a word, and neither had Meghan.

Soon Laura arrived with wrapped sandwiches, small bags of chips, and bottles of iced tea. She led them into a small room connected to the entrance foyer.

Andi immediately noticed the lighthouse décor. Over the fireplace, a big wooden sign read, *Hope is our anchor.*

"Look at that, Megs. Remind you of anything?"

Meghan's puffy, red eyes opened wide. "Ava," she replied softly. "I need to talk to Ava."

Laura unwrapped the sandwiches and set out plates and napkins. "You both look exhausted. Are you sure you couldn't stay in town tonight?"

Without a thought, Andi responded for both of them. "It's definitely worth considering."

As they ate, Laura talked about Safe Haven and the help they could provide. As if on cue, a text pinged Laura's phone, and she glanced down. "Tony says we can head over as soon as we're done here."

Andi considered Meghan's current detachment, and a protective instinct kicked in. "What do you think, Meghan? We don't want to push you into something you're not ready for."

Meghan shrugged.

Laura pulled back. "I know it's a lot to think about, Meghan. You've already done one heroic thing today. You are very brave, and I am so proud of you."

Meghan set her sandwich down and covered her face with her hands. Andi dropped to her knees beside her on the right, and Laura did the same on the left.

Laura spoke first. "Meghan, I need to apologize. We haven't

asked you what you need or want. Everything happened so fast that we never considered the trauma you've just experienced. Maybe before making any more decisions, you need to process that."

Andi handed her friend a napkin. "Do you want to talk about it?"

Meghan remained quiet, so Andi didn't push her to share. When Laura excused herself to take a phone call, Andi returned to her seat. "It's okay if you don't want to talk about it. I just want you to know I am really proud of you for what you did today."

Meghan looked defeated but raised her eyes and studied the picture over the fireplace. "What exactly did Ava say about an anchor?"

"Was it 'I anchored my soul to grace'?" Andi joined her friend's gaze at the picture. "What are you thinking, Megs?"

"I'm thinking I almost made the biggest mistake of my life. I'm so ashamed of myself." She began to cry again. "Look what I've put you through. What I almost did to an innocent baby." She cried so hard her shoulders shook. Her words were incoherent.

Andi didn't ask for clarification. There would be time for that later.

Laura returned. "What do you need, girls? How can I help?"

Andi thought Meghan had made enough life-changing decisions for one day. "Laura, we appreciate everything, but I think we need to head back to Mackinac for now." She turned to Meghan. "Any objections to that?"

Meghan shook her head.

"I think that's best," Laura agreed. "Meghan, would it be okay if you and I spent a few minutes together before you leave?"

Meghan nodded, and the two walked out the door.

Andi sat down in a rocking chair and rested her head on the high wooden back. Eyes closed, she tried to pray, but no words came. The day caught up with her, and she felt exhausted. Just as she drifted into sleep, the door opened.

A man entered, half-hidden behind a large box. He was singing an unfamiliar melody. "I was lost, hope was gone when His love . . ." He slid the container onto a table and jumped when he saw Andi.

"Oh, hello there. You startled me." He had an easy smile, with a hint of embarrassment coloring his cheeks. "I apologize. I didn't know this room was still in use."

"No problem," Andi assured him. "I'm just waiting for my friend."

"I assume your friend is with Laura?" He moved around the table for a handshake. "My name is Pastor Nate. Praise God for the miracle today."

"I guess it really was a miracle," Andi observed. "Everything happened so fast I don't think it's really sunk in yet."

"You did a brave thing today too. I imagine it wasn't easy, bringing your friend to the clinic."

His words sent a ripple of guilt through Andi. "Could I ask you something?"

He nodded.

"Did I do the wrong thing? I mean, was it wrong of me to drive Meghan to the clinic? If she had gone through with it, would it be my fault?"

Pastor Nate didn't immediately answer. He exhaled loudly and sat down across from Andi. "Those are complicated questions, and I don't have simple answers. I suppose some people would say that driving her there was wrong. Was it? I don't know. But here's what I do know: Your friend planned to have an abortion today but didn't. Maybe if anyone *but* you had taken her, she would have gone through with it. You didn't drive her because you agreed with her. You drove her because you disagreed and loved her the best way you knew how. That's the way God loves us. He doesn't condone our sin or act in ways that cause our sin, but He's always right there waiting for us to turn back to Him. Maybe God used you to help save that baby."

Andi was without words. Could it be true? Had God used her to save Meghan's baby? Maybe He really could work all things together for the good, just like her dad said.

Meghan returned to the room. "I'm ready when you are," she said, her voice quiet.

Andi introduced Meghan to Pastor Nate, then followed her to the parking lot. Laura waited, holding the car door open. As Meghan climbed into the passenger seat, Andi noticed her feet.

"Hey, you're wearing shoes again."

Meghan and Laura exchanged smiles before all three looked down at Laura's bare feet. It felt good to laugh.

"If you feel too tired to drive, please stop somewhere. I am going to worry about you driving so far."

"We'll be okay, and we'll let you know as soon as we get home," Andi said.

Meghan was asleep well before they passed Cedar Springs. Andi knew she needed to rest. It had been the longest day of their lives, but they were *all* going back to Mackinac. That was more than enough. Tomorrow would be a new day, full of new challenges. If God got Meghan this far, Andi believed He would carry her the rest of the way.

CHAPTER 15

The blurred numbers on the clock came into focus—11:37 a.m. Meghan sat up and swung her legs out of her safe cocoon. As the room came into focus, a pile of rumpled clothes on the floor jolted her awake. A flashback of memories exploded, and Meghan needed to get away. Away from the walls. Away from those clothes. Away from the reminders. She dressed quickly, hiding disheveled hair under a hat and dark circles behind sunglasses.

Two blocks from home, she realized she should have checked the forecast. Or at least grabbed her raincoat. Cold. Cloudy. Stormy. The weather outside matched how she felt inside. With no destination in mind, Meghan simply walked.

The good thing about rainy days on Mackinac was a lighter crowd. The bad thing about rainy days on Mackinac was knowing that the mud-looking-puddles weren't from dirt. Usually this bothered Meghan, but today it didn't. She had bigger things to worry about than splashes of watered-down horse manure. She was still pregnant. She would be having a baby in February.

Huron Road curved past the fort and wound around the east bluff. The path to Anne's Tablet branched off the intersection.

Farther along the road, stairs led down the hill behind the inn. And, straight ahead in her field of view, rising behind the hedge of pink wild roses, stood a simple cross on a familiar steeple. Meghan locked her gaze on it and listened. What words would it speak today? Meghan braced herself, prepared to hear the words of condemnation she deserved.

The rain fell harder as she waited. And waited. Her hair was wet. Her shoes were soaked. No words came. Almost disappointed, she dared to pray. *God? Are You so angry You won't speak to me at all?* Still nothing. Maybe she deserved God's silence. Maybe He was that disgusted with her. Maybe He'd turned His back on her.

Fine. She knew how to live life alone. She'd taken care of herself before, and she could do it again. She would take responsibility, figure out the right thing to do, and make a plan. Maybe then God would see how hard she was willing to work to earn His forgiveness. Starting now.

By the time Meghan circled back to the apartment, the rain had stopped, and the sun was out. Warmed by dry clothes and a cup of coffee, she began phase 1 of her plan. Despite techie life hacks, Meghan still preferred an old-fashioned, handwritten, to-do list. She opened an empty journal to page 2—just in case inquiring minds forgot that journals are supposed to be private.

> Apologize to Andi
> Talk to Netta and Steve
> Call Ava
> ~~Call Zac Call Dad Call Mom~~ (move to Phase 2)
> Text Laura
> Talk to Father Joshua
> Schedule dr. appointment
> Email admissions counselor

Reenergized, she decided to make a nice dinner for Andi. She needed to mend the rupture in their friendship. She grabbed a pair of scissors and hopped on her bike. A huge patch of wild sweet peas grew near Mission Point. Hopefully, the vines were still bursting with fragrant red flowers.

Since it was the afternoon lull before new arrivals, Meghan stopped at the Marquette Inn. She wanted to let Steve know she could come back earlier than planned.

Today, Netta occupied her chair behind the front desk. "Meghan! What a delightful surprise."

"Hi. I stopped by to let Steve know I could come back to work tomorrow."

"I'll let him know. He went to the mainland with Andi."

Another shard of condemnation stabbed Meghan's heart. She had been so exhausted that, until that moment, she hadn't remembered they'd parked in Mackinaw City last night. Now Steve and Andi had to take personal time to move the car back to St. Ignace. It was her responsibility to get Andi's car back across the bridge. She shook her head. She would make amends later. Right now she needed to focus on the task at hand.

"That's fine. He can text me later." Meghan scanned the room to confirm she and Netta were alone. "Actually, would you and Steve be available to talk tonight? Maybe around seven?"

"Sure. Come on over."

"Thank you. I think I'll grab a treat and be on my way."

Meghan hurried to the atrium, grabbed a mini berry scone, and ducked out the side door before she could change her mind.

Next, Meghan walked her bike across the street to Sainte Anne's. Father Joshua wasn't in the sanctuary, so she wandered downstairs to the museum. Before she reached the entrance, she heard voices approaching and ducked into the tiny gift shop. As she pretended to study a display of prayer cards, one seemed to jump out at her: "Prayer for the Vulnerable Unborn." Without thinking Meghan stuck the card in her pocket and walked out of the gift shop. She made no eye contact with the elderly woman standing open mouthed at the register.

A small group of people now gathered at the nearest stairway exit. Meghan recognized the man in black who blocked her escape, relieved his back was to her. Not wanting to be seen, she spun around to face the exit at the other end of the hallway. Just then, a frantic voice called out.

"Father! Come quick!"

Meghan panicked and slipped through an open doorway. Now cloaked in complete darkness behind a solid wooden door, her heart pounded as she heard footsteps and voices on the other side of the wall.

"Oh, Father, we've been robbed! I think you can catch her if you hurry."

"Catch whom and for what?"

"A thief, probably from Chicago. She had curly, reddish hair and a green shirt. That little hooligan stole a prayer card right out from under my nose. Can you believe it? She stole from God!"

Meghan reached back to the card in her pocket.

Father Joshua spoke with a hint of playfulness. "I appreciate your diligence, Irene. I think we'll be okay if one twenty-five-cent card is unaccounted for. Maybe God thought she needed it more than we needed her quarter."

"But, Father, she broke a commandment *and* sullied my inventory."

Meghan heard the jingle of metal, then Father Joshua's voice again. "Her debt has been paid. Let it go, Irene."

Meghan waited until the retreating footsteps faded, then rushed up the stairs, out the side door, and around to the bike rack.

"Meghan, wait up," a familiar voice called.

There was nowhere to run. "Hey, Father Joshua. How's it going?"

"Well, according to Irene, we were just robbed."

Meghan hung her head. "Sorry. I don't know what possessed me to do that." She held the card out to him. "Are you going to press charges?"

"Keep it." Father Joshua pushed her hand away. "But may I ask why you wanted it?"

"Are you sure you really want to know?"

"I'm sure. Want to go back inside and talk?"

"Can we make an appointment for tomorrow?" Meghan asked. "Right now I need to be somewhere else."

After she had cut enough stems to fill her vase, Meghan texted Andi.

> First of all, I want to tell you how sorry I am. About everything. If you don't want to talk to me yet, I understand. I put you through more than any friend should endure. I was inconsiderate of your feelings and never once stopped to think about the way I was hurting you. If you decide you want to talk, please text me. I would love to make your favorite dinner tonight and have a heart-to-heart with my best friend.

Andi's reply bounced back immediately.

> TACO BAKE??

"So when are you telling Zac?"

"Soon."

Andi and Meghan secured their bikes to the metal rack at the Marquette Inn. At the same time, Father Joshua exited the side door of Sainte Anne's. "Hey, Father Joshua!" they called in unison.

He returned their greeting with a wave and waited as they crossed the street. "What are you two up to tonight?"

"We're going up to visit Steve and Netta." Andi answered.

"If you're not busy, could you please join us?" Meghan asked. She was certain the Schmidts wouldn't mind an uninvited guest.

Father Joshua didn't hesitate. "Why, I do believe I will crash your party. Is Netta serving treats?"

"Chances are very good." Andi laughed.

They crossed back to the inn and climbed the tall exterior stairway to Steve and Netta's private quarters.

Steve answered after Father Joshua rang the bell. "C'mon in and make yourselves at home. I've been instructed to keep everyone out of the kitchen." With a twinkle in his eyes, he added, "Netta is experimenting with a new recipe and needs her personal space."

"I heard that!" Netta called from the kitchen. "Be careful, or you won't be included in my focus group."

"I'll take his sample too," Father Joshua called back.

They seated themselves on a mismatched assortment of well-cushioned chairs arranged around a circular antique coffee table that Netta had prepared with fresh flowers, candles, and coordinating tableware. Steve poured ice water and lemonade from cut-glass pitchers as Netta entered, carrying a wooden serving tray.

"I'm at your service and ready to do my part," Father Joshua announced. "What are we sampling tonight?"

Netta named each item. "Strawberry shortcake kabobs. Nectarine and brie tartlets. Mini Greek yogurt parfaits."

After everyone was served, the room grew quiet. Meghan took a breath. It was time. "Thank you for meeting with me tonight. You've all been very patient and supportive. What I have to say is hard, so I'm just going to say it."

She made eye contact with everyone in the room. Then she closed her eyes, exhaled deeply, and quietly confessed, "I'm ten weeks pregnant."

When she opened her eyes, everyone was staring at her. Steve's hand was frozen in place even as it held a kabob partway inside his open mouth. Netta's eyes opened wide as she sank onto an ottoman. Father Joshua looked calm but sad. And Andi, sweet Andi, came to the rescue.

"Please say something. Tell her you aren't mad at her. Because she could've had an abortion. I mean, she almost had an abortion. But she didn't. But I thought she was going to. You should have seen her. We were there. And then I left and then she was calling my name . . . and . . . then Laura and Tony came . . . and the security guard wouldn't open the gate . . . and . . ."

Netta held up her hand. "Whoa, Andi. Slow down. Take a breath." Then to Meghan, she said, "Of course we aren't mad at you, dear. We're just surprised."

Steve still hadn't said a word, but at least Andi's monologue gave him time to finish chewing.

Meghan was most afraid to hear Father Joshua's response. Timidly she looked his way, ready for whatever he had to say. "I'm sorry, Father Joshua. You must think I'm a terrible person. First to get pregnant and then almost have an abortion."

Before he could reply, Netta observed, "You don't look surprised."

He smiled at Meghan and shook his head. "I knew. I've known since the day we met."

Now it was Meghan's turn to be surprised. "How? How could you have known?"

"When you're in my line of work, you learn to see things people think they are hiding."

"Why didn't you say something?"

"Oh, I wanted to. And I almost did. But I didn't feel my words were being led by God. So instead I prayed. A lot."

"Did Ava tell you?"

"No, not outright. She wouldn't betray your confidence. But I know my sister, and I did pick up on a few crumbs she may have dropped."

Steve finally spoke. "I'm completely lost. How about if you start at the beginning?"

So Meghan did. Andi added the missing pieces, and by the end of the evening, everyone in the room had the complete picture.

"What's next, Meghan?" Netta asked.

Meghan almost laughed. "Only figuring out the rest of my life. One step at a time, I suppose. I guess my first step is figuring out what to do about school."

CHAPTER 16

Week 12

Rushed for time, Meghan composed an email before she left for work.

> *Dear Professor Hamilton,*
>
> *My name is Meghan McPherson. We met when I visited campus in April. I am enrolled to begin classes this fall, and you have been assigned as my advisor. I am writing today to let you know I am pregnant. My baby is due early February, so I will be able to complete the first semester as planned but may need to rethink the spring semester. I was hoping you could help me plan my classes and discuss options. Please let me know when you are available to talk. Thank you.*
>
> *Sincerely,*
>
> *Meghan McPherson*

She hit the Send button and crossed one more item off the to-do list. She was confident her fall classes would go well. Even if she missed the spring semester, she could take summer classes to catch up. She didn't give it another thought until a reply arrived a few days later.

> *Miss McPherson,*
>
> *The committee has reached a recommendation. Please call the admissions office to schedule an appointment. We will do our best to reach an agreement beneficial to both parties.*
>
> *Dr. E. Hamilton*
> *Professor of History, Department Chair*
> *Michigan Christian University*

Meghan was confused by the formality. Why did a committee need to meet? She dialed the office and scheduled an appointment, then texted Andi. In order to make the most of her time off the island, she decided to stay overnight in Traverse City and finish her to-do list.

Meghan wanted to make a good impression, so she arrived at the university fifteen minutes early. The receptionist was polite but not friendly. Meghan sat near a window and looked through a course catalog. Each time she glanced up, the receptionist looked away.

Thirty minutes later, an office door opened and an unfamiliar woman called out, "Miss McPherson?"

Again, so formal. Since when? Every other interaction had been casual and easygoing.

Meghan set the catalog down and hurried into the office. She took the only open seat at the glass-topped workstation. Awkward silence hung in the room. Meghan smiled but the effort was not reciprocated. Someone had to break the ice. "Thank you for meeting with me, Ms. . . ."

"Perkins. *Mrs.* Vivian Perkins."

Did she just emphasize the "Mrs."?

"Thank you for meeting with me, Mrs. Perkins."

"Let's get right down to business, shall we?"

Meghan guessed this wasn't going to go well.

Mrs. Vivian Perkins glanced at her computer screen and continued. "You have put the university in a rather awkward situation, Miss McPherson. Legally, we cannot bar you from attending here based on your"—she paused and raised her eyebrows at Meghan—"condition. But we would like to propose alternatives."

Alternatives? The words came as a shock. Meghan was prepared to be stared at or gossiped about but had never considered the university wouldn't want her on campus.

"What are you suggesting?"

"The committee has three proposals for you to consider. First, a full refund and penalty-free withdrawal of enrollment. Second, continuation with classes, but housing off campus. Third, switch to online classes, also off campus. Of course, a penalty-free adjustment would be made to your student account."

"Off campus?" Meghan interrupted. "Where would I live?"

Mrs. Vivian Perkins wasn't finished quite yet.

"And should you decide to choose the first option, the university is prepared to offer you a generous scholarship of two thousand dollars to be used at another institution of higher learning."

As the words sank in, Meghan couldn't believe what she was hearing. *Did she just try to bribe me to go somewhere else?*

"But the baby isn't due until February. Why can't I live in the dorm and attend classes for the fall semester?"

"As I said, *legally* we cannot deny you that option. We cannot discriminate based on your condition. But we do ask you to consider the ramifications for the university. Your predicament is a blatant violation of the student handbook."

Meghan read between the lines. *They don't want me to be associ-*

ated with them. I would be an embarrassment. A spotted sheep. No, a wolf among the sheep.

Mrs. Perkins didn't elaborate. "You have until Monday to decide."

"Monday? That's only three days, and this is a big decision. I was planning to live on campus. Where am I supposed to go? Plus, I might not be able to enroll for classes somewhere else. This changes everything."

Mrs. Perkins's icy stare bored directly into Meghan's soul. "What do you expect when you don't do things God's way?" She motioned toward the door. "We'll need to hear from you by end of business Monday. Good day, Miss McPherson."

Meghan walked robotically out the door, past the receptionist, and down the steps. As she stepped outside, the intensity of her reality felt hotter than July's heat index. She moved toward a shaded bench under a huge maple tree. How could she have been so naïve? Of course she shouldn't attend here. Imagine. An unmarried, pregnant girl walking the straight-and-narrow path of a Christian college? Like the proverbial woman at the well, she didn't belong.

What am I supposed to do? There's no plan B.

Just then she heard her name.

"Meghan? What are you doing here?"

It took a moment to place the man walking toward her. "Hi, Pastor Nate. I had a meeting. What are you doing here?"

"I teach a summer class and I'm heading to the library to do some research." He studied her, then asked, "Is everything okay?"

How am I supposed to answer that? "Let's just say I need to figure some things out very soon."

"Want to walk with me to the library?"

As they sat in an air-conditioned study room, Meghan recounted the meeting.

Pastor Nate couldn't hide his frustration. "When are we going to learn we are not called to play the Holy Spirit? When are we going to stop shaming one another? Throwing stones? We are called to speak the truth in love. We are called to point people to Jesus."

Meghan stared in disbelief. She had never heard a pastor criticize other Christians. "In all fairness, I deserved it. I am the one who broke the rules, not them."

"That may be true, Meghan, but let them without sin cast the first stone."

"Is that in the Bible?"

"Yes. The very words of Jesus. He came upon a group who wanted to stone a woman caught in adultery. He knew it was wrong. She knew it was wrong. They knew it was wrong. And stoning was the legal punishment of the day. They would have technically been keeping the law. But Jesus didn't demand justice according to the law. He called for mercy. He asked them to look at themselves before condemning someone else."

"What did they do?"

"Jesus told them to go ahead with it. He instructed anyone without sin to throw the first stone."

"They killed her?"

"No. They walked away. Jesus exposed the fact that none of them were innocent. Furthermore, Jesus didn't condemn her either. Instead, he told her, 'Go and sin no more.'"

"What does that even mean?"

Pastor Nate paged through his Bible. "It means Jesus takes sin seriously but offers mercy and forgiveness instead of punishment. He didn't say, 'I've got you covered. Go and continue to sin.' He also didn't say, 'Go and live a perfect life.'" Pastor Nate turned his Bible around and pointed at words printed in red. "Look right here in John eight, verse eleven. Jesus instructed her to turn from her sin and move forward free of condemnation for her past. His very words? 'Neither do I condemn you. Go now and leave your life of sin.'"

"But, Pastor Nate, how can I do that? I can't turn from my sin because I literally carry the effects of it."

"Meghan, contrary to the message you may receive, a baby is not an 'effect' of sin. Every baby is a gift, a miracle. Every baby is a precious human being created in the image of God. Your baby isn't an accident. No matter what the circumstances, God has a plan and purpose for your baby."

Meghan's thick layer of shame cracked. *My baby is not a sin. My baby is not a mistake.* Just then her phone beeped. It was time to meet Laura. "Thanks, Pastor Nate. You've given me some things to think about."

The words were still on her mind as she drove away from campus. *A baby is not an 'effect' of sin. A baby is a miracle.* Meghan parked her car behind Safe Haven Pregnancy Support Center and massaged her throbbing temples. The day had become more stressful than anticipated. Maybe she should have rescheduled. Her eyes caught movement in the side view mirror as a black minivan pulled up beside her. Too late to change her mind now.

Laura stepped over to Meghan's car and opened the door. "Are you feeling okay? You look tired."

"I am tired. It's already been a long day." Meghan pocketed the keys and followed Laura through a side entrance. "Hopefully, this appointment goes better than my last one."

The name on the office door read *Elaina Kent.* Meghan felt at ease the moment the door opened. Elaina was kind, friendly, and didn't exhibit an ounce of shock or shame as Meghan shared her story.

Instead, she beamed with joy. "You're my hero. You did a very brave thing."

"I sure don't feel brave," Meghan replied. "A firefighter isn't a hero if he's the one who started the fire."

"Meghan, a hero is someone who gives up their interests for another. This is especially true when the someone else is a baby."

Meghan wasn't convinced, but she wanted to believe.

Elaina gave Laura and Meghan a tour of the facility. There were programs to help with healthcare, housing, food and nutrition, diapers and baby supplies, and even daycare. Meghan had no idea such assistance existed. Maybe she could do this after all. Maybe, with help, she could go to school and raise a baby. But first she needed to have some difficult conversations.

Equipped with a new sense of hope, Meghan said goodbye to Elaina and Laura and began the journey home. Home to Traverse City.

CHAPTER 17

Meghan parked curbside in front of a familiar two-story home. Twin lilac trees stood tall under the upper corner window. One for Andi. One for her. She couldn't remember which was whose anymore. They were so young the day they'd transplanted the tender shoots under Andi's bedroom window.

Meghan was always welcome at the Thomsons', no questions asked. She rapped lightly, then pushed the door open and stepped into the entryway. Andi's mom was coming out of the bedroom with a load in her arms.

"Hey, Mrs. T. Mind if I crash in Andi's room for the night?"

Mrs. Thomson dropped the overflowing laundry basket and embraced Meghan. "You know we always enjoy your company. But now that you're officially an adult, please call me Suzanne."

Meghan laughed. "That might take some getting used to. I've called you Mr. and Mrs. Thomson forever."

"And call me Matt." Mr. Thomson joined them in the entryway and pointed to Meghan's backpack. "You packed light. Short visit?"

"Just one night." Meghan looked to Suzanne. "Do you guys have time to talk?"

Suzanne looked at her husband, then back to Meghan. "I'm sure we do. The kids won't be home until dinnertime."

Around a small table in the breakfast nook, Meghan cradled her head in her hands and poured out the whole story. The breakup with Zac, the pregnancy tests, the scheduled abortion, the news from the university, the reason she came home today.

"I am so sorry I disappointed you." Silence. "I know you must be so ashamed of me." Silence. "If you don't want me around anymore, I understand." Silence. *Say something!* Andi's father cleared his throat. Meghan timidly raised her head.

The couple sat close together as tears streamed down their faces.

Finally, Matt spoke. "Oh, Meghan, we are not disappointed in you. We are proud of you. Thank you for not having the abortion. Thank you for giving your baby the gift of life."

Stunned, Meghan waited for more. A wagging finger, a frown, a condemning lecture. Something. These were good, godly people. Matt was a pastor. The closest thing to being "her pastor" she had ever known. More than that, he was a second dad to her. In some ways, more like a father than her own.

"'Thank you?' That's it? Aren't you going to tell me what I did was wrong? Get mad at me or something?"

Suzanne reached across the table and cradled both Meghan's hands in her own. A mother's hands, strong yet soft. Manicured nails painted pink.

When was the last time my mom held my hands? Surprised by the thought, Meghan pulled away and tucked her hands under the table.

"Meghan, please look at me. There is something important I need you to understand."

Meghan had never felt so exposed. So vulnerable. Here, with them, she'd always felt safe. Accepted. Before now. Now she wanted to run but chose to stay. Chose to trust.

"Meghan," Suzanne repeated. "You don't need us to tell you

what you already know. Deep inside, we all know where we have fallen. I know when I sin against God. So does Matt. That's the work of God's Spirit alive in us. If we didn't see it, we couldn't ask Him to forgive it." Fresh tears fell, and Matt stepped in.

"The Bible promises God will forgive our sins and never hold them against us. Jesus died to take the punishment for our sins so we don't have to be separated from God. When we trust the work of the cross, our debt is paid in full, and God sees us through the righteousness of His Son."

Suzanne continued. "Meghan, do you believe Jesus is God's Son?"

"Yes, of course."

"Do you believe He came to earth as a baby, lived a perfect life, died on the cross, and is the risen Savior of the world?"

"Yes, of course."

"Do you believe He died for me?"

Meghan nodded her head.

"For Matt? Andi?"

Meghan nodded again.

"Do you believed He died for you?"

Her head dropped. *I don't deserve to be forgiven. I don't have an excuse. I knew better. I knew. And here I am anyway. I deserve to be punished. Not Jesus. Not my baby. Not even Zac.* Too embarrassed to speak this truth, Meghan told them what she thought they wanted to hear. "Sure. Jesus died for the whole world, so I guess that includes me."

The timer on the stove chimed, and Matt got up. "Andi told us about a girl on the island who was pregnant. We didn't know it was you, but we've been praying. Praying for you. And we rejoiced when she told us the baby wasn't aborted. We rejoiced for you. For your baby."

The front door opened, and the entry filled with loud voices. The rest would have to wait for another time.

Suzanne quickly closed the conversation. "Thank you for trusting us. We're always here for you." With that, she called, "Everyone, wash up! Dinner will be ready in ten minutes."

After the meal, Meghan excused herself. "I have some visits to make." By the time she made the quick drive to Zac's, she had a text from Suzanne:

We love you and are praying for you.

Meghan reached to push the doorbell. She needed all the prayer she could get.

Meghan knew Zac would be home with Abuela Maria. Every Friday, Zac took his grandmother to Mass. And every Friday after the service, Abuela Maria prepared the exact same home-cooked meal.

Meghan inhaled the familiar smells drifting from the house. Cheese empanadas served with Spanish rice, refried beans, homemade guacamole, and tortilla chips. Fridays had always been her favorite day to visit the Sanchez home. It was odd no one came to answer the door. Maybe she should have called first.

She heard footsteps, and Zac appeared on the other side of the screen door. Meghan's courage waned when she saw him wearing his trademark cap. They stared at each other through the mesh barrier but said nothing.

Abuela Maria appeared beside Zac and smiled. *At least someone's glad to see me.*

"Buenas noches, mi niña."

"Buenas noches, Abuela." Meghan replied, though her eyes were again locked on Zac.

Abuela Maria rapped Zac with her wooden spoon. "Déjala entrar, mi nieto."

Zac pushed open the screen door. "Grandma says to let you in."

"Thanks." Meghan stepped over the threshold and stooped to give Abuela Maria a hug.

Her greeting was returned with kisses on both cheeks and a look of irritation directed toward Zac. With that, she returned to the kitchen.

Left alone in the entryway, Meghan wiped her sweaty palms on her shorts. "Is your mom home?"

Zac narrowed his eyes. "You know she's working."

Yes, Meghan knew. His mom worked the night shift at the hospital. An awkward silence hung between them as she rocked back and forth on her heels. "So how's your summer going?"

Zac leaned in, almost nose-to-nose. "Why are you here?"

Small talk wouldn't accomplish her purpose. "I'm pregnant."

Under different circumstances, Meghan would have laughed at the look on Zac's face as he stumbled backward. She had never seen someone so shocked and confused. The look quickly changed to anger.

"Not funny, Meghan. Not funny at all."

"I'm not joking, Zac. I am twelve weeks pregnant with your baby."

He pulled Meghan into the living room and shut the French doors. When he turned, his dark eyes blazed. "Well, what are you going to do about it? What do you want from me?" Before Meghan could answer, his look of anger changed to desperation. His tone of accusation changed to panic. "You need money. Sure, not a problem. How much does an abortion cost?" He pulled out his wallet. "I have two hundred dollars, but I can get more."

Meghan put her hand over his mouth to stop him. "No, Zac. I've decided not to have an abortion. I almost did, but I changed my mind. I am going to carry our baby."

Zac threw up his hands. His voice got louder with every word. "Oh, so now you've decided for both of us? You think you can come here and make demands of me?"

"Shut up, Zac! I'm not making any demands. I just thought you should know. This is your baby too."

"No. This is your problem. I have a full-ride scholarship. I leave for training camp in two weeks. This is my ticket out of here and you can't stop me."

Meghan got caught up in the moment and shouted back just as loud. "Don't you want a say in what happens to our child?"

"So now it's 'our child'? If you were going to have an abortion on your own, then I'm sure you can figure the rest out on your own too. Don't think you can win me back with this, Meghan. Don't think you can use this to keep me in your life."

"Keep you in my life? Win you back? Hah! I feel sorry for whoever you end up with. It's over for us, but I am going to carry this baby. I am going to be responsible for my choices. Now you need to decide if you're going to be responsible for yours."

"¿Un bebé? ¿Vas a tener un bebé?"

Meghan turned to see Abuela Maria standing in the doorway. They had been talking so loudly, neither had seen her enter the room.

"No, Abuela. *We* are not having a baby. *She* is." Zac said nothing more. He made no eye contact with Meghan or Abuela Maria as he stormed out of the room, out of her life.

Meghan was almost sorry he didn't look back. If he had, he would have only seen his grandmother's love and compassion. They both knew him so well. Nothing good would come if they followed.

Meghan kissed Abuela Maria on the cheek and walked toward the door. As her hand turned the knob, she saw Zac's hat thrown to the floor. This time, the "G" shouted, "Guilty." Maybe she shouldn't have told Zac. The list of names on her guilt list grew longer each day. How many more people would she hurt? How many more people would she disappoint?

Barely above a whisper, Meghan heard Abuela Maria say, "Por favor ayúdanos, Señor." She knew just enough Spanish to translate. "Please help us, Lord."

CHAPTER 18

Meghan had a strange, unwelcome sensation as she walked up the front steps of her house. It didn't feel like home anymore. She didn't know if she should knock or just walk in. With apprehension, she turned the doorknob. It was locked. Had her dad changed the code?

She punched in the four-number combination and heard a click. "Hello," she called into the empty foyer. "Dad? Are you home?" A pair of women's shoes sat on the edge of the entry rug.

She called out again. "Hello. Anyone here?"

She passed the open door of her dad's office and continued down the hallway. Voices and soft music came from the kitchen. She pushed open the swinging door, and the conversation immediately stopped. Her father stood at the stove with his arms around a strange woman.

"Dad?"

"Meghan? What are you doing here?"

"I need to talk to you." Her eyes darted back and forth between her father and the woman.

"Sure." He nudged the woman toward the dining room. "I won't be long, hon."

Hon??

Meghan led the way to her father's office and sat opposite his desk. When she swiveled around, he planted his feet just inside the doorway. Shoulders squared. Arms folded. Right foot tapping the hardwood floor.

Meghan needed to know. "Who is she?"

"Paula."

"How long have you two been together?"

"A few years."

"*Years?* How come I never knew about her?"

"I met her through work. She lives in Chicago but . . . I . . . we . . . she just agreed to move in with me."

Meghan tried to make sense of it all. *There goes any chance of moving back here.*

"What did you need to talk about?"

Always down to business with Dad. How many times had she felt like an employee instead of a daughter? "I'm pregnant."

"Pregnant? That's what happens when I let you go away for the summer?"

Just breathe. "No, Dad. I was pregnant when I left. I just didn't know it at the time."

"So I suppose you want money to take care of it?"

Dad too? Stay calm. "No, Dad. I am going to have the baby. I just wanted you to hear about it from me."

"Well, um, okay. I guess that's it then?"

"Yeah, Dad. That's it."

He turned his back and walked out the door. Just like that, he was gone. Just like that, someone else walked out of her life. Didn't he care at all? Didn't he understand this was his grandchild?

Two conversations. Two total disasters. One more to go. Meghan sat in the car and worked up the courage to go through it once more.

The call went straight to voicemail. "Hi, Mom. It's me. Meghan. Please call me back when you can talk."

Not yet ready to face the Thomsons, Meghan circled back to Zac's house. The driveway was empty, and the house was dark. She drove past the high school, the movie theater, and Memorial Park. Everything looked the same, but nothing was the same. Each of those places represented a part of her past. She was not the same girl who'd walked those halls with Zac, sat in those seats with Zac, or played on those swings with Andi. Her childhood was over. Now she was responsible for the lives of two people. A ringtone pulled her away from her thoughts. It was Mom.

"Hello?"

"Your dad told me you got knocked up. What are you going to do about it?"

Straight to the point. Wow.

"I'm going to have the baby."

Alone apparently.

"Meghan, what are you thinking? You better not lose your scholarship. Everyone has high hopes for you."

Who was "everyone"? Where was "everyone"?

"I can still go to school, Mom. I'll figure something out."

What other choice did she have?

"Well, you can't come live with me. I have one bedroom, and the cats don't like kids."

Nothing had changed.

"Sorry I disappointed you." How many more people would she have to say that to?

Mom talked, but Meghan only half listened. At least one of them knew what they thought. Finally, a pause in the lecture.

"Thanks for calling me back. Bye."

Meghan rummaged through her purse and pulled out the list she'd made for this trip:

~~Talk to Zac~~
~~Mom and Dad~~
~~College~~
~~Safe Haven~~

Completely exhausted, Meghan returned to the Thomsons'. She heard voices coming from the basement. Family movie night. If it hadn't been too late to make the last ferry, she would have driven straight back tonight. Instead, she snuck into Andi's room.

A text buzzed on her phone. It was from Zac.

You're ruining everything.

Her mind told her it was a lie, but her heart didn't believe it. It would have been better if she hadn't come home at all.

The house was still quiet when Meghan pulled out of the Thomsons' driveway well before dawn. She would be back on the island early enough to take over at the inn so Andi didn't have to work for her. A twinge of guilt indicated it was rude to leave without saying goodbye. She justified her decision with the excuse that Saturday was the family's only day to sleep in.

Meghan had until five o'clock Monday afternoon to make her decision. In sixty hours, her future would once again change. Living on campus was no longer an option. Living at home was not an option. Attending classes on campus was an option, but where would she live? Online classes were an option, but again, where would she live? If she got a job, she could pay rent, but then could she be a full-time student? Should she take the refund and forget about going to school until after the baby was born? So many questions. So many unknowns. So little time.

⟨⟩

Andi, Steve, and Netta were surprised to see Meghan back so early. No one asked about the trip. In fact, everyone gave her an extra amount of space.

After work, Meghan crossed the street to Sainte Anne's. Evening Mass was over, and the sanctuary was quiet. She chose a seat near the front and stared at the mural on the ceiling. The picture of

Mary drew her attention. Like her, Mary had faced an unplanned pregnancy. Unplanned to Mary but part of God's plan from the beginning.

Meghan tried to place herself in Mary's position. She was young. Unmarried. Surprised. Unsure. How did she handle it? Meghan couldn't remember what happened between the time of the angel's visit and the starry night in Bethlehem. She needed a Bible.

Looking around, she saw nothing but Mass books. "Where do Catholics hide their Bibles?" she wondered aloud.

"Ask and ye shall receive."

Meghan jumped at the sound. "Oh! Hi, Father Joshua. I didn't know you were there."

"So I gathered." He walked down the center aisle. "What do you need a Bible for?"

"I was trying to remember Mary's story. I thought maybe her decision would help me make mine."

"Here. Use this." He held out a small edition encased in wrinkled brown leather. "I suggest starting in Luke, chapter 1, verse 26."

Matthew. Mark. Luke. All those summers of backyard Bible clubs paid off sometimes.

She scanned the verses and summarized the highlights. "So . . . Mary was greatly troubled. The angel said, 'Do not be afraid.' Nothing is impossible with God. She went to visit her cousin." With a look of defeat, she turned the book upside down on the wooden bench.

"Not the answers you were looking for?" Father Joshua observed.

"No. But I guess it's different when you're pregnant with the Son of God."

"Sure, it's different in some ways, but think about it." Father Joshua sat on a pew arm and dangled one leg over the edge. "Mary lived in a time when getting pregnant out of wedlock was a dangerous predicament. Who would believe she was a virgin, let alone chosen to carry the Messiah? Joseph had every right to have her severely punished, or at least run out of town. With that in mind, why do you think they obeyed the angel's instructions?"

Meghan wanted to say, "I don't know," but suspected Father Joshua wasn't going to let her off that easy. She picked up the Bible and glanced through the verses again. This wasn't a Bible trivia question with an easy answer. "Because they trusted God more than they needed answers?"

A wide grin crossed Father Joshua's face. "Exactly! None of it made sense from an earthly perspective. A young virgin, an ordinary carpenter, a tiny town in Israel. This was God's plan to save the world? When it came time for Jesus to be born, His earthly parents were poor, far away from home, and camping in a cave. Life wasn't easy just because it was God's idea. Life is never easy, but God is always good. He is worthy of our trust because He sees everything we can't and knows everything we don't."

"How does this help me?" Meghan handed back the Bible. "God told them what to do. Where's Gabriel when I need him?"

Father Joshua gently traced the embossed letters on the cover. "Meghan, God still gives us answers. Maybe not through angelic visitation, but through His Word. Through prayer. Through His Holy Spirit."

That wasn't enough for Meghan. "How am I supposed to know what He wants me to do? I know I'll just mess up. Again."

"I wish I had easier answers. Sometimes, we just have to do the best we can and trust nothing is impossible for God."

Meghan stared at him for a moment. "Can you talk less like a priest and more like a normal person?"

"I can try." He laughed. "Until you know the answer, keep your options open. It's perfectly okay if you waver—for now. You're going to have to make a decision, sure, but you don't have to do it today. Breathe. Pray. Seek." Father Joshua stood up and motioned for Meghan to as well. "Remember, we are here for you too. We'll listen, ask questions, make suggestions—but ultimately, the choice needs to be yours. Not everything in life comes down to a simple matter of right versus wrong. God isn't confined or defined by our choices."

"Hmmm, I think I understand," Meghan responded as they walked toward the exit. "If I trust God, then I am trusting Him *with* my decision just as much as *for* my decision?"

"Wise words, my young padawan."

"Padawan? What the heck is that?"

Father Joshua shook his head. "You have no idea what your generation missed."

All day Sunday, Meghan thought, prayed, and debated her decision. Just when she thought she had a definitive answer, doubt crept in, and the cycle began all over again. By the time Monday morning came, she was sick of thinking about it.

Over extra-strong coffee, she prayed. "Okay, God, I can't think of one more angle to consider. Please just tell me what to do. What am I supposed to do?" She waited, not sure what to expect but holding out hope for something. Anything. "So are You saying I need to make this decision on my own? Aren't You going to help me at all?" She waited longer, but nothing out of the ordinary happened. "Fine. Let's go over the facts one more time: College plans? Out. Dorm room? Out. Go back home? I guess as a last resort." At least there was one option. "Classes? Online since I have no idea where I will be living. Yay, me. Two decisions before eight in the morning. That's enough for one day."

Meghan opened her laptop and composed an email:

Mrs. Perkins,

I have considered the choices you presented to me on Friday. For the fall semester, I have decided to remain enrolled at the university and to take my classes online. Thank you for being so very clear in your explanation of my alternatives.

Have a wonderful Monday,

Miss Meghan McPherson

Meghan glared as she hit Send. I hope she can read between the lines.

CHAPTER 19

Week 15

Meghan opened the microwave and inhaled the citrusy aroma of lemongrass. She placed the warm compress at the base of her neck and returned to her desk. Why did Zac have to ruin a perfectly good day? The first actually good day in a long time? His simple text, the only one since her return to the island, read,

> I did some research online. Do whatever you want but don't name me as the father.

What did that even mean? How could Zac so casually walk away from any responsibility? Meghan had so many other things to do, she didn't have the bandwidth for anything else. Especially for Zac.

Her original list was now complete:
1. ~~Apologize to Andi~~
2. ~~Talk to Netta and Steve~~
3. ~~Call Ava~~
4. ~~Call Zac Call Dad Email Mom~~
5. ~~Text Laura~~
6. ~~Talk to Father Joshua~~
7. ~~Schedule dr appointment~~
8. ~~Email admissions counselor~~

And a plan was in place for the fall semester. When Andi left at the end of August, Meghan would stay on the island. Steve and Netta had invited her to move to the inn and work through the end of the tourist season. God really had made a way. She could take her classes online and stay with the Schmidts. After that, she probably could move back home. An unpleasant thought, but these were desperate times. Her dad hadn't said she couldn't come back. He hadn't said anything, actually, since the night she'd told him about the baby.

Nearly mid-August, the air was cooler and the weekday foot traffic lighter. A continued sense of peace confirmed Meghan's decisions. With one more trip to Grand Rapids, she could purchase a car, visit the campus bookstore, and stop at home to pick up warmer clothes for the fall. *If they even fit*, she mused. Her last doctor's appointment had revealed a healthy pregnancy and her first significant weight gain. The nurse laughed when Meghan stammered, "Six pounds? It's only week fourteen."

"Oh, honey," she'd said, "you just made my day. At least you have a good reason. Wait until you hit my age."

After lunch on a quiet Tuesday, Steve poked his head out of the office. "Feel up to doing me a favor? I would do it myself, but I have a meeting."

"Of course," Meghan replied. "It'll be quiet until check-in time."

Steve handed her a sizable stack of outgoing mail. "Don't let Netta see you with these. I was supposed to send them last week."

Outside, Meghan eyed the shallow basket attached to the inn's utility bicycle and decided to walk instead. The packages were bulky but not heavy, and the post office was only half a mile away. By the time she reached Marquette Park, she regretted her choice and rolled the tower of boxes and padded envelopes onto the grass. She sank to the curb and deliberated going back for the bike. Before she could make up her mind, a shadow covered her. From the look of the shoes, the silhouette belonged to a first-time visitor. Only rookies wore heels to Mackinac Island.

Meghan looked up with a forced smile. She expected to see a tourist gazing in awe at the limestone fort built into the bluff behind her.

Instead, the woman in silver pumps glared down. At her.

Startled, Meghan quickly analyzed the intruder. *Definitely tourist. Cruise-ship lanyard. Coordinating designer outfit—bright pink at that—complete with jumbo jewelry. Big, expensive handbag. Probably mad her tour group left her behind.*

Smile still adhered, she spoke first. "Welcome to Mackinac Island, ma'am. May I help you with anything?"

The woman snorted. "Unless you can help the way these horses smell, I doubt it. This is the worst cruise port I've ever been to."

Meghan fought the urge to defend her beloved island. "I'm sorry you're not happy here. The charms of the island aren't for everyone."

"Charms?" the woman huffed. "This place is anything but charming."

"Perhaps you would enjoy browsing the shops?" Meghan ventured.

"That took all of five minutes," the woman replied. "Nothing here I would waste my money on."

Well, lady, I'm done wasting my time on you. Suddenly motivated to continue her errand, Meghan gathered and restacked the packages. When she stood, the bottom of the tower rested on her slightly rounded abdomen.

The woman looked her up and down. "Aren't you a little young? You'll never get off this godforsaken island." With that, she turned up her nose and walked away.

As her high heels clicked down the sidewalk, Meghan wished the woman could hear her thoughts. *Sorry, God. Those ideas were all mine. How about we compromise, and You let her step on a nice, fresh horse apple before her visit is over?*

That picture was enough to keep Meghan entertained for the next block. But as her muscles fatigued, a familiar ache crept into her heart. *"Aren't you a little young?"* It shouldn't matter what a snooty, judgmental, narrow-minded woman thought. But it did. Somewhere inside, she still tallied her failures, imperfections, and ways she disappointed others. This time, though, she had a comeback. *Better toughen up. The bigger this baby grows, the more you're going to face the critics.*

Meghan wished she could turn to God when she felt the all-too-familiar shame. But she pulled away instead. God was so perfect, and she was such a mess. Maybe if she tried harder, she could figure out how to clean herself up. Surely God wouldn't turn her away if He could see how much she was willing to change. She couldn't do anything over, but she vowed she could do everything better. No more mistakes. Moving forward, she would always try to do the right thing.

The first right thing was to finish the trip to the post office. Everyone on the island had a PO box, and, in addition to residents, a steady stream of visitors flowed through the lobby. An unfamiliar elderly man held the door and took the tipsy boxes from Meghan's load.

"What happened to manners?" he asked. "In my day, no gentleman would allow a young lady in your condition to bear such a burden."

Meghan's face grew hot. She wasn't offended by his kindness. She was embarrassed.

She stared at his windbreaker jacket. The many symbols printed on the glossy blue fabric indicated he was an army veteran. "You're very kind, sir. Thank you. And thank you for your service."

The stranger walked her to the service window and set the packages on the counter. He cupped a wrinkled hand on her cheek. "Babies are a gift from God. Don't ever doubt it."

Before Meghan could respond, he walked out the door. She watched him leave, then turned back to the postal worker. "Who was that man?"

"No clue. Never saw him before." Then it was back to business. "Charge these to the inn's account?"

Meghan left the post office with a bagful of mail. Since they didn't check their boxes every day, there was quite a bundle to sort back at the inn. She kept an eye out for her angel in disguise and entertained herself with an image of Hot Pink Lady maneuvering the gauntlet of horse droppings on her way back to her prim and proper cruise ship.

Back at her desk, Meghan arranged the mail into three piles. One for Andi. One for the Schmidts. One for herself. There were two letters from Abuela Maria. A yellow envelope underneath caught her attention. Her name was written in small block letters: *M. L. McPherson.* The return address was familiar, but the handwriting was not something she saw very often. Dad? Dad had sent her a card?

Two hands were enough to count the times in her life her father had written her anything. Most of that correspondence took the form of letters from Santa. Meghan guessed this was a birthday card. Nothing else made sense, but even that was weird, because her birthday was weeks away.

Before she could open the envelope, the bell over the front door rang. She tucked the card into her backpack and refreshed the computer screen. She was ready to check in new guests.

No one appeared around the corner. Maybe it had been a delivery. After a few moments, she heard muted voices and stepped into the hallway to investigate.

"Surprise!"

Simultaneously, Meghan jumped, screamed, and covered her hammering heart. "What are you doing here?" she asked Andi's family. "Besides giving me a heart attack."

The commotion brought Steve out of his office. He awarded the group with a round of applause. "You got her good! Major score for Team Thomson."

"Team Thomson-slash-McPherson," Matt corrected.

All eyes turned to a solitary figure standing on the other side of the screen door.

Now Meghan was completely shocked. "Dad?"

Suzanne broke the awkward silence. "You didn't think we'd forget our annual visit, did you?"

Meghan was too perplexed to reply.

Steve jumped to the rescue. "Come on in, Peter. Is the last Thomson out there with you?"

"We dropped Isaiah off in St. Ignace," Matt answered. "Apparently he's too cool for Mackinac now that he has a driver's permit." A dramatic eye roll got the laugh he was looking for. "He may or may not be coming over with Ray and Jenna tomorrow."

"I told them to leave a long list of chores if he decides to skip out," Suzanne added.

Becca, Andi's younger sister, tapped her mom's shoulder. "Gabe's coming too, right?"

"He sure is," Suzanne assured. "He and Nikki should be here soon. They had a long drive from Green Bay."

"Yeah, Becca, that's all the way in Wisconsin!" Austin, age seven, poked his sister's side. "Gabe's a Cheesehead now."

Professional football did not impress ten-year-old Becca. She ignored him and focused on the arrival of Gabe's girlfriend. "Wait till you meet Nikki," she told Meghan. "She's awesome. She braids my hair and paints my nails." She turned back to Suzanne. "Mom, can we go for a horseback ride? Are we going to the fort?"

Becca was a chatterbox, so when she took a breath, Meghan jumped in.

"Does Andi know you're here?"

"Nope," Matt answered. "We wanted to drop off our luggage before surprising her."

"Try not to scare her half to death," Meghan advised. "She might throw a pie at you if you do."

"Cool!" Austin chimed. "Food fight!"

Suzanne took his chin in her hand. "No food fights, young man. You got messy enough on the ride here." She turned back to Meghan. "Would you mind showing us to our room so he can change into clean clothes?"

Meghan looked to Steve for direction.

"I think you all know the ropes around here." He handed Meghan a set of keys. "The Thomsons will be staying in the bunkhouse. How about you walk over with them while I get your dad set up in the Dubois Suite?" He moved toward the door, where Meghan's dad still stood. "Sound okay, Peter?"

Meghan's dad spoke for the first time since arriving. "Sure. Thanks."

CHAPTER 20

While Becca and Austin unpacked their small suitcases, Meghan pulled Suzanne aside. "Why is my dad here? How did you talk him into coming?"

"It was his idea, Meghan, not mine. He told Matt he wanted to see his daughter."

Before Meghan could ask another of her many questions, Austin pointed and said, "Meghan, your tummy is fat."

Both parents swooped in. Matt clapped his hand over Austin's mouth while Suzanne scolded, "Austin! That is very rude."

Hot tears filled Meghan's eyes. She ran out the door, down the steps, and back to the inn.

Matt must have released Austin, because he loudly called after her, "No offense!"

Meghan wasn't upset with Austin. *He's just a kid*, she reminded herself. *Why do I run whenever I am embarrassed? When will I learn to stay in it?* She recalled Ava's words from their last phone conversation: *"Feel the feeling but don't become the feeling. Don't base your choice on feelings but on truth."*

Feel the feeling. Don't become the feeling. Feel the feeling but don't let it define my truth.

From the front desk, Meghan saw her dad in the atrium. She pretended to be busy behind the counter but looked up when he spoke.

"Maybe I shouldn't have come."

"No, it's fine. I'm glad you came," Meghan lied. "Well, the truth is, I'm confused. Why did you come? We haven't talked, and then you just show up here?"

Her dad swallowed hard and looked away. "I'm sorry about what happened."

"I don't know what you want me to say, Dad. I get that you have your own life and don't want my problems to get in the way. How does Paula feel about you coming here?"

Father and daughter locked eyes. Meghan's flashed with pain, but her dad's gaze conveyed sorrow. "Paula? Now I'm the one confused. Didn't you get my letter?"

"Letter? What letter? No. Since when do you write lett—" She stopped as she remembered the yellow envelope in her backpack. She reached down and pulled it out. "Is this it?"

He nodded, and Meghan's anger deflated. "Sorry. We hadn't been to the post office in a while, and I just picked up the mail today. I haven't had a chance to open it."

"How about if I go for a walk and we try again after you read it?" Instead of waiting for her answer, he exited the room.

When the door latched behind him, Meghan slid a letter opener across the top of the envelope and removed the card. The picture on the front showed a little girl walking on a beach. She was walking away, leaving a trail of tiny footprints in the sand. Not sure what to expect, Meghan opened the card.

> *Meghan,*
> *I'm sure you're surprised to receive this from me. I didn't want to put you on the spot with a phone call.*
> *First of all, I want to say I'm sorry. I'm sorry for so many things, I don't even know where to begin. I'm*

sorry I wasn't there for you when Mom left. I'm sorry she and I couldn't resolve our differences. I'm sorry I made my job more important than you. I'm sorry for all the times I left you alone or made you responsible for things that weren't your responsibility. I'm sorry for being so hard on you and expecting you to be an adult instead of a child.

I'm sorry for not telling you about Paula. She's not part of my life anymore, but that doesn't mean I shouldn't have told you. I'm sorry I pushed you away. I'm sorry I was blind to your feelings and needs. I'm beginning to see them now.

Matt came over the day after you told me about the baby. We had (as he calls it) a "come to Jesus moment." He helped me understand how selfish and uncaring I have been. I wish I could go back and do better, but I can't. I can only try to do better moving forward. If you'll let me.

You are my daughter, and I love you. The baby you carry is my grandchild. I don't want you to go through this alone or feel like you have to figure it out alone. You will always have a home with me.
Dad

Becca bounded into the room, oblivious to Meghan's tears. "C'mon, Megs. Time to go surprise Andi. I bet she won't look as funny as you did."

Meghan slouched in her seat so Becca couldn't see her over the countertop. That kid asked too many questions and didn't need more reasons. "Gee, thanks, Becca. You'll have to go without me. I'm working."

"No, you're not," Steve's voice called out from his office. "You are officially off duty. Get outta here."

Eager to see her dad, Meghan hid the letter behind her back and the tears behind her sunglasses. "Whatever you say, Boss," she called back, then held out her other hand to Becca. "Lead the way."

The whole crew waited outside, Meghan's dad included. Like a soldier at attention, he didn't move until Meghan walked over and gave him a hug.

"Thanks, Dad. I love you too." She felt his chest relax as he exhaled deeply. For the first time, Meghan noticed what he was wearing. Khaki shorts and a red golf polo shirt with a white logo. Maybe he wasn't so predictable anymore.

Before she could comment on his wardrobe change, Austin ran up.

"Meghan, I'm sorry I called you fat. Mom told me you're not fat. You just have a baby growing in there." He tapped her abdomen with one finger.

Meghan reached out for a fist-bump. "That's okay, kiddo."

Austin returned the fist-bump and called out, "Mom, I 'pola-gized. Can we get ice cream now?"

Everyone laughed as Austin skipped down the sidewalk. What was it like to be so carefree about making mistakes? Deal with it and move on? She could learn a few things from that kid.

The trek to the Somewhere in Thyme coffee shop officially began. Gabe and Nikki waited in the park and joined the group as they continued down Main Street. Meghan peeked in the front window then texted Netta so she could send Andi to the back room. As soon as Andi was out of sight, the group snuck in and lined up.

"Andi, we just got busy. Can you come help?" Netta called.

"Coming." Moments later the curtain opened, and Andi appeared. She did a double take and dropped the box she was carrying. Her hands flew up, and she let out a squeal of surprise.

Their plan worked perfectly and, this time, Gabe captured the whole thing on video. "This could go viral," he teased.

Becca ran over to her big sister and lunged into a hug. "Did we surprise you?"

"You got me good," Andi assured her as she scanned the smiling faces.

Becca was talking again. "You looked funny, but not as funny as Meghan. We got her real good, didn't we, Austin?"

Austin didn't answer. He was too busy deliberating over the cooler of ice cream flavors. "Can we get our treat now?"

"Yeah, Andi, get back to work. The service here is lousy," Gabe teased.

The sibling banter continued as Netta and Andi began to serve their customers. Meghan made her way to the cooler and debated between lemon-poppyseed and key lime.

Austin joined her. "What flavor does your baby want, Meghan? I think he would like cotton candy crunch like me."

The room grew quiet as Matt reached for Austin.

Meghan suppressed the familiar urge to run. *Feel the feeling. Don't become the feeling.* She took a deep breath, turned around, and faced everyone. She gently pushed Matt's hand away and bent to Austin's level.

Already a sticky mess, he took another sloppy lick of his ice cream. "Am I in trouble again?"

"No," Meghan assured him. "You didn't do anything wrong. You asked a very smart question that shows you're a good thinker."

Her compliment was rewarded with a huge blue grin. Blue lips, blue teeth, blue tongue. Showcasing his burgeoning sibling-rivalry skills, he skipped over to his sister. "Did you hear that, Becca? I'm a good thinker."

Meghan's dad wrapped his arm around her shoulders. "I'm proud of the way you handled that. My little girl is changing so much."

Meghan tugged the collar of his shirt. "Maybe we both are."

After dark, Meghan and her dad sat on the wraparound porch while everyone else played games in the great room. Father-daughter time was new and uncomfortable. A haze of uneasiness rose between them.

"Dad, can I ask you something?" When he didn't respond, she continued. "What was that 'come to Jesus moment'?"

He cleared his throat. "The day after you were home, Matt dropped in unannounced. He asked to speak to me alone, but Paula insisted on being part of the conversation." Dad rose from his chair and stepped to the edge of the porch. "Matt got right to the point and told me I wasn't a good father. He said the Peter he once knew would never have lacked compassion for anyone, especially his own daughter. He said he should have confronted me long ago but kept thinking I would snap out of it. He told me it was bad enough that your mom had abandoned you, but what was worse is that I had too."

Meghan cringed. She felt bad for being the cause of her dad's obvious discomfort, but at the same time, it felt good to know Matt had stood up for her.

"That didn't go over well with Paula," her dad continued. "She gave Matt a piece of her mind and told him . . . well . . . let's just say they exchanged words. Paula left before Matt did, and I haven't seen her since."

Great. Now she was responsible for their breakup too? "I'm sorry you and Paula broke up because of me."

Her dad sat back down and reached for her hand. "No, Meghan. Don't ever say that again. I was so caught up in my anger I couldn't see straight. I was angry at your mom, at God, at the world. You paid the price for my anger, and that was wrong. I was so wrong."

Was Dad crying? Meghan couldn't be sure because the moonless sky offered no light. "I forgive you, Dad. We can close this chapter and start a new one. Right now."

CHAPTER 21

When Meghan arrived for work the next morning, Steve surprised her with a day off. "Andi should be here soon." He slid into her place behind the counter and waved her away with the flick of his wrist. "Your dad is having breakfast. Get something to eat and then go do something fun."

Meghan leaned on the doorframe to the atrium as her brain deciphered the bewildering scene across the room. *Is that really my dad?* Instead of isolating himself, he was seated at a small table with Austin and Becca. *Andi's not gonna believe this.* The three were involved in an animated, none too quiet conversation. Dad's eyes met hers and he winked. *Winked.*

Meghan walked over to the table and ruffled Austin's hair. "Good morning, rug rats."

Austin dipped his head back and looked up. Faded-blue lips framed a crumb-filled, toothless grin.

"You're up early this morning, kiddo." Meghan handed him a napkin.

"Mom said we hadda if we wanna ride the horses." He stuffed the rest of a blueberry muffin into his mouth.

"It's gonna rain later," Becca added.

Now Austin spooned a bit of oatmeal into his mouth. "Meghan, are you coming too?"

Meghan and her dad exchanged smiles. "Not today. I am going to spend time with my dad."

Matt and Suzanne entered the atrium. Suzanne took one look at her youngsters and hurried over.

"Peter, we're so sorry the children are bothering you." Suzanne pulled Austin's chair away from the table. "Come with us, kids."

Before Mother Hen could gather her chicks, Meghan's dad protested. "They aren't a bother at all. In fact, Austin and Becca were just about to share their knowledge of ancient 'care-in' construction." He looked to Becca for confirmation he had pronounced the word correctly. She approved with a thumbs-up while licking frosting off the top of a cinnamon roll. "Being a novice cairn builder myself, I was really looking forward to their expertise on this Celtic custom."

"Yeah, Mom," Austin confirmed. "We were just getting to the most important part."

"You have to let us, Mom," Becca chimed in. "Mr. McPherson is Scottish, and no one ever taught him about cairns. It's his heritage, Mom. And"—Becca went all in—"it's a Mackinac tradition."

Her mother was out of objections. "All right, you may continue, but please don't use the inn's dishes as visual aids. Unlike real rocks, they will break if you drop them."

The youngsters continued their lesson in ancient rock piling, as the Thomsons wove through the breakfast buffet.

Meghan fixed herself a cup of coffee and followed them outside to the sunny porch. "Mind if I crash your romantic breakfast, Mr. and Mrs. T?"

"Not at all," Matt said.

"It's nice to see your dad happy," Suzanne commented. "That's the Peter I remember."

Meghan glanced back toward the atrium. "It's been a long time. I think I gave up hoping."

"God's time is always on time," Matt added. "I think we sometimes forget life is more like a crockpot than a microwave. We want God to hurry up and fix it already, but that would interrupt the process of His work."

"That's good . . . Matt." Meghan was still getting used to calling him by his first name. "I am going to try and remember that." After a sip of coffee, she added, "Dad told me his side of your conversation. Did you really get in a fight with Paula?"

Suzanne rose from her chair. "I'm going to check on the kids."

Her reaction knotted Meghan's stomach.

Matt watched his wife disappear around the corner. "Don't worry about Suzanne. She's still dealing with the whole Paula thing." He pushed aside the antique porcelain plate and brushed crumbs onto the wooden slat floor. "Maybe I did the wrong thing, but I was very angry with your father. For five years I stood on the sidelines, watching him move further away. In the beginning I tried to help him but gave up when nothing changed. I figured he would come around eventually. When you shared your story, I realized I failed you both. I'm just sorry it took so long."

Meghan reached over and squeezed his hand. "You never gave up on me and I am so thankful. I just don't understand the sudden change in him."

"I don't understand it myself," Matt confessed. "Everything happened so fast. Honestly, there was a lot of yelling, mostly between Paula and me. But as your dad watched, it was like he woke up from a deep sleep. From the outside, I could see something was happening on the inside."

"What was happening?"

"I think he was remembering. Remembering who he really is and what really matters."

Before he could say more, Suzanne, followed by Meghan's dad, appeared with a pair of to-go coffee cups. "The kids are eager to get to the stables. Peter witnessed my maternal skills in action when I got the kids to brush their teeth in spite of their but-mom-it's-vacation strategy."

"I was impressed with your quick thinking," Dad laughed. "Meghan was always so responsible I never had to rise to the challenge."

Meghan was always so responsible. Ouch. *If I was so responsible, would we be here right now?* She caught herself before the spiral of shame went any further.

"Well, Dad," she said, changing her internal focus as she grasped the foam cup he held out to her, "what are we going to do today?"

"Totally up to you. I defer to your vast knowledge of the island. The only orders I am bound to carry out involve afternoon cairn building—rain or shine—with Austin and Becca. Until then, I'm all yours."

Meghan turned to Suzanne. "Since you're going trail riding this morning, want to meet for a late lunch?"

"Sounds good. How about the pizza place? The kids are already begging to go there."

With a solid plan, Meghan turned back to her dad. "I know just where we'll go first. How do you feel about butterflies?"

"Butterflies are good. Lead the way."

Meghan looped her arm around her dad's elbow and pointed across the street. "Let's go learn about caterpillars."

After they'd purchased admission tickets, Meghan led her dad to the same bench she'd shared with Ava and told him the story of the butterfly.

A light of understanding washed over Peter's face. "I've never heard grace explained that way before. It seems too good to be true . . . after all the things I've done wrong."

"I know, Dad. It's hard to understand." Meghan held out her hand, hoping to attract a hovering monarch. "I think it's something we have to trust. Kind of like, you fake it till you make it. You know?"

"I've missed out on so much with you. I can never forgive myself."

"We've both made mistakes. Both been hurt. Both hurt each other. My friend Ava said when we learn to trust God's grace, we can be free. Maybe that's all we need to understand for now."

Dad looked at her for a minute, then without a word, stood up and walked away. Meghan let him go. She knew he needed time alone. She'd wait for him in the gift shop—it was the only way out of the butterfly garden.

Meghan was focused on the jewelry display when Dad spoke from behind. "I expected to find you by the books, not the jewelry."

"That was my first stop." Meghan laughed, then pointed to a row of necklaces. "Look at these. Aren't they cool?"

Dad leaned down to get a better look. "What are they?"

She pointed toward two signs on the counter, and Dad lifted his glasses to read the bright, bold letters on the first sign. "We love butterflies! No butterflies were harmed in the process of creating these wearable works of art." He moved on to the second. "Original. One of a kind. Each of our unique items is crafted from real butterfly wings. The butterflies are raised on specialty farms and recycled after the completion of their normal life cycle. Preserved in resin and designed specifically for our collection, a portion of every purchase is reinvested in the protection of these beautiful creatures."

He straightened. "That's fascinating. I've never seen anything like this. Which one do you like best?"

Meghan pointed to a small, oblong pendant. "This one. The *doxocopa Cherubina*."

Dad studied the object. "Why that one?"

She shrugged. "The shape reminds me of the island and the aqua blue of Lake Huron."

He gestured to the salesperson. "We'll take this one. I'm buying a gift for my daughter."

The rain held off until the next morning. Andi and Meghan shared the canopy of a big, striped umbrella as they walked to the dock.

"I still can't get over the change in your dad," Andi said.

Megan's hand reached for the pendant as she let out a breath of astonishment. "I know, right? Only God. There's no other explanation."

Andi stopped suddenly, and Meghan's head collided with the scalloped edge of the umbrella as momentum propelled her forward.

"Hey!" She ducked back under and pulled the handle away from Andi. "Some of us aren't wearing raincoats."

"Sorry." Andi laughed. "It just came to me. Your baby is the reason for your dad's change. It's like she brought you back together."

"Or he," Meghan corrected. "I hadn't thought of that, but I guess maybe you're right."

"And," Andi continued, "she's also the reason you're choosing to trust God's grace."

Meghan took that to heart. "Yeah, that's true. God took my mess-up and turned into something good."

"My dad has a word for that. I can't think of it right now."

"Speaking of dads," Meghan pointed to an oncoming carriage. "I see the whole gang coming down the street."

"They're such trolls." Andi teased, using the nickname for below-the-bridge visitors. "Only true islanders walk instead of ride in a taxi just because of a little rain."

Meghan glanced down at their dripping, brown-splattered rain boots. "I'm not so sure I blame them."

Meghan and Andi followed the troupe onto the ferry for St. Ignace. Ray and Jenna had invited everyone for a goodbye brunch. According to Jenna, they had extra time to prepare a meal since Isaiah had completed all their chores for them. On the trip across the lake, the rain stopped. By the time the ferry reached the mainland, the sun was peeking through the clouds. The group divided, and Meghan wound up seated between the two youngest Thomsons in the back of a minivan.

"Just like Uber. Only better," Becca declared.

It was a quick ride to Ray and Jenna's where Meghan was surprised to see her dad's small SUV parked in the driveway. "You didn't ride here with the Thomsons?"

"No, but I'll be hitching a ride back with them." He tossed Meghan a pair of key fobs. "I'm leaving the Red Baron here for you."

Meghan was surprised he remembered her nickname for the cherry-colored vehicle.

"I remember," Dad said, as if reading her mind. "During your *Peanuts* craze, you called your mom's white car 'Snoopy' and mine the 'Red Baron.'"

"Just like the cartoon," Jenna observed.

"What's a red bear ride in?" Austin asked.

"Not 'red bear ride in,' doofus," Becca corrected. "Red Bar*on*. Don't you even know who Snoopy is?"

"No. So what if I don't? You don't know anything about football." With that, he took off chasing his sister.

"It's going to be a long ride home," Dad lamented.

CHAPTER 22

Week 16

The young dock porter picked up Andi's last tote and placed it on the dray. Meghan knew all the porters who delivered to the inn, but this one was unfamiliar. He was practically drooling over Andi. "You want these loaded on the St. Ignace ferry, right?"

"Yikes. I almost forgot," Andi replied. "Mackinaw City, please."

"Maybe you should give me your number in case there's a mix-up."

Meghan choked back a laugh and moved to the front of the dray. She rubbed the nose of a chestnut Belgian draft horse and waited for Andi's reply. She knew that look. Andi was not impressed.

"Everything is clearly labeled, so I think you're good to go." Andi spun and walked away.

Meghan handed the guy a ten-dollar tip. "Hope the rest of your day goes better."

Andi waited at the bike rack and wagged her finger at Meghan. "I know what you're thinking. Don't even go there."

"Fine, I won't. But only because it's your last day on the island."

"And this is our last bike ride. Ready?"

"Lead the way," Meghan said.

They pedaled through town, around the bend at Mission Point, and past Arch Rock. Just beyond mile marker 2, they stopped on a quiet stretch of beach. Meghan lay back on the loose pebbles and shielded her eyes from the sun.

"Look at that cute little baby bump!" Andi reached over and patted Meghan's belly. "You've been wearing baggy clothes, and I hadn't really noticed until now."

"It won't be long until everyone will know," Meghan replied, her arm still over her eyes. "It's finally starting to feel real."

Andi hesitated. "Can I ask you something?"

"Of course." Meghan sat up. "No more secrets between us."

Andi took a deep breath. "If you don't want to tell me, I understand, but . . ." Her voice trailed off.

"But what?" Meghan nudged. "It's okay. Really. After everything you've done for me, the least I can do is answer a question."

Andi scrunched her forehead. "What happened that day? At the clinic? What changed your mind?"

Meghan's shoulders fell.

"I'm sorry. It's probably too painful to talk about," Andi said.

Meghan hugged her knees to her chest and stared out over the turquoise waters of Lake Huron. Yes, it was painful to remember, but it was time. If anyone deserved to know, it was Andi. *Feel the feeling. Don't become the feeling.* She gathered her courage and allowed her mind to drift back to that day, back to the long drive to Grand Rapids.

"I don't remember everything. I was so scared. At the same time, I just wanted it to be over. I wanted to put it all behind me and pretend it never happened. Every time I felt it was wrong, something inside me told me it was already too late to turn around. I never wanted to be someone who had an abortion, but I didn't see any other way."

The pressure building in her chest constricted her breathing. "Do you remember the signs?" She looked at Andi for confirmation. "I was scared because the news always says how nasty those protesters are. But when I got out of the car, I looked back, and there was a man looking at me through the fence. We locked eyes, and for a second I felt this strange sense of peace. The next moment, the umbrella blocked him, and the fear rushed back."

Meghan closed her eyes and replayed the scene in slow motion . . . the people, the towering clinic building, the barricaded entrance. To the right, she saw the gatehouse. To the left, she saw a sign—be pro-love. It all happened in slow motion, yet so fast.

"Once I got inside, I was . . . numb. I didn't feel scared or sad or even confused. I didn't feel anything. I just put one foot in front of the other and did what they told me. Once I finished the paperwork, they took me to an exam room and gave me a gown. And a pill. A painkiller, I think. Maybe an antibiotic." Meghan trembled. "Then I had to wait. Alone. There was nothing to do but look at posters on the wall and listen to the voices in my head. As I waited, I thought about Zac. I thought about my parents. I was so angry. At them. At God. At myself . . .

"Then suddenly, I remembered the man at the fence. Something about him was different. He didn't look like he wanted to hurt me. He looked like he wanted to help me." She stopped, remembering.

Andi took her hand. "I'm right here. Keep going."

"It was something about his eyes. Like they were speaking to me. Calling to me."

"Calling to you?"

Meghan stood. The memories were as clear as if they were playing on a movie screen. "They were saying, 'Run. Run to me.' And I did. I grabbed my clothes, threw them on, and ran. People were shouting and chasing me, but I kept running." Turning to her friend, Meghan gasped. "Andi, I didn't know it until this very moment. I think it was God's voice. God told me to run to Him."

Tears ran down Andi's face.

In that instant, Meghan felt more loved than she ever had before. She was free! God hadn't turned His back. An urge rose from someplace deep within. She wriggled out of her sweatshirt, shook off her shoes, and walked into the water.

"What are you doing? Are you crazy?" Andi called. "Those rocks are sharp."

Meghan kept walking.

"And the water's cold."

She didn't turn around. She didn't want anything to distract her or change her mind. She continued into the cold, clear water. The rocks beneath her feet weren't sharp. They were white and smooth. The foamy edges of the waves broke against her skin. When she was knee deep, she prayed, "God, You called. I ran. You saved me from myself, so now I give myself to You."

She held up her arms. She was like a child, reaching for her Father. She lowered her arms into the water, then brought them back up with an exuberant splash. Her wet clothes clung to her as she walked back to shore. The evidence of her condition was never more obvious. Some might call her pregnancy a mistake, but Meghan knew her baby was a miracle.

Andi set their empty teacups in the sink. "Where did the summer go? We waited so many years for this, and now it's over."

Time was running out.

"Andi, I truly am sorry for what I put you through." Meghan picked up one of Andi's last two tote bags, and they walked out of the apartment together for the last time.

It was a short trek to the dock. Their summer on the island had come down to its final minutes, not even hours. Was there enough time to say everything she still needed to say?

"I feel so ashamed for the way I handled everything. For not being honest with you. For asking you to drive me to the clinic. For expecting you to bear responsibility for my mistakes. But today I realized something else. If you hadn't been there, I think I would have gone through with it."

"Wow, Megs. I don't know what to say. I was feeling so guilty for driving you there. It was like I was supporting your decision." Andi tilted her head. "Growing up, I always heard the adults say, 'God moves in mysterious ways.' I kind of get it now."

Meghan gave her a quick hug. "What am I doing to do without you?"

"Holland's only half an hour from Grand Rapids. We'll still see each other."

"If I don't end up living at home with Dad," Meghan said. "At this point, moving back to Traverse City seems to be the best plan."

Andi waved her hands excitedly. "Oh! I just had a great idea! How about I meet you in Grand Rapids when you pick up your textbooks? We can go to the mall, get pretzels and pedicures, and look at baby stuff. Can I help you make your registry?"

Baby stuff? Registry? Meghan had been so wrapped up in other decisions, she hadn't given thought to all the things her baby would need.

"Sure. That sounds fun." Meghan had more reasons to be grateful. "I just realized something. Because Dad gave me his car, I can use my savings to get things I'll need for the baby."

"Another one of God's mysterious ways?"

"Definitely. And it won't be long until we see each other again."

Andi checked her phone. "Fourteen days starting right now. But we'd better walk faster, or I'll miss my ferry."

"If you do," Meghan teased, "I know who to call. He would gladly come to your rescue."

"Just for that," Andi scolded, "you get to buy me a soda for the ride over. Make it a large, please."

While Andi sipped her cola, Meghan studied the people waiting at the dock. So many were her age. She smiled at the familiar faces, though her heart was heavy. She was supposed to be one of them. This was supposed to be her ride home to pack for college.

The ferry from the mainland emptied, and the departure line inched forward. After one last hug, Andi boarded and disappeared into the belly of the boat. Probably for the best.

For the first time, Andi was leaving her behind. It would be two weeks before Meghan traveled to Grand Rapids. Two weeks of working full time while her friends moved into dorms and began classes. Two weeks of meeting new people and making new friends. The summer hadn't turned out as she planned, but maybe it was better than she could have imagined.

CHAPTER 23

Week 19

Meghan walked into Grace Baptist Church and looked for Laura. As she scanned the sanctuary, her heart jumped when she recognized a familiar face staring at her. That was all it took. The dark cloud of shame headed her way.

Vivian Perkins pursed her lips, crossed her arms, and marched directly to the front of the room. Pastor Nate was talking with the keyboardist, but Vivian didn't wait for him to finish before she tapped him on the shoulder. Meghan could see Vivian's mouth already moving as Pastor Nate turned around. A moment later Vivian motioned toward the back of the room.

Maybe it had been a mistake to come. Maybe she should sneak out before the service started. Maybe she should text Laura and say she wasn't feeling up to it. Maybe . . . too late.

Pastor Nate saw her and gave a little wave. He was probably going to ask her to leave. She would save him the trouble.

She turned and pressed her way upstream toward the exit. When she reached for the door, someone tapped on her shoulder.

"Good morning, Meghan. Leaving so soon?"

"I'm not sure I should be here. No offense, Pastor Nate." Straight to the point.

Pastor Nate laughed as Meghan turned to face him, hand still gripped on her only escape. "No offense taken. I'm not sure I'm ready either." His tone shifted from playful to serious. "Are you leaving because you saw me talking to Vivian?"

Meghan felt her face grow warm as she tried to sound calm. "Vivian?" The word erupted from her throat with a nervous squeak.

"Yes, Vivian Perkins. You know, from the university?"

"Oh, *that* Vivian." Meghan didn't recall revealing the name of her nemesis.

"I asked her to come today because I want her to hear what I have to say. I asked you to come for the same reason. Please stay. Just give it a chance, okay?"

The call to worship began. With no cause to doubt Pastor Nate, Meghan let go of the door and followed him back to the sanctuary. He continued toward the front as she slid into a back pew, close to the exit. Just in case.

If Meghan hadn't been so worried about Pastor Nate's sermon, she might have enjoyed the service. After announcements, prayer, and a couple of blended hymns, Pastor Nate greeted the congregation.

"Please open your Bibles to Romans three, starting in verse nineteen: 'Now we know that whatever the law says, it says to those who are under the law, so that every mouth may be silenced and the whole world held accountable to God. Therefore no one will be declared righteous in God's sight by the words of the law; rather, through the law we become conscious of our sin.' Skipping to verse twenty-two. 'This righteousness is given through faith in Jesus Christ to all who believe. There is no difference between Jew and Gentile, for all have sinned and fall short of the glory of God, and all are justified freely by his grace through the redemption that came by Christ Jesus.'"

Meghan kept her eyes glued to her bulletin. The words blurred together through her tears.

". . . accountable to God . . . No one will be declared righteous . . . all have sinned . . ."

Pastor Nate was right. Those words described her. Meghan's legs itched to run, but fear pressed her down. If she stood, everyone would see the evidence and know those words were meant for her. She squeezed her eyes shut and wished she could close her ears too. But then, Pastor Nate's voice reached out and, with one word, pulled her back to the present.

Grace.

That one word was enough to open Meghan's eyes and focus her heart on the present instead of the past.

"According to these verses," Pastor Nate said, "there is not one person here today who is good enough to be declared righteous before God. Every single one of us is guilty. Some sin is flaunted. Some is buried. God sees it all. And He wants to bring the light of grace and truth into all of our hidden places."

He stepped off the platform and began walking down the main aisle. "Some sin is outwardly visible. Some is completely internal. There is nothing we can do to pay for our sins or earn our righteousness."

He continued moving toward the back.

"But the good news of the Gospel proclaims our redemption has been paid in full. Through the blood of Jesus, shed upon the cross of Calvary, our debt is wiped out. When we freely receive this gift of amazing grace, God no longer sees us as sinners. Instead, He sees us through the perfect righteousness of His Son."

Can this be true? Meghan wondered. *Does God really see me that way, after everything I've done wrong? Even though I'm pregnant and not married?*

Halfway from the front, Pastor Nate turned around. "I know

this can be a hard truth to trust. We Christians put a lot of effort into looking like we have it all together. We put a lot of effort into making ourselves look righteous. But the truth is, no matter how much we dress up the outside, every one of us is still dying inside. Until we get to Heaven, we will continue to fall short of the glory of God."

Suddenly, a man in front raised his hand. "Pastor Nate," he called out. "If we continue to sin, how can we know we're truly saved?"

Surprised at the interruption, Meghan waited to see how Pastor Nate would respond, but he answered as though this was a completely normal occurrence. "Okay, Joe. Let me rephrase your question. How can we call ourselves Christians if we keep on sinning? Aren't Christians supposed to live without sin? Unfortunately, that's the message we often receive—from ourselves and from each other. Deep down we all know the truth. We know we still sin. Sometimes a little, sometimes a lot. But here's the greater truth—God's truth. Even on the days we fail, we are fully loved. We are still fully accountable for our choices, but God doesn't give up on us."

What? How is that possible? I disappoint God on a daily basis. Don't I?

Meghan listened intently, hoping Pastor Nate would answer her questions. Instead, he stepped back onto the platform.

"I've invited a few people from our congregation to join me. Please listen to their stories. Our past doesn't have to define us. It will affect us. It will remain with us. But it can never disqualify us from God's redeeming grace."

About a dozen people lined up beside Pastor Nate. Meghan was surprised to see Laura standing with them. One by one they passed a microphone.

A college-age woman: "I'm over my head with credit card debt, but I've been redeemed by God's grace."

A college-age man: "I struggle with addiction to video games, but I've been redeemed by God's grace."

A middle-aged man: "Sometimes I'm impatient with my wife and kids, but I've been redeemed by God's grace."

A teenage girl: "I lied to my parents, but I've been redeemed by God's grace."

A young boy: "I hit my sister. I kicked her too, but I've been redeemed by God's grace."

That got a laugh from the congregation.

Laura: "I got pregnant when I was eighteen, but I've been redeemed by God's grace."

Laura? Laura was pregnant like me? Meghan didn't hear the rest of the group. Her head was spinning with questions. Were Christians even allowed to admit they sinned? Didn't that make God look weak?

As the stage emptied, Pastor Nate picked up a guitar. "If we were all as honest and brave as our brothers and sisters, every one of us could stand here and confess how our sin has separated us from God." He strummed a melody. "First John one, verse nine says, 'If we confess our sins, he is faithful and just and will forgive our sins and purify us from all unrighteousness.' When we receive forgiveness, we receive redemption through Christ."

Silence filled the room. "This is between you and God. Don't worry about the football game. It's just preseason anyway." The lights dimmed. "Don't worry about the person next to you. Think about your own struggles. The obvious sin and the hidden sin. Confess it to God and receive the grace He freely offers. Trust the redeeming power of God at work within you. Trust He is great enough to fully see your sin and fully love you still."

Meghan closed her eyes. Through the sounds of people whispering and even sniffling, Pastor Nate's voice was the only voice she heard.

"While you spend time reflecting, I want to sing a song. Let the voice of grace speak louder than the voice of condemnation." Accompanied only by his guitar, Pastor Nate proclaimed truth through music:

I was bound and without freedom
Deep down inside my soul
I was lost, hope was gone,
When His love broke through.

He heard me in my pleading
He saw me in despair
Picked me up, made me clean;
He made me new.

Oh how great, His grace
Emptied out for me
Though I don't deserve it,
He is my victory.

Oh this debt I could not pay
It was completely washed away
Now I'm free, no more chains
Oh how great, oh how great, His grace.

My past does not define me
I am not my mistakes
I am loved, I am His child.
A child of God.

Pastor Nate repeated the bridge of the song, and Meghan hurriedly wrote the words on the back of the bulletin: *My past does not define me. I am not my mistakes. I am loved, I am His child. A child of God.*

God Himself declared His grace was sufficient to wash away the stain of her guilt, her mistakes, her failures. Her past created consequences she would have to own, but it didn't define who she was. It might disqualify her from relationships, opportunities, or acceptance, but it didn't disqualify her from God's love.

Megan's hands cradled the child growing in a hidden place. *Little One, my past does not define us. You are not a mistake. You are loved. You are my child. A child of God.*

CHAPTER 24

Meghan sat in an oversized armchair and paged through a photo album as Laura said goodbye to her family. Last week, when Meghan texted that she'd be coming to town, Laura had invited her to spend the afternoon. After lunch, Laura's husband and two sons left to go kayaking with the men's group.

As her eyes studied the images under the smudged plastic, her heart bounced back and forth between the extremes of shame and grace she'd experienced at church. She recalled Laura's admission as she studied the pictures of Laura's seemingly picture-perfect life. Most of the photos captured images of her sons' activities: Basketball, soccer, fishing, camping. Others were a surprise: serving food (complete with plastic gloves and paper hairnets), playing cards at a nursing home, picking up debris strewn among palm trees. The last page held an older family photo. The fake winter background, matching holiday sweaters, and tacky props screamed box store photo shoot. Meghan couldn't help but laugh.

Laura turned from loading the dishwasher. "What's so funny?"

Meghan held up the picture, and Laura sucked in her breath. "I take it out, and Mark keeps putting it back. I need to start hiding it better. Or get rid of it altogether."

"It's adorable," Meghan said. "Adorable in an embarrassing, cheesy, vintage kind of way."

"Is that supposed to be a compliment?"

"Absolutely!" Meghan studied the picture again. Joel and Tanner were preschoolers with curly blond hair, blue eyes, and chubby pink cheeks. They were seated in a red plastic sled, pulling apart fuzzy fake snowballs. Laura and Mark each sat on upturned logs, knees turned inward, hands unnaturally cupped over their outer knees. Between them stood a boy, maybe fourteen or fifteen years old, with the same hair and eye color as Laura. His pinched smile seemed to say, "See what I put up with?"

Laura stepped out of the kitchen. "I imagine you have a few questions for me."

"I had no idea. Why didn't you tell me before?"

"I was waiting for the right time. I didn't want my story to complicate your story." Laura walked to the fireplace and removed a frame from the mantel. Without saying a word, she brushed her fingers over the glass before she placed it in Meghan's open hands.

A very young woman stared back from the past. She cradled a tiny bundle of blue close to her heart. Though time created obvious change, there was no mistaking the same dark-brown hair, same hazel eyes, same smile. "Time has been very good to you. You're even prettier today." Meghan handed the picture back. "Your hair was bigger then."

Laura laughed. "It was the nineties. Those were some good times, but I shudder to think about all the hairspray I inhaled."

"Well, on you it looked good." Meghan pointed to the frame. "Umm, will you please tell me your story?"

Laura returned the picture to the mantel before she began. "I got pregnant when I was eighteen. Still in high school. When I told my boyfriend, he said, 'Well, I guess we'd better get married.' Not a rom-com proposal, right? Back then, it was what you were supposed to do. What everyone expected us to do. We never considered alternatives, and we certainly didn't have a clue how hard it would be."

Meghan already had a mental list of questions but didn't want to interrupt.

"After the wedding, we moved away from our hometown, our families. He was in his second year of college, so it seemed like the right thing to do. I worked part time as a waitress. We had one car, and it was the only job I could find that I could walk to. Every day I thought of more reasons we were completely unprepared for what was coming. As the weeks went by, we began to consider adoption. Well, I should say I considered adoption. It felt like the weight of the decision was all on me. Even my then-husband said it was my choice. My delivery date drew near, and I still wasn't sure. Everyone said the same thing: 'We'll support whatever you decide.' Even as we set up the crib, I was still talking with the adoption agency."

Meghan hadn't expected that. "You mean you were considering placing the baby *and* getting ready to bring the baby home at the same time?

"Exactly. I didn't know what we were supposed to do. Part of me couldn't imagine giving my baby to someone else, but the other part of me wasn't sure we were ready to raise him. If keeping him would be selfish or irresponsible."

Why would keeping a baby be selfish? "So what happened? How did you finally decide?"

"I don't remember anything significant or earth shattering. I didn't hear God's voice or see a miraculous sign. When the time came, I just knew in my heart he was mine forever. He was meant to be with me. After Arik was born, we brought him home and should've lived happily ever after. Except we didn't."

Laura paused, and Meghan was afraid that was the end. "What happened?"

Laura took a deep breath and looked over to the photo.

"Life was hard. We were young, poor, clueless, and alone. But we did have everything we needed, and we loved and adored our baby. Time passed, and we seemed to be figuring things out. Our beautiful son was healthy and thriving. At the end of the academic year, we moved closer to our parents. I also enrolled in college the following fall. We were still young and poor but no longer clueless or alone. We had a plan. We could've lived happily ever after. Except we didn't. When Arik was two, my husband left. After that, he only saw him during the summer. Even though I was hurt and angry and scared, I tried to provide stability for Arik. I didn't always succeed."

Laura paid a price in sharing her sacred story. Meghan could see the pain it was causing.

"I ended up switching from the university to a technical college so I could begin working sooner. The fall Arik started preschool, I began working full time. After that, things got easier because I had a steady income and regular schedule. Arik was an absolute joy and the love of my life. Never once did I ever regret the pregnancy, painful divorce, or hard years. I never saw Arik as anything but a gift from God. And going through all of that was worth it because he is worth it."

Meghan weighed Laura's words and delivered a question. "So the moral of your story is, all's well that ends well?"

"Noooo. I would say it's more like, with God all things are possible. But even that doesn't guarantee happily ever after, at least not how we'd define it."

A phone alarm hummed in the background. Time always seemed to run out too soon. Still seated, Meghan tried to wiggle her bare feet into her shoes. The bigger the baby grew, the harder it was to bend over.

Standing on the front porch, Laura pointed to the sun's position in the western sky. "It's going to be late by the time you get back to Mackinac. Why don't you stay here tonight?"

"Thank you for your kindness," Meghan replied. "Pastor Nate arranged a place for me to stay. Tomorrow, I'm supposed to pick up my textbooks and meet Andi at the mall."

"Did he say who you'll be staying with?"

Meghan checked her phone. "Glenn and Lucinda Maxwell?"

A smile spread across Laura's face. Meghan wasn't sure what it meant.

"Is that a good smile or a 'What was Pastor thinking' smile?"

Laura wrapped Meghan in a hug. "It's a 'God is good' smile," she answered.

"Okay, 'cause I'm supposed to meet them at Monte Cristo in twenty minutes."

"You'll be fine," Laura assured her. "Better get going, though."

Two couples were already seated when Meghan arrived at the Italian restaurant. To her relief, Glenn and Lucinda Maxwell turned out to be a very normal-looking middle-aged couple. Pastor Nate introduced his wife, Beth. She looked familiar, but before Meghan could ask Beth if they'd met before, the couple excused themselves. Glenn and Lucinda picked up their menus, but Meghan rested her elbows on top of the glossy pamphlet and cupped her chin in her open palm.

"I've seen Beth before. I just can't remember where."

Glenn replied but didn't look up. "She was the keyboardist at church this morning."

Before Meghan could consider the possibility, Pastor Nate and Beth returned. Over salad and breadsticks, the Maxwells shared their story. Similar to both Meghan and Laura, Lucinda and Glenn had once faced an unexpected pregnancy. They married soon after the discovery and began the hard work of raising a baby and alternating between working and going to school. It took a while, but they both finished college and built a wonderful, successful life together.

By the time the entrées arrived, the story concluded with details of their recent anniversary trip to Disney World.

"Thirty-three years?" Meghan asked incredulously. "Oh! I don't mean to imply you're lying. I've just never heard a story like yours end with a real-life happily ever after."

Lucinda and Glenn exchanged a smile before Glenn confessed, "Don't think happily ever after doesn't come without a lot of blood, sweat, and tears."

"Along with that," Lucinda added, "we both know we wouldn't be here today without the Lord. It hasn't been an easy road—there were plenty of times I didn't think we'd make it this far."

Pastor Nate, who had been quietly eating his lasagna, interjected. "In those early days, were people ever rude to you or treat you badly because of the pregnancy?"

"Hmmm, how much time do we have?" Lucinda leaned in. "Unfortunately, the answer is yes. And sadly, the worst treatment we received was from our church."

Glenn reached for another breadstick. "It was pretty bad. When our pastor found out about the baby, he basically bullied us into making a public confession. In front of the whole congregation." He turned his head to directly face Nate. "Would you do that?"

Nate shook his head. "I can't speak for that pastor, but I am very sorry you were treated like that."

Beth set her glass down hard. "I'm sorry, but this really bothers me. Where does the church get off calling certain people out when we all have logs in our eyes? If you're going to call out one, be fair and call out everyone. What if the entire congregation had to parade up to the front and publicly confess their sins? For real. Every person. Every sin. We'd be at church twenty-four seven. Do we believe in grace, or don't we? Heaping shame on people won't cause repentance. Throwing stones never won a heart for Jesus. It just causes hiding and lying. Which, in turn, leads to more sin." When she realized they were all staring, she looked down.

Nate leaned over and kissed her cheek. "What she said." He looked around the table. "That's exactly what prompted today's sermon. This is a big issue. One Beth and I have been dealing with frequently in our own congregation."

Beth's face was red. "Excuse me," she said as her chair slid away from the table.

Meghan watched her walk, almost run, toward the front of the restaurant.

Lucinda pushed her chair back also. "Is she okay? Should I go after her?"

"No, she'll be fine," Nate gestured for Lucinda to scoot back in. "She just needs some space. Carry on with your story."

"Yes, please. What happened next?" Meghan asked.

When Glenn nodded, Lucinda continued. "We did what we were told. It was humiliating and embarrassing. I have never felt so exposed or ashamed in all my life. To make matters worse, then the pastor told the congregation to basically shun us. When one of the women asked about having a baby shower for us, he outright told her it would be a sin."

Meghan stopped her there. "A sin? To have a baby shower for someone who is having a baby? I don't understand how that would be a sin."

"He said if the church rewarded us for getting pregnant, it would send a message to the other girls they could get presents if they got pregnant too."

Before Meghan or Nate could respond, Glenn rose and scanned the dining room. "When's Beth coming back? I would love to hear her thoughts on that one."

Lucinda grabbed her husband's arm. "Sit down. You're not helping."

The laughter brought much-needed lightheartedness to the situation. Lucinda continued. "I know you're probably thinking of all the reasons that pastor was wrong, and I would probably agree. Looking back, though, I don't think he was trying to be mean. I think he just didn't know there was a better way. Years later he actually came to us and apologized. He had matured enough to see the error of his ways and was genuinely sorry. It was horrible at the time, but God wasn't done writing the story."

Beth came back in time to hear Lucinda's last statement. "As the saying goes, 'If it's not the best thing, then it's not the last thing.'" She sat down and looked at Meghan. "Sorry. I just needed some air."

The compassionate look in her blue eyes stirred another feeling of familiarity in Meghan. *Come on, think. Where have I seen her before? Her hair was up, away from her face, not down like it is now.* She still couldn't place her.

Pastor Nate was speaking again . . . to her. "As I was saying, the reason I wanted you to meet Lucinda and Glenn is because part of their incredible story is how they serve the Lord. When they built their home, they designed the basement to be a separate apartment. They use their home to help others who are starting out or starting over. Up until a few weeks ago, a missionary family on furlough was staying there. But now . . ." He turned to Lucinda. "Take it from here."

"Gladly," she said. "Now, Meghan, we would like to invite you to consider staying with us."

Meghan couldn't believe what she'd heard. Had Lucinda just offered her a place to live?

"Obviously, you don't have to decide here and now. You can stay with us tonight as sort of a trial run and then take your time to decide."

Glenn picked up a small menu. "Speaking of time. I think it's time for dessert. Who wants to share tiramisu?"

Nate and Beth raised their hands as Glenn responded. "Good! You two share, because I never share when it comes to tiramisu."

The conversation took a new direction as Glenn and Lucinda told stories from their many travels. Over her first-ever piece of tiramisu, Meghan tasted something even sweeter than dessert. Hope. God was for her, not against her. He hadn't released her of responsibility, but He was providing a way to move forward.

As the waitstaff cleared the rest of the dishes, Nate said, "I guess we should call it a night. Starting tomorrow, Beth goes back to full time."

Beth looked directly at Meghan. "The students will swarm campus tomorrow. You know how the college schedule goes."

The scattered pieces came together in Meghan's mind. "Oh! You work at MCU, don't you? Admissions office?"

That explained why Beth looked familiar and also how Pastor Nate knew Vivian Perkins.

Beth walked Meghan to her car. "I almost said something earlier but didn't want to invade your privacy. I'm so sorry for the way the university treated you. Please know that's not the heart of everyone there."

An all-too-familiar lump formed in Meghan's throat. "Thank you" was all she could manage.

As she followed Glenn and Lucinda to their home, she remembered Beth's earlier words. "If it's not the best thing, then it's not the last thing." *It's not the last thing until it's the best thing. Lord, help me remember to let You define what's best for me and my baby.*

CHAPTER 25

Meghan was on the south side of Petoskey when her phone rang. The digital dash screen read "Wireless Caller." She dismissed the call and ignored two more. When the fourth came, she answered. Even robocallers weren't that persistent.

It was Zac. An angry Zac. He must have gotten a new number.

"Meghan, what were you thinking? You shouldn't have gone to my house. You didn't need to drag them into this."

Word traveled fast. After her night in Grand Rapids, Meghan had stopped to see her dad in Traverse City. Together with Zac's grandma and the Thomsons, he had surprised her with a special birthday lunch. It had already been a long day, and she didn't feel like playing nice.

"Is that you, Zac? It's been, what, six weeks since I've heard from you? How nice of you to call and ask how your baby and I are doing. Or were you calling to wish me Happy Birthday?" Her syrupy response only fueled his fire.

"Knock it off. I told you to leave me out of it. Apparently, you couldn't figure out that means to leave my family out of it too."

"They have a right, Zac. This baby is part of their family too."

Zac ignored the statement. "I'm texting you my address. Again. Get me those papers to sign and let's get this over with. I want out for good, Meghan, and I want out now."

Meghan was just as angry and returned fire. "Oh, does your new girlfriend not like the idea you got someone else pregnant?"

Beep. Meghan looked at the screen. *Call Ended.* No matter. She continued her side of the conversation. "You're such a jerk. Must be nice to get your way all the time. Thanks for only thinking about yourself. As usual."

A gentle voice interrupted her. *He is still the father of your baby.*

Zac wasn't going to let this go. He'd been pushing her to find out how he could revoke parental rights. Why didn't he figure it out himself? How had that become her responsibility? Right now she had more pressing issues, such as where to live when her job ended next month. Grand Rapids or Traverse City? Her dad continually reminded her he had two extra bedrooms. And Zac's mom had practically begged Meghan to live with them. That would sure stick it to Zac. Then again, maybe cutting ties with Zac would make life easier for everyone.

Over dinner that night, Steve and Netta were astonished by how much had changed in only three days.

"Just think," Netta said. "When you left you didn't have any prospects, and now you have a two-bedroom apartment in the home of a loving Christian family."

"It gets even better." Meghan added. "They insisted they wouldn't take rent from me. Instead, they want me to build up my savings for when I move out."

That caught Steve's attention. "Hey, we'll be leaving here in November. Maybe we can stay rent-free in your second bedroom."

"Steven, you're terrible," Netta poked him playfully. "That room will be for the baby." She held out a stack of dirty plates. "How about you take these to the kitchen and clean up so Meghan and I can look at her baby registry. I doubt you are interested in such things."

"If it will get me out of dish duty, I suddenly feel very interested in diapers and wipes."

"Speaking of wipes"—Meghan laughed—"don't forget to wipe off the table when you're done."

"Two against one. Doesn't seem fair." He grabbed the stack of dishes and left the dining room with his head down.

Meghan followed Netta to the living room. "I hope I didn't hurt his feelings."

"Hah. He's totally faking, for attention," Netta said, loud enough for Steve to hear.

Tears erupted uninvited. *God didn't answer my prayers as far as my parents getting back together, but He brought some awesome people into my life to help fill the empty places.* "You and Steve have been so good to me."

Netta reached over and hugged Meghan. "We love you, sweetie. You are every bit as much a gift to us."

After a thorough look at all the cute baby things on Meghan's registry, Netta relocated to the empty, and clean, dining room table. "No peeking while I do some shopping."

Meghan stretched out on the sofa and reached for an envelope on the coffee table. It was a birthday card from Zac's mom. She included a check and handwritten note. The updates on work and home were now mostly old news since Meghan's drop-in visit. There was no mention of Zac until the very end. *Keep the faith. Deep down, my son is afraid. He has been running from his pain for a long time. Putting up walls thinking they will protect his heart. We are praying God will use this baby to bring healing, but it's up to him to surrender. That is not something any of us can choose for him.*

Wise words. As she considered them, Meghan found a little room for compassion. It wasn't much, but it was a start.

Week 24

It was Meghan's last day on the island. She easily pedaled her bike up the hill to Huron Road. Turning east, she rode along the east bluff, taking in the view of historic homes high above Lake Huron. The cooler fall temperatures created an ombré palette of blues. Set against the bright-colored leaves of maple and birch, mixed with the soft-green cedars, the sight was glorious.

"God, only You could paint such a picture," Meghan declared. Two blue jays sitting on a nearby stump squawked in agreement.

Meghan continued her journey along of Huron Road. The tree tops reached for one another and created a canopy over the pavement. Sunbeams filtered through the openings, creating a kaleidoscope of movement and light. She parked her bike at Arch Rock and recalled a story her dad had recently told her.

"Your mother and I were sitting right here when she told me she was leaving. She had it planned down to the very last detail. I never saw it coming. She told me and then left me sitting here. She left the island and never looked back." Five years and the wound was still raw. *"We told you she was called away for work. Do you remember?"*

As if she could ever forget. The missing pieces fell into place and now everything made sense. Why they extended their stay on the island. Why they'd rented a car twenty miles away in Pellston. Why her mother's things were gone when they got home. Why Dad stopped going to Mackinac.

Before she continued her journey, Meghan climbed to the overlook. From there she spied the rocks where Andi had shown her the picture of Zac. The place where her future had fallen apart. She imagined the place around the bend where she'd walked into the water. Where she'd surrendered her future to God.

From Arch Rock, she cut through the woods to Skull Cave, then rode past the cemeteries and looped around to Fort Holmes. The highest point on the island offered an unobstructed panorama.

From her bird's-eye view, even the Mighty Mac bridge looked tiny. *God, is this what You see when You look down on us? We are so small and I am one of so many. Can You really see me?* How could God be so vast and yet so personal? How could He watch over the whole world and the single sparrow? He was big enough to tower over the galaxies . . . yet became small enough to be cradled in the womb of a teenage girl from Nazareth. It was a beautiful mystery.

Meghan took the long way back, not yet ready for the ride to end. She retraced the path along Garrison Road to where she'd started on Huron Road. Leaning her bike against a tree, she walked along the ridge to Anne's Tablet. It was here she and Andi had formulated their original summer-on-Mackinac plan so many years ago. Very little had turned out the way they'd expected. Meghan laughed as a long-forgotten detail emerged, then snapped a picture and texted Andi.

> Do you remember dreaming of cute boys from far-off lands who would marry us and take us back to their mansions? LOL. Not exactly the life we planned for, right?

She leaned against a cedar tree and thought of the unexpected life within her. She placed her hands protectively over her baby. "Thank God His plan prevailed, Little One."

Little One must have heard, because at that moment, Meghan felt the first kick. She began to cry, not from sorrow but joy. "Did you hear me, Little One? God has plans for you, plans to prosper you and not to harm you, plans to give you a future and a hope." Meghan pulled out her phone and sent a group text:

THE BABY JUST KICKED!!

Then she hopped on her bike and rode to the coffee shop to tell Netta. They waited twenty minutes, hoping the baby would kick again, but nothing happened.

"Don't fret," Netta assured. "She's probably sleeping. There will be many more to come."

Meghan was disappointed. "Maybe if I move around?" She glanced at the wall clock. "How about if I go for a walk and come back at closing time to help you clean up?"

"Sounds great," Netta answered. "It's your last day to hit all the fudge shops."

"Thanks for the reminder. I want to get some to take to Grand Rapids. Plus, if I don't bring some for Andi, she might unfriend me."

As she passed Marquette Park and turned onto Market Street, Meghan remembered the lady in hot pink. *Would I respond differently if that happened now?*

Not sure how to answer her own question, she continued past the post office and thought of the kind man who'd held the door. He was so different than hot-pink lady. *I want to be like him. I want to treat people with dignity and respect. He didn't assume he knew my story. He didn't judge my choices without knowing the options I had.*

The next stop was her favorite fudge shop.

"Meghan!" the staff chimed in unison.

The manager did a double take. "Meghan?"

"Yes. I'm pregnant. It's okay to talk about it." Her up-front response broke the tension and set off a barrage of questions.

"When are you due?"

"Is it a boy or girl?"

"How are you feeling?"

"Are you staying on the island?"

No one asked, "Who's the father?" or "Won't this ruin your life?" They seemed genuinely happy for her and insisted on celebrating with a gift of fudge.

"We need to fatten you up. Choose three slices. Whatever kind you want."

"I'm doing just fine fattening myself up." Meghan laughed. "But I do need to stock up because tomorrow I'm leaving."

Meghan exited the shop with four pounds of Mackinac Island fudge. *Good thing it freezes well.* Then her mind shifted to Mary's parting words: *"Please say you'll be back next summer. We want to meet your baby."* Next summer? She couldn't even fathom what next summer would look like.

On her way back to Netta's, Meghan stopped at Marquette Park. Everywhere she looked triggered a memory of people and places. She touched her butterfly pendant, a symbol of the ways God used His people in those places. The steeple of Sainte Anne's stood high above street level, commanding its dominant place as an icon of the island. The shadow of the cross no longer cast shame. It had become a symbol of God's love. The cross had become her anchor to grace.

CHAPTER 26

Week 26

Meghan climbed the stairway from the basement apartment to the kitchen and closed the door behind her.

"Glenn and your dad sure hit it off." Lucinda pointed a chunky chef's knife at the two men hunched over a small table in the next room. "They have a best-out-of-five cribbage tournament going strong."

Meghan strained to reach four bowls from the cupboard. Her arms seemed to grow shorter as the baby grew bigger. "It's funny they both graduated from Ohio State but ended up in Michigan."

Lucinda resumed chopping. The knife hit the cutting board in rhythm with her words. "Probably [thump] another reason [thump] they bonded [thump] so quickly [thump]. Not many admit to being an Ohio State fan in Wolverines' territory. 'Buckeyes beware' is a real thing here."

"Speaking of Wolverines," Meghan began, "Zac goes to U of Michigan. He got a full football and academic scholarship package."

"Good for him," Lucinda beamed. "His little wolverine will be proud."

Four metal forks rattled as Meghan carelessly dropped them into the stack of bowls. "That's not going to happen. Zac doesn't want anything to do with me or the baby. He wants to terminate his parental rights."

Lucinda stopped chopping, leaving the knife blade stuck inside the striped, green rind of a large watermelon. "He's just walking away? Leaving you to raise the baby alone?"

Alone. Could she really handle it alone? Before Meghan could fully consider that possibility or answer Lucinda's questions, Glenn and Peter walked into the kitchen.

"It was close, but I prevailed," Glenn declared. "If Peter hadn't—" He stopped and looked back and forth between Meghan and his wife.

"Uh oh," Dad began. "It seems we interrupted something." When no one replied, he handed Meghan a cable-stitch poncho. "I thought we should get going."

Meghan slipped the soft woolen garment over her head. Zac's mom was an accomplished needleworker, and when the gift had arrived in the mail, Meghan declared it too beautiful to wear and told her so.

"You're the mother of my grandchild," she had responded. "I will knit you as many as you want. Think of it as my way of giving you a hug each time you put it on."

Meghan relented and was increasingly grateful as the temperature dropped.

Lucinda reached over to touch the intricate stitches. "I can't even imagine making something so beautiful. You called it Aran knit? And the color . . . it's perfect on you."

"Thank you, and yes, it is called Aran, after the Irish islands this pattern came from." Meghan pulled the hem diagonally over to one side and secured the two leathery buttons nestled at the collar. "The color is called 'marine mist.'"

"And here all along I thought the sweater was blue." Glenn hand-ed Meghan a covered container of watermelon for the road.

Dad opened the front door and swept his arm toward the shiny late-model, full-size SUV parked outside. "Your chariot awaits."

When he'd arrived yesterday morning, Meghan asked why he'd bought something so big. He simply answered, "Precious cargo."

Meghan grabbed the handle above the doorframe and pulled herself in. Before long she would need a stepladder to climb into the front seat.

She secured her seat belt and waited for her dad to close the door. When she looked up, he was watching her. Was it hard for him to see his daughter pregnant? Looking through his eyes, she imagined it would be difficult.

"Ready or not." Dad didn't break eye contact as he shut the door.

Ready or not, this was going to be a long day. A busy day. An emotional day. Since their time on Mackinac, Dad had developed a protective posture over his daughter. He insisted, as often as his schedule allowed, on making the trip to Grand Rapids to visit. He was also quick to open doors, offer his arm, and anticipate Meghan's (real or imagined) needs. Each time she caught herself ready to say, "Okay, Dad, that's enough," she remembered how it used to be and flipped the negative feelings into prayers of gratitude. Her father was showing love the best way he knew how, and helping his daughter obviously brought him joy.

So Meghan patiently waited. Waited in traffic. Waited as her dad drove slowly across the bumpy parking lot of the health clinic. Waited for their turn to pull up under the maroon covered entrance. And waited as her dad walked around to open her door. She took his offered hand and stepped out to see a wheelchair waiting on the side-walk. "Oh no. Not happening," she insisted. Even love had its limits.

This appointment would be Meghan's introduction to her new obstetrician's team as well as another round of intake paperwork and routine procedures. The measurements and tests sent from Mackinaw City confirmed she was twenty-six weeks along in a healthy pregnancy. That meant she was about to enter the third, and final, trimester. The first ultrasound, at fourteen weeks, had revealed no concerns but was unable to determine the baby's gender. Today, her second ultrasound was the last item on the appointment checklist, and she wasn't certain she wanted to know.

Before the procedure began, the nurse, she introduced herself as Erin, responded to Meghan's hesitation. "It's okay to be surprised. For most of human history, mothers have survived not knowing what color to decorate the nursery. That's why mint green and yellow will never go out of style, right, Gabby?"

"Do most people find out?" Meghan asked the sonographer.

The young woman squirted clear jelly unto the wand. "It really varies. Most couples I work with want to know. I'm not sure what their reasons are, but that has been my experience."

"It might have something to do with gender reveal parties and social media ratings," Erin suggested as she pivoted the large monitor.

Meghan wasn't interested in either of those things. The more she drew attention to herself, the more opportunities for people to insult her. The cold sensation on her belly interrupted her thoughts and turned her attention to the screen.

As the wand rolled around, Meghan couldn't help but squirm. Gabby lifted the transducer. "Does something hurt?"

"No. It just feels really weird."

"I know it does." Erin patted her hand. "You're doing great. Just try to hold still a little longer, okay?"

As the cold jelly dripped down her side, Meghan tried to relax by mentally rearranging the letters of the sign hanging on the far wall. *Ultrasound. Ultra. Sound. Star. Rat. Rats. Sun. Son.*

Gabby soon interrupted her game. "We've got a good picture today. Baby isn't hiding anything. What's the verdict, Mom?"

Torn, Meghan wished someone else would decide for her. This was a big decision. The kind of decision you couldn't take back. Out of nowhere, Father Joshua's words came to mind. "Keep your options open." Based on that advice, Meghan made her decision. "Mint green it is. Don't tell me. Not today anyway."

"My lips are sealed." Gabby handed Meghan a handful of paper towels.

"Mine too," Erin added. "I won't print any pictures that will ruin the surprise."

After a much-needed bathroom break, Meghan scheduled her next ultrasound, then followed the exit signs down the long hallway. As she walked, she stared at the tiny face on the glossy paper. True to her word, none of the pictures Erin had printed revealed the baby's gender.

"Well?" Dad asked when Meghan returned to the waiting room. "How's my grandchild doing? Will I have a grandson or granddaughter?"

"He"—Meghan paused for effect—"or she is doing great. Want to see a picture?"

With just one look, Dad was transformed into a proud to-be grandpa. He snapped a photo of the sonogram image and spent most of the time over lunch texting it to his contacts. Meghan was almost finished with her sandwich before he finally set his phone down.

"Did you send a picture to your mother?"

Meghan didn't know what to say, so she said nothing.

"Meghan, did you send a picture to your mother?"

"No."

"Do you think you should?"

"I don't know."

"Would it be okay if I did?"

"It's a free country."

"I'll take that to mean you would prefer I didn't."

"I would prefer not to discuss it. Let's not ruin this perfectly beautiful day."

After lunch, Dad took Meghan grocery shopping. Walking up and down the aisles of the mega-store took more time and energy than it used to. If it was up to him, they would still be browsing the baby section. Her plea of "Dad, we're going to be late if we don't get moving" was the only reason they weren't still there. For once, Meghan didn't mind waiting in line at the checkout. If offered a ride in a wheelchair now, she wouldn't turn it down.

Settled in the car, Meghan reclined the seat and closed her eyes. By the time Dad unloaded and returned the cart, she was half-asleep. Shortly after backing out of the parking space, she had the sensation of being on a merry-go-round. Confused, she sat up.

Her dad also looked confused. "Remind me where we're going next."

"Dad . . ." Meghan laughed. "How many laps have we taken on this roundabout?"

One more loop and they were on their way to meet with Elaina at the pregnancy center. Safe Haven had a room full of maternity clothes, and Meghan's wardrobe was shrinking. People from the community donated everything from maternity swimwear to formal dresses and business suits. Clients were encouraged to take whatever they needed, free of charge. The items from the room-sized closet were borrowed like library books and returned after they weren't needed anymore. Meghan had been getting by with leggings and baggy sweatshirts, but it would be nice to have some real clothes again. It also gave her a good reason to introduce her dad to Elaina.

While a volunteer led Dad on a tour of the classrooms and various storage areas, Meghan briefed Elaina on school, the move, and her doctor's appointment.

"Who's your OB?" Elaina asked.

"Dr. Caygen," Meghan answered. "Do you know her?"

A reassuring smile spread across Elaina's face. "Candace is a wonderful doctor and a sister in Christ. She often steps in to help when a girl seeks to reverse a dose of mifepristone."

This was news to Meghan. "What? You mean a baby can survive the abortion pill?"

"In the first trimester, yes. As long as the mother hasn't taken the second set of pills and receives a counteracting dosage of progesterone within seventy-two hours. Obviously, the sooner the treatment is given, the better chance the baby has to live."

Meghan was shocked. If this was true, why hadn't the doctor told her? Why didn't the information provided with the pills include this option? If she would have taken that first pill, it would have been too late for her baby. Her ignorance would have cost her the chance to change her mind. The option to make a different choice.

The weight of this realization pulled her down into a nearby glider rocker. "How did I not know this?"

"It's surprising how many people don't know. If each one tells one, the truth will spread, and somewhere down the line, some baby will have a second chance."

Elaina pulled open a desk drawer and handed Meghan a thin brochure. The cover photo featured a young woman holding a sign. On the ground next to her feet was an empty infant car seat. The words on the sign read, *It's Not too Late: Bella's Second-Chance Life.*

Meghan folded the brochure and tucked it into her purse. "There's so much I have to learn."

"That reminds me." Elaina quickly stepped out of the room and came back with another brochure. "In two weeks, Saint Bridget's is hosting an event you might be interested in. Take a look at this and let me know if you'd like to go. Many of our clients find it very encouraging."

Meghan glanced at the cover of the brochure. "Be Pro-Love" stood out in bold, red letters. "Sure, I'll think about it." Later. Right now, all she wanted to do was go home and put her feet up. Between the doctor's appointment, shopping, and the fact she still had to pick out maternity clothes, she was ready to call it a day.

Meghan walked around the lobby as she waited for her dad. The walls were covered with pictures. Mothers and babies, groups and families, events and honors. She stopped when she recognized Laura in one of the frames. The setting looked like some sort of award ceremony because everyone was dressed up and holding a plaque. Meghan's eyes scanned the others in the group picture. She let out a little gasp as another face caught her attention. Where had she seen that man before?

CHAPTER 27

*M*eghan circled the block twice before turning into parking lot of Saint Bridget's Catholic Church. With the push of a button, the ignition shut off, but Meghan made no move to exit her vehicle. The minutes passed as she watched people going in and out the main doors. If she waited much longer, she'd be late. So far, every girl her age was with a guy who reminded her of Zac. Or, more specifically, they reminded her of Zac's absence.

Once Meghan had registered for the event, she'd texted Zac a picture of the brochure and invited him to come. She knew he didn't have the excuse of football. The team had an away game at Penn State, and freshmen didn't travel that far. The venue was a two-hour drive from Ann Arbor, but she still hoped he might come.

9:50 a.m.

The lot was almost full. A bunch of people showed up at the same time and hurried inside. No one looked her way. *If I wait until the event starts, I can drive away, and no one will even know I was here.* Meghan reached for a tissue, surprised by the feeling of sadness. For some reason, the urge to escape wasn't holding the same power it once had. Still, it was getting harder to find the motivation to keep walking into places pregnant and alone.

Maybe I should just forget it and go home. Maybe Andi isn't busy, and I could visit her for the weekend. She opened the brochure again.

9:50	Welcome	School Auditorium
10:10	Morning Breakout Sessions	
	• Expectant Mothers	St. Aaron Room
	• Expectant Fathers	St. Benedict Room
	• Family and Friends	St. Catherine Room
	• Clergy/Lay Leaders	St. Damien Room
	• Prayer/Counselors	St. Francis Room
Noon	Lunch/Break	Cafeteria
1:15	Afternoon Breakout Sessions	
	Same Groups/Same Rooms	
2:30	Event ends. Expectant Mothers. Please pick up a gift bag on your way out	
9:30-3:30	Resource and Information Tables	Cafeteria and Foyer

10:08 a.m.

Keep your options open. Funny she should think of Father Joshua's words while she stood in front of a Catholic church. "Here goes nothing," she told herself. Then she pulled open the door and walked into another unknown.

A table designated *Registration* sat directly across the entryway. Meghan took a deep breath and walked toward a friendly looking woman who stood to greet her. "Good morning. We are so glad you're here. May I have your name, please?"

Meghan tended to talk fast when she was nervous. "I'm sorry I'm late. If I missed registration, I can go. No problem. It's my fault."

The woman wasn't deterred. "You haven't missed anything. We're glad you're here. My name is Patrice. What's yours?"

"Meghan. Meghan McPherson."

Patrice scanned her clipboard. "Here you are, under the M for McPherson." She followed her finger across the page and added, "Looks like your group is meeting in the St. Aaron Room. My husband will escort you there. And I will look forward to seeing you later."

Meghan took the folder offered and turned in the direction Patrice pointed. Twenty feet away, stood a man looking directly at her. Or more like directly through her. Meghan dropped her folder, her purse, and her phone. Was that *him*? The man outside the abortion clinic?

Patrice hurried to retrieve Meghan's belongings. "Are you okay, dear? Do you need medical attention?"

Meghan couldn't move or speak as the man walked over. No doubt. It was definitely him. Those were his eyes.

A moment of silence passed between them before he spoke. "Are you all right? Do you need to sit down?" Without waiting for an answer, he led Meghan to a folding chair and sat opposite her.

Patrice handed her a bottle of water. "You're looking a little better now. The color is returning to your cheeks. Do you think we should take you to urgent care?"

"No, thank you. I'm fine. Sorry to have troubled you." Fighting tears, Meghan cautiously glanced toward the man.

Patrice saw the tears welling up in Meghan's green eyes. "This is my husband, Tony. Tony, meet Meghan McPherson."

Tony. His name was Tony.

His voice was kind. "It's nice to meet you, Meghan. If I'm not mistaken, we may have seen each other once before."

Meghan could only nod.

"Do you want to rest here, or shall I escort you to your group?"

Meghan quickly assessed her body's strength, then stood and said, "I'm ready."

10:21 a.m.

It was a quick walk down the hall to the St. Aaron Room. Neither spoke as Tony held the door open and quietly shut it again after Meghan passed through the threshold.

That got everyone's attention. Meghan scanned the room. Small round tables were arranged in rows. Groups of two or three girls were seated at each table. She spied the perfect spot, ducked her head, and made a beeline straight through the middle of the room. A table of one was okay with her.

The speaker stood behind a lectern and addressed her directly. "Welcome. We're so glad you can be with us today. We've just finished introductions and are about to begin the presentation. If you don't mind, we'll move on and save time at the end to formally meet you."

Meghan didn't mind at all.

She scanned the paper on the table. The speaker's name was Yasmine Phang. She worked for Saint William Adoption Assistance Services located somewhere downtown. According to Yasmine's introduction, the first session would focus on various support resources available to anyone experiencing unexpected pregnancies. Each organization had representatives available at information tables set up in the cafeteria.

"As I was saying earlier," Yasmine said, "there are many wonderful gifts that have been donated today. Each booth you visit will earn you one entry for a chance to be the recipient of those items."

"So you're basically bribing us to visit the booths," one girl cheerfully observed.

Busted.

Yasmine took it in stride. "It depends on how you look at it, Bryonna. I call it incentive."

Bryonna followed with, "Oh, no complaints here. I'm not above bribery."

Their playful interaction made everyone laugh and lifted the tension in the room. For the first time since arriving, Meghan felt herself relax.

Yasmine explained how her organization helped women explore and create personalized plans for adoption. "We walk with you from the beginning of the process until you decide you don't need us anymore. A woman's journey doesn't end when the adoption is complete. Carrying a baby creates a bond you will carry with you the rest of your life. Choosing to place your baby is a courageous decision but also difficult and, at times, painful. Deciding to let someone else raise the baby you've carried is an incredible act of sacrificial love."

Meghan thought of Ava's story and how, even as a teenager, being adopted by the Renick family had changed her life for the good.

Yasmine lowered the lectern and stacked her papers. "Whether you choose to place or parent your baby, we want you to know there is a lot of help available. Everyone here cares about both you and your baby. We want this to be a place where you feel safe and supported. No one will judge you or the circumstances of your pregnancy. You made the courageous decision to give your baby life, and we are so thankful. We also understand some of you may have chosen a different path before this. Again, we are so glad you're here. If you struggle with a past abortion, there are women here who have walked in your shoes. They would love to talk with you. This day is about you. We want to meet you wherever you're at, however you need us."

All doubt melted away under the covering of sincere compassion. No one was hiding from the truth or manipulating it to advance an ideology. Meghan believed what Yasmine said. She felt neither judged nor belittled. *Lord, obviously You're here. I lay down my agenda and trust You will guide me through this day.*

As Yasmine concluded the first breakout session, Meghan felt empowered and encouraged. Safe Haven wasn't the only source of assistance for so-called crisis pregnancies. One group offered rides and delivered meals. Another sponsored baby showers. There was a car seat giveaway, nutrition assistance through the government, and a variety of other support and education programs.

Yasmine assured the girls there was no shame in accepting help. "That's what it's there for," she said. "These opportunities are available to all who qualify, even married couples who purposefully conceived every one of their children. Don't fall into the trap of thinking you are somehow inferior if you utilize these programs."

An electronic chime drew all eyes to the overhead speaker. It was noon. The sound of shuffling papers, scraping chairs, and immediate chatter reminded Meghan of her middle school years. Instinctively, the group formed a line and moved toward the door. Yasmine's arm stretched across the doorframe and blocked their exit.

"One more thing. Remember—how people treat you speaks of their character, not yours. I wish I had understood that when I was your age."

As the procession spilled into the busy hallway, Bryonna raised the same question Meghan found herself asking. "Where did that come from?"

No one had an answer.

12:15 p.m.

Meghan balanced her plate and drink, not sure where to go next. *This is so awkward. It really does feel like a middle school cafeteria. I don't have anyone to sit with.* Rather than waiting for someone to invite her to sit with them or risk the humiliation of sitting alone, she decided to eat in her car. As she edged along the wall toward the back of the room, someone called her name. She searched for the one person who apparently knew her.

"Meghan, over here." Beth waved from the opposite side of the room.

Relieved to see a familiar face, Meghan zigzagged her way to Beth's table. "What are you doing here?"

"Nate and I are both here. He is attending the sessions for pastors, and I am helping run the booth for Moses' Basket."

"What's Moses' Basket?"

"It's a ministry for pregnant single women. They help them finish their education, find jobs, get to doctor appointments, and things like that."

"I'll stop by later," Meghan promised.

Beth looked at her watch. "I wish I had more time to visit, but I need to get back in ten minutes."

Ten minutes? I'll eat fast.

As Meghan took the first bite of her salad, Beth asked, "Have you seen Laura? She said she was coming."

Meghan swallowed too quickly and struggled to reply. "Laura Garrick?"

12:25 p.m.

Meghan was still hungry but didn't want to eat alone. She wrapped some food in a napkin, picked up another water bottle, and returned her tray. It felt good to stretch her legs as she walked the perimeter of the large room lined with decorated tables. Not all appealed enough to warrant a stop, even if it meant losing out on prizes. Bryonna, on the other hand, was speedily making her way from booth to booth. After a quick sign-up, she was off to the next one. Meghan's eyes widened when she saw Elaina at Safe Haven's table. She might have missed it if not for Bryonna's race to the finish.

"Meghan," Elaina greeted warmly. "So glad you made it today. I was worried when I saw you hadn't checked in."

Unsure how to respond, Meghan shrugged.

"How was your first session?"

"It was good," Meghan replied. "Thank you for inviting me. This is a really nice event. Everyone is so friendly and nonjudgmental. I feel like they genuinely want to help."

"We are thankful for all who participate. Too often, people criticize the pro-life movement for only being anti-abortion and not caring about what happens to a mother after she chooses life. As you can see, there are many people who do care."

"No doubt," Meghan agreed. "Maybe you should invite the haters next time."

Others approached the table, so she said goodbye to Elaina and continued down the row. Beth supervised the Moses' Basket table but was busy with someone else. Meghan dropped her ticket in the bucket and moved to the next booth in line. No one was there at the moment, but she stopped to study the trifold display board. Then she added her ticket to the fishbowl and turned around.

Once again, she stood face-to-face with Tony. The familiar brown eyes behind his wire-rim glasses were the same ones that had watched her walk into and run out of the abortion clinic.

It was the voice that was unfamiliar. "Glad to see you're feeling better. I'm sorry I gave you such a fright."

The memory of their earlier interaction dropped like a stone in a pool of calm water and created a ripple of anxiety. Meghan reminded herself to feel the feelings and stand strong in the moment. "I was just caught off guard. You didn't frighten me."

"I'm sorry if I embarrassed you by mentioning we had met before."

"No, it's okay. It's just that I never expected to see you again . . . you know, after that day."

"It's a day I will never forget." Tony patted his hand over his heart. "Never experienced anything like it. I've stood outside that clinic for twelve years and prayed as young women walked in pregnant and walked out . . ." His voice trailed off. "We pray and we hope, but I've never seen someone run toward life like you did that day."

"I'm sure it was a spectacle."

"No, Meghan. It was a miracle."

Meghan wanted to tell him. She wanted him to know the role he played in that day. But she couldn't bring herself to do it. Not yet. She would cry in front of all these people, and they would think she was crazy.

1:00 p.m.

As the group trickled back into the room, a girl about the same age walked up to Meghan's table. "Hi. My name's Jada. Mind if I sit with you?"

Meghan replied by pulling out the chair beside her.

Jada was thirty-six weeks pregnant and due the first week of December. "Brady, my boyfriend, and I are getting married this Friday. Not a real wedding or anything. We're just going to the courthouse to make it official."

"That's exciting. Congratulations." Meghan mostly meant it, but a little part of her was jealous.

"Thanks," Jada said. "We rented a little one-bedroom apartment in Allegan. When Brady heard the big factory there was hiring, he quit school and got his GED. We'll get along fine as long as they don't lay him off."

Before they could visit more, Yasmine began the session. "Now that you've had time to learn about all of the support available in our community, I would like to introduce the director of Safe Haven Pregnancy Support Center. I know many of you are already familiar with this wonderful organization, so please help me welcome Elaina Kent."

Yasmine quietly exited after Elaina stepped to the middle of the room.

"Good afternoon," she began. "It's so good to be with you today. I think I know all of you, so let me begin by saying 'Congratulations.' Congratulations on the expectant arrival of the new life God has placed inside you. Congratulations for choosing life and allowing us to walk with you. Inviting us to be part of your journey."

Elaina wove through the maze of tables, making a personal connection with each of the participants. "I have worked at Safe Haven for almost forty years and know the power of story. Not fairy tales or dramatical romances, but real stories from real people who have been where you are now."

Elaina walked to the back of the room and opened the door. "Today we have two women who have graciously agreed to share with us. As you listen, remember these are *their* stories. You can learn from them. You can question them. You can put yourself in their shoes. But remember, their story is not your story. Try not to compare yourselves to others. Please welcome Karissa Butler and Laura Garrick."

Meghan was surprised but not as much as she would have been had Beth not already mentioned Laura's presence.

Meghan gave a little wave as Laura took a seat in the row set up behind the lectern. Karissa spoke first, but Meghan had a hard time following her story because she kept comparing it to her own situation. *Doesn't apply to me . . . Easy for you to say . . . Must be nice to have a supportive mom . . . How can you be so nonchalant about sharing these personal details?* So much for Elaina's instruction.

Karissa's next words, however, caught Meghan by surprise.

"That's when I decided to place my baby for adoption."

The internal chatter stopped. Karissa commandeered Meghan's full attention.

"Even after eight years, not a day goes by that I don't wonder if I made the right choice." With that, she sat down.

As though the group held its collective breath, a reverent stillness encircled the room. Laura stepped up to the podium and bluntly shared the basics of her story. Nothing about it was new to Meghan, until Laura said, "While I loved my son and gave him the best I could, he still paid the price for things he had no control over. He didn't ask for parents who didn't stay married. He didn't ask to be raised by a single mom. He didn't ask for stepfamilies. He didn't ask for only every other weekend with his dad. Our choices have caused him deep pain. Despite me doing the best I knew how, he will carry the effects of those realities the rest of his life. So many times I have felt incredible guilt. Would he have had a better life if I'd given him up for adoption? Was I selfish to keep him? Is he being punished for my mistakes?"

Laura and Meghan locked eyes, and she felt Laura's next words to her core.

"I don't tell you this to scare you or shame you. No one can walk this journey for you, but you don't have to walk it alone. Your path isn't going to look exactly like anyone else's, but that's okay. It's not supposed to. God has a unique plan for your life and for your baby's life. He's not done writing my story. He's not done writing my son's story. And, no matter what you choose, He's not done writing yours either."

A shaky voice called out from somewhere behind Meghan. "How are we supposed to figure out what to do?"

Compassionate tears flowed from Laura's eyes. "You keep searching. This is the time to focus on taking care of yourself and exploring all the possibilities. Don't look for an easy way out, because there isn't one. Don't let what others think or say cause you to doubt your worth or your faith."

The girls sat in silence as Laura sat down. Then someone asked, "Miss Laura? How can I know which decision will give my baby a better life?"

Laura returned to the podium slowly. "Mmm," she said. "Great question. It shows you are thinking about what is best for your baby. But you already know, there are no guarantees in life. Sometimes things fall into place. Sometimes they don't. Sometimes people get married and stay married. Sometimes they don't. Sometimes adoptions are smooth rides, and sometimes they aren't."

The girls grew restless in their seats.

"The fact is, no one is guaranteed a fairy-tale happy life. We could be born into the most perfect circumstances imaginable and still grow up unhappy or unhealthy. That's why we so desperately need God. He is the light in the darkness, the hope in the brokenness."

Elaina stepped in. "Girls, the very fact you are here today shows you are already seeking answers. You care about making the best decisions you can. You aren't asking, 'How can I get out of this? What's best for me?' You're here asking, 'What is best for both me and my baby?'"

Karissa also returned to the front. "We don't mean to cause you pain or make you afraid. We want you to understand the real-life implications of whichever choice you make. We know this is hard to hear. Hard to comprehend. But we also wish someone had told us these things before we learned on our own, the hard way. We care about you and your babies. We want to walk with you."

Afterward, Laura approached Meghan. "You doing okay?"

"That was intense," Meghan admitted. "At the time I was sorry I was hearing it, but as it sinks in, I have some new things to think about."

"Anything I can help with?"

"Actually, there is. I set up an appointment with Yasmine to learn more about adoption. Would you maybe want to go with me?"

"Absolutely. Are you leaning in that direction?"

Meghan shrugged. "I don't know. I'm exploring my options. Just like everyone keeps telling me to do."

"Good. That's very wise." Laura exhaled loudly. "I sure could use some chocolate. I heard there's quite a spread in the cafeteria. Care to join me?"

"Sure," Meghan agreed. "I'll meet you there. I need to do something first."

10:49 p.m.

Meghan was tired but having trouble falling asleep. A whirlwind of the day's events spun in her mind. There was so much to think about. *How do I sort this out? How do I know which option is the right one?*

She would never forget the look of shock on Tony's face. His tears fell freely as she recalled that day at the clinic.

"Thank God. Thank You, God," he'd kept saying.

Meghan couldn't get over the fact that Tony had spent twelve years praying outside the abortion clinic before he'd witnessed a single answer. She was pretty sure she wasn't the first person impacted by those prayers, but Tony's dedication had taught her an important lesson: Trust God and don't give up.

Okay, God, I'm trusting You to have the answers. Until You show me what they are, I'll keep moving forward one step at a time.

CHAPTER 28

Week 30

Saint William Adoption Assistance Services shared a two-story brick building with a dentist and realtor. The soft gray walls of Yasmine's office were accented by pearl and golden-yellow furnishings. A few turquoise accent pieces added a pop of contrast to the otherwise drab color-scheme. This room was very different than the monochrome, impersonal classroom she and Laura had sat in two nights ago.

Meghan circled the perimeter, studying the picture-perfect images of smiling faces adorning the walls. There were pregnant women, chubby babies, and joy-filled couples. Collectively, the photographs reflected people of various ages, appearances, and ethnicities. Laughing children in the arms of adoring parents, apparently including some birth parents. No one looked as though the journey had been hard.

She moved to a large collage frame. One photo caught her attention. A young woman with raven-black, silky-smooth hair leaned over a bassinet. Meghan stepped in for a better look. The baby bed was not the modern mesh and plastic variety. It seemed to be woven with thin wood or cord or something. It looked more like a basket than a piece of baby furniture. The woman's shoulder-length hair obscured her face as she gazed into the basket. The only evidence of what the basket held was a tiny hand reaching up to grasp the woman's outstretched index finger. The picture was no doubt real, but the anonymity of the mother and child represented every young woman who had ever sat in this room. Every young woman just like her. She turned away from the image as well as the ache she felt for the woman and her baby.

As her eyes swept to the next photo, Meghan recognized the face from one of the videos she'd completed only minutes before. That young woman's name was Olivia. She lived in Indianapolis and had become pregnant when she was twenty years old. The circumstances of her story echoed most of the others. She was young, single, unprepared, and uncertain. She and the baby's father had been high school sweethearts and had already been planning to get married after college. When their parents learned of the pregnancy, both sides advocated for immediate marriage. In the end, Olivia and her boyfriend had instead placed their baby with adoptive parents.

Meghan was surprised. She wanted to ask Yasmine more about Olivia. If they were planning to get married anyway, why would they place their baby for adoption? Did they stay together after the baby was born?

Each of the birth mothers in the video had spoken about not being ready to parent. Each had believed they weren't able to provide their child with the life they wanted for them.

There were differences too. Some birth mothers spoke openly about sadness and regret after the adoption. Others felt complete joy and peace. Some chose to be involved in their baby's life. Others shared no information in either direction. It seemed like each story began the same way, yet in the end, each one was as unique as the woman telling it.

Meghan wished she knew the story behind every picture. She turned as Yasmine entered the room and pointed to the walls.

"All of these pictures show families matched through our agency."

"I know people who are adopted, but I don't know anyone who placed a baby for adoption." Meghan glanced once more at the young dark-haired woman reaching into the baby basket. "I'm not even sure where to begin thinking about this."

Yasmine nodded as she set a file on the table. "I hear that more than you might think. The good news is you don't have to decide anything today. This is simply another step in learning about adoption." She motioned for Meghan to take a seat at the table.

"Another step?" Meghan repeated. "How many steps are there?" She moved toward the table.

"Simply put, there are three—the adoption plan, birth plan, and post-adoption plan." Yasmine turned off the TV and settled into the chair opposite Meghan. "You are in charge every step of the way, and we are here to support your choices for as long as you want us to be. While it is helpful to gather information, do research, and get input from others, it is critical that your choices come from within you and not because you were pressured or persuaded into something." She opened Meghan's file. "Would it be okay if we start by talking about the forms you filled out?"

Meghan handed her more papers to add to the records—medical charts, behavioral inventory, school transcripts, personal background, and family history. The information was straightforward.

"Have you discussed this with the baby's father?" Yasmine asked.

Meghan looked away. "He isn't interested in me or the baby." Talking about Zac caused an undeniable mixture of anger and sorrow. Her voice broke as tears threatened. "Does he have to be part of this?"

Yasmine handed Meghan a tissue but continued the hard conversation. "Legally, the answer in Michigan is 'sometimes.' But,

Meghan, it really is best for everyone if you talk to him. Before your next appointment if you can."

⌒

Three days later, Meghan sat in Elaina's office. Unlike the serene atmosphere of the adoption agency, Safe Haven was adorned with bright colors and buzzed with constant activity. A young woman struggled to balance a large box and Meghan moved to open the door for her.

A yellow knit beanie and two brown eyes appeared over the box top. "Meghan?" It was Jada, the girl from the event at Saint Bridget's.

"Uh. Hi." Meghan immediately regretted her unenthusiastic response.

Jada set the box on the floor. "Are you okay?"

Meghan leaned in to receive a quick hug. Her heart softened as she felt Jada's baby pressed against her own. "Sorry. It's just been a tough few days."

"Let's talk." Jada took Meghan's hand and led her into an adjoining room.

Meghan offered Jada first choice of the two chairs. "Pick whichever is more comfortable for you." Unlike the large, open lobby, this room was quiet and dim.

Jada sank into a padded glider and exhaled loudly. "Ohhh. That feels good." She dropped her bag on the floor. "So what's going on with you?"

Meghan deflected. "How was the wedding? Do you like your new apartment?"

Jada lifted her bulging shoes onto a matching footrest. Meghan's eyes grew wide as she pointed. "What happened to your feet?"

Jada followed Meghan's finger, then laughed. "Don't look so scared. It's just fluid. My feet swell up like balloons when I stand too long."

Meghan breathed a sigh of relief and made a mental note to elevate her legs whenever possible.

The young woman enthusiastically recalled the events of her and Brady's wedding. "It wasn't the princess day I always dreamed of, but it was still special. Plus, I'm glad we have our little nest to bring this little chick home to." She patted her abdomen. "Any day now, Deiondre."

"You're having a boy." Meghan concluded. "Congratulations. Are you glad you know?"

"Yes. I couldn't wait to find out." Jada shifted uncomfortably. "Are you having a boy or a girl?"

Meghan shrugged. "I don't know."

"You don't know, or you don't want to know?"

Meghan shrugged again. "Can I ask you something?"

"Shoot," Jada replied.

"How did you know what to do? I mean, did you ever consider adoption?"

Jada stood up and rubbed her lower back. "So much for putting my feet up. This kid has been giving me backaches," she explained. "Hmmm. Did we ever consider adoption? Honestly, no. As soon as we knew we were pregnant, we wanted to get married and raise the baby together."

Meghan was confused. "Then why did you wait so long to get married?"

Jada turned the plain silver band on her left ring finger. "Practical reasons. Financial reasons. Insurance reasons. Our parents suggested we wait until Brady got a full-time job with benefits. We cut it close, didn't we?"

Before Meghan could ask more questions, Elaina opened the door.

"Here you are." She smiled. "I'm glad you two found a quiet place to talk, but I need to steal Meghan for our appointment."

Meghan was quiet until Elaina shut her office door behind them. Then she asked, "Do you think Jada and Brady will beat the odds?"

"Honestly, I don't know." Elaina motioned for Meghan to sit at a small glass-top table, then took the opposite chair. "Statistically speaking, they have a mountain to climb, but it certainly isn't insurmountable."

"Do you think getting married is the right thing to do?"

"It's a brave thing to do. I admire their commitment to their baby and truly hope they make it."

"But?"

Elaina smiled sadly. "But marriage is hard. Even under the best of circumstances."

"You don't sound very confident."

"Time will tell. We will certainly do our best to walk with them and help them to strengthen their relationship."

"You mean even after the baby is born? I thought you were a pregnancy center."

"We are." Elaina handed Meghan a thick booklet, pages folded and stapled together along the middle crease. "But our services don't end once the baby is born."

Meghan opened the cover and scanned the table of contents. Sure enough. Post-pregnancy resources included parenting classes, marriage mentors, ways to earn diapers and baby clothes, early childhood development workshops, post-abortion counseling, grief support groups, and even financial education.

"As you can see," Elaina said, "we are so much more than just an abortion alternative. We aren't just pro-life, but pro-family."

Meghan's initial question still wasn't answered. "If Jada was your daughter, would you tell her to get married?"

Elaina hesitated, drumming her fingers on her lips and staring so intently at the ceiling that Meghan fought the urge to turn around and look. Instead, she studied a small corkboard on the wall overflowing with letters, pictures, and cards. If she squinted, she could read some of the words. She was partway through a note from a thankful grandmother when Elaina broke the silence.

"That's a hard question, Meghan. Traditionally, most Christians would say yes, pregnant couples should be legally married before the baby is born."

"Shotgun weddings, right?" Meghan couldn't imagine her dad even thinking of defending her honor in such an archaic, politically incorrect way.

"Thankfully we've moved past the idea of forcing marriage at gunpoint." They grinned at each other, then Elaina continued. "But, in some ways, I think now maybe we've tipped too far the other direction."

"What do you mean?"

"Marriage, babies, families. They no longer have the esteem and value they once had. For centuries they were the bedrock of civilization. Now they seem to be the exception instead of the rule."

Meghan steered back to her original question. "So would you or wouldn't you want your daughter to get married?"

"You're not letting me off the hook, are you?"

"Nope."

Elaina laughed. "Okay. Then, here's my personal answer—I don't think I would vote for getting married. Not right away, and for sure not unless they had already been planning to get married."

"Really?" Meghan had to rewind the words to make sure she'd heard them correctly. "Whoa. I wasn't expecting that answer."

"Honestly, it wouldn't have been my answer five years ago. And there are many good, godly people who would heartily disagree with me. And the reasons for their opinions are just as valid as mine. We're all on a journey and, sometimes our thinking changes even if our core beliefs remain the same."

"So what changed your mind?"

"Well," Elaina began. "I guess I would say I simply no longer view marriage as the automatic solution I once believed it to be. To think marriage alone will somehow fix deeper issues is an illusion. I would rather see a couple enter marriage from a place of strength than desperation or obligation. Marriage isn't the first step toward health and healing. Jesus is. And, married or not, any couple who thinks raising a baby together is enough to create and sustain a healthy marriage is in for a rude awakening."

Part of Meghan wanted to dive deeper into the discussion, but marriage didn't apply to her current situation. She had her own life to figure out.

"I met with Yasmine on Tuesday."

Elaina showed neither surprise nor disappointment.

"I'm considering adoption."

Hearing herself speak the words wasn't as terrifying as Meghan had imagined it would be. Considering that Safe Haven wasn't an adoption agency, however, she half expected Elaina to push against it. She didn't, so Meghan continued.

"Honestly, I'd not even thought of it before that day at Saint Bridget's. I guess I'm just trying to get as much information as possible." Meghan shrugged and picked at the fuzzies on her sweatshirt. "It's what everyone keeps telling me to do."

Elaina rose from her chair and pulled a book from a honey-stained oak shelf. "Here. You can borrow this. It's filled with stories of women who've walked in your shoes. It will give you a wide-lens picture of the reasons behind the choices they made. Both parenting and adoption."

"Thanks." Meghan turned the book over in her hands then flipped through the pages. "I watched some videos at Yasmine's office, but a book will give me more time to think."

CHAPTER 29

Week 32

Meghan's heart pounded as she stared at Yasmine's computer screen. She wondered if Andi and Laura could hear it. Ten hopeful couples. Twenty smiling faces. Forty arms longing to hold a child they could call their own. All ten fit the parameters Meghan had set for prospective adoptive families.

Andi unclenched Meghan's fist and slid her hand under Meghan's clammy palm. "Breathe, Megs. It's okay."

"What if I choose the wrong couple?" The images on the screen blurred as tears welled up and spilled over. "I can't. I can't do this. They're all hoping—" Meghan turned from the faces on the monitor and pushed her chair back.

Laura stepped out of the way but quietly asked, "Would you rather not see the pictures? Maybe just read the words?"

"That might help. I'm so afraid I'll choose by judging how someone looks in a photo."

"We can scroll down to their stories first." Andi moved the computer mouse and minimized the open file. "Who do you want to begin with?"

Meghan returned to her chair, closed her eyes, and listened as Andi slowly and reverently spoke the names of potential parents of her baby.

"Pedro and Gianna . . . Kevin and Hope . . . Jack and Jackie . . . Chivish and Rebekah . . ."

Meghan's eyes popped open. "Wait. Go back."

"Chivish and Rebekah?"

"No, the one before."

"Jack and Jackie?" Laura asked.

Andi scrolled back to find them. "Do you think those are fake names?"

"Read their bio, please." Meghan closed her eyes again as Andi read.

> "Dear Birth Mom,
>
> Thank you for considering us as adoptive parents. In case you were wondering, yes, our names really are Jack and Jackie. If you choose us, we will raise your child in a committed, stable home built on love and faith. Your baby will always know how they came to be part of our family and the love you have for them.
>
> We hope to maintain a relationship through open adoption, but if you prefer a closed adoption, we will respect your choice and commit to raise your child with the knowledge of your sacrifice for them. We are praying for both you and your baby as you prepare to make this difficult decision."

Andi stopped there. "What do you think, Megs? Do you want to hear more?"

Now that the faces were gone, Meghan could concentrate the information. At her request, Andi read the rest of the bios. Meghan noted three she felt drawn to. But it was a lot to take in. A lot to consider.

Her heart was still pounding in her chest and then, out of nowhere, an unexpected question came to mind. "Which couple has been waiting the longest?"

<hr>

Meghan opened her bedroom door and noticed a soft light coming from the kitchen. *Andi must've left it on when she went to bed.* She tiptoed past the closed guestroom door and was surprised to find Andi, wrapped in a fuzzy blanket, seated at the kitchen counter.

"Can't sleep?"

Andi swiveled her stool. "Sorry if I woke you. My mind is racing."

"Welcome to my world." She squeezed her friend's shoulders. "Thanks for coming with me today."

"I'm really proud of you, Megs."

Meghan pulled out the other stool. "I'm still blown away by the whole thing. I mean, the details of it all."

"How can people deny God is real?" Andi moved to the couch and grabbed the afghan stretched over the back. "I was sitting here thinking about it. All of it. Not just today, but everything. Don't get me wrong. Today was incredible too." She handed the blanket to Meghan. "You're shivering."

Meghan draped it over her legs as she balanced precariously on the seat. "Would you mind reading the bio one more time? I think I'm ready to see their picture."

"Sure." Andi reached for Meghan's laptop. While the adoption site loaded, she slid a photo in front of Meghan, bottom side up.

Meghan spread her fingers over the glossy white rectangle. Underneath her hand were the faces her baby might call "Mama" and

"Daddy." The people who might be taking her baby home from the hospital.

"Meghan, are you sure about this?"

Meghan considered the question before she verbalized her response. "Pretty sure."

Andi chuckled. "That wasn't too convincing."

"There's a lot of pressure here. They gave me a multiple-choice test. You know, like age, location, family dynamics, occupation . . . What do I know? Based on my answers, they matched me with potential couples, and here we are."

"Is there something about this couple that's a deal-breaker from that list?"

"No. Not really." But Meghan was harboring second thoughts. What if she'd picked the wrong answers or missed important details? Or was she expecting too much, being too picky? Maybe her hesitation was God's way of telling her she was making the wrong decision. Maybe she should look at more profiles. Or maybe she shouldn't return to the agency at all.

"So what's wrong?" Andi closed the laptop.

Meghan dropped her head to her hands. "I don't know. I don't know if it's them or me. I'm probably overthinking things. As usual."

"Well, what isn't right? What's bothering you?"

"It's probably not a big deal." Meghan tapped the back of the picture with her fingertips, then pushed it to the side. "But . . . I think maybe I should have checked the box for siblings."

"Siblings?"

"A preference for couples who already have children in their home."

Andi didn't have to think long. "Because you're an only child?"

"Yeah, I guess. But maybe that's a selfish reason. It's probably best I left it blank. I mean, if a couple has children, why would they be adopting?"

That realization quieted the nagging reluctance. Meghan laid her palm on top of the picture and pulled it back across the countertop. Then she tapped the computer. "Now that I hear myself say it, I don't think it's a big deal. Let's keep going."

Andi adjusted the position of the screen and found her place again. "Jack and Jackie. Ages thirty-four and thirty-three. Live somewhere in the Midwest. Married eight years. Been on the waiting list six years . . . Six years? That's a long time."

Meghan laid her hand on the photo. It was a start.

"She's a hospice nurse. He's—I still can't believe this—he's a history teacher. High school American history."

Meghan slid her thumb under the bottom edge.

"Large extended family."

She lifted the bottom left side corner.

"They live on a lake. Love the outdoors. Active in church and community. Enjoy traveling . . ."

Meghan inhaled deeply and closed her eyes as Andi's voice faded into the background of her mind. Her fingers pinched the corner and lifted just enough to see a hint of color. There she hovered, not sure if she should rip off the bandage or peel it slowly. She exhaled loudly and turned over the photo. When she opened her eyes, three faces looked back at her. She gasped.

Andi reached for the photograph now clutched to Meghan's chest. "What's wrong? Don't you like how they look?"

Between tears and laughter, Meghan couldn't answer. Instead, she passed the picture to Andi.

"What? No way!"

"I know, right?"

The girls looked back and forth between the image and each other. Finally, Meghan found her words. "God did it anyway. Even though I didn't check the box, He did it anyway."

Andi scrolled back through the family's information. "How

did we miss this? Jack and Jackie have a four-year-old son named TJ. How is that possible?"

"Didn't you say they were the couple who'd been waiting the longest?"

Andi reset the search criteria and refreshed the page. "Yeah. It says Jack and Jackie have been waiting six years."

Neither girl could think of a possible reason for the improbable math. Their best guess landed on *typo*. Meghan didn't care who had made the mistake or why. She was elated to discover her baby could be raised with two parents and an older brother. A sibling to play with. An extended family to make traditions with.

She held the photo, staring down at the smiling faces.

Andi spoke into the wonder of the moment. "What are you thinking? How would you describe what you see?"

Meghan didn't hesitate. "Radiant."

Andi looked at her quizzically. "Did you say 'radiant'?"

Meghan searched for another word, but everything else fell short. "Yeah. Radiant. Their faces radiate . . . love. Joy. Hope. I see that in their faces."

"Are they who you want to adopt your baby?"

"Yes, if I decide to place the baby. I'm still not sure which choice is right. But I'm going to move forward with them until I know for sure."

After another hour of talking, Meghan was finally ready to sleep. She took the picture to her room and set it on the night-stand. Jack and Jackie. And cute little TJ. Jackie had sandy-blond hair and glasses. If Meghan had to guess, she would say Jackie's eyes were light blue. Jack was the opposite. He had a darker skin tone and short brown hair. There was no mistaking his dark-brown eyes.

TJ wore a little red baseball cap, but white-blond hair peeked out from under the rim. His skin was tan, but lighter than Jack's. Meghan's gaze lingered on the little boy. She wondered where he was born, who his birth mother was, and why she'd chosen adoption.

The picture was taken next to a lake. Not a big lake like the Great Lakes, but big enough for boats to dot the background. Meghan pulled the photo closer as she looked for clues. Blue sky, wispy white clouds, clear water, trees. Nothing hinted to the location. If the picture was taken recently, then the family didn't live anywhere near Michigan. Meghan gave up searching the background and inspected the family.

Jack wore cargo shorts, a purple shirt, and no shoes. Jackie sported athletic capris, sandals, a T-shirt, and a tan safari hat. In addition to the red baseball cap, TJ wore shorts covered with colorful fish and a royal-blue shirt. That caught Meghan's attention. The shirt was the same as Jackie's. Meghan took a screenshot so she could magnify the logo printed on the front. Under a cartoon drawing of a kayak were the words "Let the day unfold before you. Philippians 3:12–14."

Though Meghan read Scripture more now, that particular reference was unfamiliar. She pulled up the Bible app on her phone and scrolled to the verses. "Not that I have already obtained all this, or have already arrived at my goal, but I press on to take hold of that for which Christ Jesus took hold of me. Brothers and sisters, I do not consider myself yet to have taken hold of it. But one thing I do: Forgetting what is behind and straining toward what is ahead, I press on toward the goal to win the prize for which God has called me heavenward in Christ Jesus."

Meghan's brow furrowed. Most of the passage didn't make sense. She read it again. What was the writer trying to take hold of? What had he not already obtained? She didn't understand the meaning or context. Except for one part. "Forgetting what is behind and straining toward what is ahead." The past was the past. It was time to press on toward the future.

CHAPTER 30

Week 33

Meghan had asked Laura to meet for coffee before Sunday service and now they sat in Laura's warm car, talking. They had made it as far as the church parking lot but would definitely be late going inside. Time was the last thing on Meghan's mind. She was still struggling with questions and Laura seemed like the right person to ask.

When Laura's answers came, they sounded exactly the same as everything she had already heard before. Her anger boiled and spilled over before she could snap the lid on.

"Blah, blah, blah. I get it. Keep my options open. Wait for God to open a door. When it's time to know, I'll know." The windows were fogging up now. "Seriously, Laura! Did that advice help you when you were me?"

Laura's face pinched as she inhaled through clenched teeth. "I guess it does come off sounding like nothing but clichés, doesn't it? I—"

When she paused, Meghan shot an arrow at the heart of all the questions. "How do you know that you made the right decision?"

Bullseye. "If you knew then what you know now, would you still have decided to keep your baby?"

Laura took a long swallow from her disposable cup and set it back in the beverage holder. Then she laid her head on the seatback and closed her eyes. It got so quiet Meghan noticed pellets of sleet hitting the windshield. Finally, Laura spoke.

"Honestly, there's no way I can answer that. Hindsight isn't going to work because I cannot imagine my life without Arik. I can't imagine living in a world where he isn't part of our family. He's an integral part of me—of my yesterday, today, and tomorrow." Laura's voice cracked as tears squeezed out from her still-closed eyes.

Meghan was sorry her question had upset Laura, but she needed to walk through to the other side. She needed someone to shine a light on her path so she would know which way to go.

"Then I guess you have your answer." But Meghan didn't have hers.

Laura sat up straight and placed an open hand over her heart. "Meghan. You're right. I didn't even realize it until this very moment. All these years, I've wondered, worried even, that by choosing to raise Arik, I kept him from a better life with someone else. Someone who would have spared him the pain my choices have caused him."

The tears now flowed freely. "I was blind, but now I see. When we had Arik, I never once thought it wouldn't be forever. At the time, there was no reason to think we couldn't give him everything we wanted for him. I knew it would be a challenge—that we'd have to sacrifice. But I was all in. Committed to him. And that has never changed."

Meghan didn't doubt the accuracy of Laura's conclusion. But it wasn't going to help her with her own choices. She sighed.

"Don't get me wrong," she began. "I'm glad you have found a sense of peace. But I still don't understand how to choose what's best. Does Zac's absence automatically make the decision for me?"

"Of course not," Laura assured. "If you decide to raise your baby, you will be a wonderful mama. And even if Zac isn't part of the picture, you have a community of friends and family who will always support you."

"But at the same time, knowing from the start the baby wouldn't have a father is a reason to keep moving forward with adoption." Meghan growled in frustration. "There are just so many unknowns. So many questions."

Laura reached for Meghan's hand. "Let's begin by asking the One who has the answers."

Meghan and Laura made it into church just as the sermon was wrapping up. As soon as Pastor Nate gave the benediction, Beth hurried over, arms waving. "What did you decide?"

Laura touched Meghan's arm, then extended her two outer fingers, held them to the side of her head, and mouthed, *Call me.* Meghan affirmed with a thumbs-up. She must have missed something Beth said. "Decide about what?"

Beth tilted her head and studied Meghan. "The shower. You're less than two months from your due date, and it will come fast with this being the holiday season."

Meghan didn't want to appear rude or ungrateful. "I'm sorry I keep putting you off," she began. "It's just that I am still not sure if I will be bringing the baby home or placing her for adoption."

Beth's eyes lit up, and she gave a little clap. "You said 'her.' The baby's a girl?"

Beth's excitement was touching. "I don't know. I switch pronouns because it feels weird to call a baby 'it.'" She circled back to the question. "I would feel terrible if you gave me a shower and then I couldn't use the gifts."

"Don't let that stop you. Everyone would understand. Believe it or not, it wouldn't be the first time that happened."

Meghan doubted everyone would understand, but Beth responded before she could protest. "Really. No one would be upset. The point isn't to guilt you into deciding either way. The point is to *celebrate* both you and your baby."

"But what happens to the gifts if I choose adoption?"

"It would be up to you. Sometimes, gifts are passed on to the adoptive family. Other times, they're donated to Safe Haven or given back to the church. No one is out anything, Meghan. The gifts are freely given with the understanding the baby may or may not use them. Everyone involved with Moses' Basket knows that going in."

Meghan opened to the idea. It might be fun. "Okay, if you're sure, I accept the offer."

Beth was elated. "I'm sure. It'll be great—you'll see."

Meghan set the empty basket on the counter and reached for a pair of oven pads. The first semester was over, and it felt good to have a break after an exhausting finals week. Tuesdays were still laundry and baking days. Cooking with Netta ignited a passion Meghan hadn't recognized before and she enjoyed the satisfaction of watching others enjoy the fruits of her labor.

While she'd waited between loads, she'd mixed up another of her favorite recipes from Netta. Before the first load was dry, it was time for a taste. Taking a sharp knife from the counter, she cut into the warm loaf, set the first piece on a checked cloth napkin, and slid it toward Lucinda. Then she sliced another for herself.

"Mmmm. This is the best banana bread I've ever tasted," Lucinda declared. "And a nice change of pace from all the sugary holiday treats."

Meghan nodded as she finished her first bite and walked around the island counter.

"Believe it or not, the secret ingredient is sour cream." Meghan chose the lowest stool. It was the easiest one to sit down on. "But don't tell Netta. I forgot to swear you to secrecy before discussing her recipe."

Lucinda eyed her suspiciously. "Sour cream? Are you messing with me?"

"I know it sounds weird, but it works. The other . . ." Meghan arched her back, gasped for air, and clutched her ribs.

Lucinda jumped off her stool. "Are you okay? Is baby wanting bread, or is baby wanting out?"

"Apparently baby wants something, but I don't think it's time yet. He has never kicked that hard before." Meghan massaged her lower left rib cage and practiced her patterned breathing. "I think his little foot is wedged right here."

"He? His? He's a him?"

"I. Don't. Know." Meghan struggled to breathe the words.

Lucinda held out her hands. "Let's get you up. Maybe gravity will work in your favor."

Movement seemed to help. Little One stopped twisting, and Meghan's pain retreated. "Did you know your baby's gender before she was born?"

"Oh, honey," Lucinda laughed. "You should have seen an eighties ultrasound. Blurry little alien lifeforms printed on glossy paper. Nothing like today's imaging. Back then, there was a fifty-fifty shot the doctor would be right. We heard both boy and girl, so didn't have much to go on."

"But if you could have known, would you have wanted to?"

"Honestly, I don't know. With all the controversy surrounding our pregnancy, I'm not sure I would have wanted to because we couldn't have told anyone anyway."

"What do you mean you couldn't have told?"

Lucinda walked over to the window. "We were given direct

orders not to discuss the pregnancy with anyone from the church. And the people from church were the people we hung around with the most. We didn't have family nearby."

Meghan didn't doubt her. Before her own pregnancy, she hadn't realized how judgmental even well-meaning people could be. Herself included. "Did things get better once you decided to get married?"

"'Did things get better?'" Lucinda turned to face Meghan. The frown on her face revealed pain she still carried inside. "Let me put it this way—no and then yes. At first, no. Some of the church leaders didn't even want us to have the wedding in our own church. It created a real controversy among the congregation and elder board."

"What?" Meghan was shocked. "You were doing what they wanted, weren't you?"

"Yes, in a way," Lucinda hung her head. "That might be what hurt the most."

Meghan recalled the first time she met the Maxwells. "More than being ridiculed in front of the whole church?"

Lucinda answered without hesitation. "Yes. Definitely. Glenn protected me from that by standing alone in front of the congregation. He took full responsibility for our indiscretions and the consequences of our choices. His love has always shielded me."

Meghan couldn't imagine a love like that. Her thoughts turned to Zac. It was hard to be protective if you weren't even willing to be present.

A loud buzz from the dryer interrupted Meghan's contemplation. As she unloaded and reloaded her laundry, Lucinda's story continued to produce questions. She returned to the living room and dumped the basket of clean clothes. "If that church was mean to you, why did you keep going there?"

Lucinda gathered a pile of mismatched socks to her end of the sofa. "I guess we were like these socks. We were looking for a place to belong. It wasn't everyone in the church. I'm sorry I didn't clarify that point. One couple in particular was very kind." She stopped sorting. "I haven't thought about this in years."

"I'm sorry. It's really none of my business."

Lucinda didn't seem to hear Meghan's apology. She spoke so quietly, Meghan had to strain to hear. "I'll never forget the retreat. I felt out of place, but for some reason, I went anyway. Holly asked if I'd felt the baby move yet. I was so surprised that she'd bring it up, I answered without thinking. For a moment, I felt happy. I felt cared for. I said, 'Yes,' then shamefully added, 'but I don't think I am supposed to be talking about it.'

"Instead of being angry with me, Holly was excited. She told me about her pregnancies and asked me more questions. I felt guilty for talking with her, but it was so wonderful to have someone to talk to. To share my experience with. To feel like a normal human being instead of an outcast."

"Did you get in big trouble when the others found out?"

Lucinda shook her head. "No. That's what I was expecting, but later, during prayer time, Holly addressed the entire group. She said, 'Ladies, I have something I need to say. We have hurt our sister in Christ. We haven't loved her well. We have acted as her judge instead of loving her as Jesus would.'"

"Wow." Meghan was not expecting that. "What were you thinking when she said that?"

Lucinda wiped unseen dust from the coffee table and set the matched socks in a neat row. Then she moved back to the window and stared at the gently falling snow. "Honestly, I don't remember. I think I was almost in shock. What I know for sure is, her words changed everything. All of a sudden, all the other women were asking me questions and sharing their stories. They even hosted a baby shower for us. Holly's decision to reach out in love instead of condemnation began a chain reaction of hope and healing."

"That's an amazing story. I'm glad you shared it with me. I'm sorry if it's dredged up painful memories."

"No. Thank you, Meghan. Sharing it reminded me of God's power to redeem all things. I never made the connection until just now. Looking back, I can see how much freedom God gave me through the gift of grace Holly extended. I was finally able to move out from the shame I was living under. Yes, the church put much of that shame on us, but God is greater. He removed the shame, and we found love in its place."

Meghan pushed herself up from the sofa and walked to the window. With an arm around her friend, she leaned in close and whispered, "Lucinda, you are Holly to me."

CHAPTER 31

Week 34

Meghan eased down to the floor, careful not to spill the water or lose her balance. When she'd taken Glenn's side in the real versus fake Christmas tree debate, she hadn't thought about having to water a living pine tree.

Being pregnant gave Meghan a new outlook on the Christmas story. She saw details of the holiday through a different lens. Imagine being nine months pregnant and riding a donkey or sleeping on the hard floor of a cave. Unlike Mary, she would have told Joseph, "Have a nice trip. Bring me a souvenir from Bethlehem."

Two days before Christmas, she received a text from Zac. "Paperwork is done. Court hearing next. Merry Christmas." This was a gift Meghan had neither asked for nor wanted. In fact, it wasn't a gift at all. The short text was enough to trigger the resentment lurking around the edges of her heart. After all this time? That was it? Nothing but a disappearing act? How about, "Hey, I'm sorry for being a jerk" or "Thanks for taking all of the responsibility for our baby" or "I wish things had been different" or "I hope you're okay" or "Is there anything you need?" No. Nothing like that. *Fine. I'm better off without him. Little One, you're better off without him. We'll be fine.*

The baby wasn't even born yet, and already she was a single parent. Could she really bear all the responsibility of raising a child?

"Ho ho ho. Grandpa Claus is here."

Meghan jolted at the sound of Peter's voice and dropped the plastic pitcher. Good thing it was empty.

Peter had driven to Grand Rapids so Meghan wouldn't have to travel for Christmas. Lucinda and Glenn were celebrating the holiday in Florida, so the house was quiet. Since Pastor Nate and Beth didn't have family in the area, they'd invited the McPhersons to join them for Christmas Eve dinner. Meghan was glad the church service was in the late afternoon instead of evening. At this point in her pregnancy, she needed an early bedtime.

The church looked beautiful decorated with red poinsettias, flickering candles, and white twinkling lights. Someone had arranged a beautiful nativity display on the platform. At the foot of the cross stood a simple, wooden manger. Scratchy straw poked from between the rough boards. As she stared at the makeshift cradle, Meghan's hands caressed her baby's hiding place. She couldn't imagine laying her newborn in a bed like that.

Soon the service began. The familiar carols meant something different this year. "Holy infant so tender and mild . . . Glory to the newborn king . . . the Babe, the Son of Mary . . ."

Mary, the mother of Jesus. Did she also wonder if she was doing the right thing? Did she have doubts about her son's future? Had she wondered if she would be a single parent after Joseph heard the news? Did she fear she wouldn't be able to provide the life she wanted her son to have?

After the singing, Pastor Nate took the stage to give his Christmas sermon. Standing at the foot of the cross, he covered the usual Bible verses about Mary, Joseph, and Baby Jesus. He spoke of the angels and shepherds and the star over Bethlehem. The darkened room and somber atmosphere caused Meghan's mind to wander and, the next thing she knew, Pastor Nate had taken a detour back to the Old Testament.

". . . Genesis three, verse fifteen. God said, 'I will put enmity between you and the woman, and between your offspring and hers; he will crush your head, and you will strike his heel.'" He set his Bible down and rested a hand on the manger. "When Jesus came to earth as a baby, His destiny was already set in motion. The curse that began in a garden would be broken by the cure that began in a womb. An unmarried virgin from Nazareth surrendered to God and carried the King of the world. Who are we to say an unplanned pregnancy is a mistake?"

With those words, the mural on the ceiling of Sainte Anne's leapt into Meghan's mind. The memory was fuzzy, but she was sure Mary had been kneeling lower than Baby Jesus. Was that the artist's way of saying Mary was surrendered? She snuck out her phone and searched for an image of the mural. Sure enough. Sainte Anne was holding Baby Jesus, and Mary knelt beside them. But what was she holding in her hand? Enlarging that part of the photo, Meghan saw something she'd missed when she was sitting right under it. Mary reached out for her son's small shoe. The front of His little foot was exposed, and only the heel remained covered. What was Mary thinking? Was she trying to protect His heel from the serpent's strike? Wasn't that what a mother would do to protect her child? Or was she voluntarily removing the shoe? Exposing His heel because she trusted God had a plan? Even if His plan didn't align with hers?

Week 36

The new year brought an onslaught of lake-effect snow to Grand Rapids. This phenomenon was not new to Meghan, but thanks to Glenn's amateur meteorological skills, she now understood why. Well, sort of. If she was honest, she would have to admit she mostly only pretended to listen. Something about an uncommonly strong west wind and the temperature of the air over Lake Michigan being warmer than the air above it.

While most Michiganders grumpily prepared for another heavy snowfall, Glenn couldn't have been happier. "Oh boy, this is going to be a good one. If we're really lucky, we'll have a total whiteout." He got his wish.

While Grand Rapids dug out, Meghan focused on final preparations for the end of her pregnancy and beginning of new online classes. She registered for only six credits the second semester, anticipating busy days and sleepless nights if she decided to bring the baby home. Thankful for four-wheel drive, she navigated the aftermath of the latest snowstorm to the university.

After she paid tuition at the registrar's office, she started the precarious walk across campus to the bookstore. A few steps in, she realized walking through the heavy snow was harder with the extra bulk of Little One. Seeing the administration building ahead, she ducked inside for a rest. Memories of her last visit to that building still produced a layer of shame. *I would gladly go up to see Beth if it didn't come with the risk of running into Mrs. Vivian Perkins.* Despite the months that had passed since she'd last seen Mrs. Perkins, the thought of another confrontation was unappealing.

One bathroom break and twenty minutes later, Meghan was ready to walk the rest of the way to the bookstore. *I should've thought this through better. Or parked closer. I hope there aren't a lot of books to carry.* At the end of the hallway, she grabbed the door handle to push, but someone on the other side pulled simultaneously. The door flew outward, causing the unsuspecting door-puller to stagger and tumble backward into the slushy mess. A bubble of laughter was about to erupt, but it burst as a mittened hand reached up and straightened the buffalo-plaid trapper hat. Under the furry front, earflaps dangling, was the one and only Mrs. Vivian Perkins.

Her eyes were narrow and dark. Her mouth was pursed as her face flushed red. Meghan instinctively took two steps back.

Mrs. Perkins's look of indignity changed to surprise. Suddenly she began to laugh. First a chuckle, then a giggle, which concerned Meghan all the more.

"Did you hit your head?" Meghan questioned. "You could have a concussion." She pulled out her phone. "I'll call 911."

Mrs. Perkins kept laughing. "No, no. I'm fine. No harm done. It's just that I expected to see a big, hairy football player or a burly wrestler, and here before me is a tiny but very pregnant young woman."

Relieved she wasn't going to be sued by the school for injuring an employee, Meghan saw the humor of the situation. "I'd help you, but I'm afraid we'd both end up in the snow."

The administrator managed to stand up and brush herself off without any further mishaps. "Where are you headed in this dreadful weather?"

Meghan explained her need to get to the bookstore and stepped forward. "Again, I'm sorry."

Mrs. Perkins grabbed her elbow. No one was laughing now. "Young lady," she commanded, "you are coming with me."

That was the Vivian Meghan remembered. She was in trouble after all.

"You are in no condition to be taking risks. I'll pull some strings and get those materials brought to you."

Does she not recognize me?

"Well, why are we still standing here freezing?" Mrs. Perkins nudged Meghan toward the lobby. "Let's go to my office. I've lived in Michigan long enough to always be prepared. I have dry clothes, hot drinks, and even some leftover Christmas cookies. Let's see if we can have your order delivered before we've finished our tea party."

Tea party? Cookies? Order delivered? Externally, Meghan complied. Internally, she was searching frantically for a way to make sense of this. There had to be a logical explanation. The lady must've hit her head. Or maybe she was a twin! This was the good sister of the duo. They were probably separated at birth.

Meghan followed, more out of curiosity than a desire to avoid a trip to the bookstore. She half expected to end up in a different part of the building, but the elevator door opened on the third floor. Mrs. Perkins marched directly to the admissions office, passed Beth's desk without a word, and opened the door to her lair.

Meghan didn't follow her that far. *She's probably waiting to get me alone. Then she'll pounce.*

Meghan preferred to stay close to Beth, but Beth said, "It's okay—go on."

Meghan shook her head.

Beth motioned for her to come closer. "Really, it's okay. She's not the same Vivian Perkins you met before. I promise. And I'll be right here if you need me."

What choice did Meghan have?

"Okay. But don't leave your post."

Forty-five minutes later, a young man arrived with a bulging maroon tote emblazoned with the university's logo: HONOR-BOUND. As he left, Mrs. Perkins followed him to the door and got Beth's attention.

"Bundle up, Beth," she directed. "Miss McPherson needs an escort to her vehicle. We can't expect her to carry this load alone."

As soon as the door closed behind them, Beth pulled Meghan farther down the hallway. "Don't leave me in suspense. What happened? As hard as I listened, I couldn't hear a thing."

In her enthusiasm, Beth walked toward the elevator so briskly Meghan was left behind. "Whoa, slow down, please. Baby mamas can't walk that fast."

"Sorry." Beth held the shiny panel open until Meghan stepped through the doorway. "I am just too eager to hear your story. I'm parked right outside. How about we sit and talk in my car, and then I will drive you to your car?"

Meghan couldn't wrap her mind around the change in Mrs. Perkins. First, she described the door incident and Vivian's offer to help. "I'm not gonna lie. I had myself positioned for a direct exit from her office and my finger over your number. I fully expected her to turn on me. But that moment never came. She made me a cup of hot chocolate and fixed a little plate of cookies. Then she called the bookstore and firmly explained what she expected of them. She didn't take no for an answer. In fact, I'm not sure they had any say in the matter. I just kept quiet and nibbled on my cookies."

Beth waved her hands in a hurry-up-and-get-to-the-good-part motion. "And? What next? I can't take it. She had to have said something."

"Hmmm, let me think . . . what did she say?" Beth was about to burst, and Meghan relented. "Okay, no more teasing. She told me God—how did she say it?—'had His way with her.' Apparently, the weekend of Pastor Nate's sermon about grace, she saw how prideful and spiteful she had been. She said Pastor Nate confronted her the day I was at her office but that had made her angrier. She only came to church that Sunday because she has to work with you. Then she saw me there, got all riled up again, and told Nate exactly what she thought. Apparently, he stayed calmer than the first time they'd talked and simply thanked her for sharing her view."

"Oh, I can vouch for the fact Nate was not calm that day," Beth interjected.

"Mrs. Perkins was fully prepared to call me out in front of the congregation. She said, at the time, she felt it was her 'Christian duty.' Then Nate preached his sermon. She said the teaching convicted her, but it was the song that broke her. Her exact words were, 'God showed me I was defining others based on their past because I was defining myself based on my own.'"

"Wow, that's powerful." Beth leaned back against the headrest. "Did she explain what that past was?"

"Yes," Meghan said. "But it's not my story to tell."

Beth didn't press. "Understood."

"Apparently she wanted to find me right away and apologize for the way she treated me. But Pastor Nate advised she give herself time to deal with her own heart first and trust God would bring us together when the time was right."

"Nate always says, 'The more grace we receive, the more grace we can give.' But it is funny that God's timing involved a tumble in the snow. He does move in mysterious ways."

"Is that in the Bible?" Meghan asked.

"No, but it's true all the same."

CHAPTER 32

Week 37

Meghan sat on the floor of the spare room—what could be the nursery room—and unpacked diapers, toys, clothes, and blankets. Beth was right. The Moses' Basket baby shower was a blessing. Andi drove from Holland to surprise her and brought an adorable stuffed giraffe for the baby. But perhaps the biggest surprise of the day was when Vivian Perkins walked in carrying a huge box of diapers. Adorning the top of the box was a child-sized buffalo-check trapper hat. While everyone cooed over the cute little cap, Meghan and Mrs. Perkins exchanged a look acknowledging its deeper meaning.

The group played silly games and ate themed foods such as baby carrots, mini sausages, and cake pops decorated like rattles. It felt good to be surrounded by people who celebrated the life within her. People who loved and accepted her. Meghan felt as though grace had rained down on her thirsty soul and caused new life to bloom.

She was surprised then, when she found herself suddenly angry with her mother. Maybe it was a normal byproduct of pregnancy hormones. Maybe she was simply tired. Or maybe it was the growing list of reminders of her mother's deliberate absence and disinterest. Something inside her longed for a mother to share this with. While so many other women cared, her own mother acted as though Meghan didn't exist.

She picked up a gift bag. And another. Tiny nail clippers and washcloths. Bibs, a bottle brush, and a diaper bag. Everything needed to welcome a new baby into the world. As she laid out the gifts, she prayed God would continue to heal her own childhood wounds. The more she trusted her identity in Christ, the less anger controlled her thoughts and feelings. The more she trusted God's grace, the less she feared being rejected by people.

When she—if she—brought her baby home, she would make sure he grew up knowing his mother would never abandon or reject him. That thought hit her like a slap in the face. She hadn't considered it before. If she chose adoption, would her baby feel abandoned? Rejected? Was that a risk worth taking? Meghan knew what it felt like to be left behind. Unwanted. Unseen. Unloved. Was she repeating the sins of her mother?

Before her thoughts could begin a chain reaction of anxiety, Meghan picked up the phone. Yasmine had said to reach out anytime she needed help. The phone rang twice before the call was answered.

"Hello, this is Bonnie. Thank you for calling the Adoption Support Helpline. May I have your first name please?"

Meghan felt vulnerable. "Rachel."

After a few general questions, which she answered honestly, Meghan got to the point of her call. "If I place my baby for adoption, will she think I abandoned or rejected her?"

"First of all, Rachel, thank you for caring so much about your baby to ask." Bonnie's friendly mannerisms softened the blow of her next statement. "The honest answer to your question is that no one can say for certain. Some adoptees do struggle with those feelings."

Fear gripped Meghan. "I can't do that to my baby. I can't—"

"Everything surrounding adoption is so much different than it used to be," Bonnie said. "Our agency works diligently to ensure the healthiest outcome for everyone involved."

"What does that even mean?"

"There are many ways to validate the truth to the child. Ways to age appropriately reinforce the reality they were very much loved."

"Like what?"

Bonnie listed more examples than Meghan could count. "Adoption-friendly language, for one. We tell children they *were* adopted instead of *are* adopted. We use words such as *parents* and *birth parents*, *placed for* instead of *given up for* adoption. We help families communicate in the way that best meets their child's need for information. We encourage birth parents to write their children letters affirming their love, affirming they chose adoption because they loved them. Because they wanted the child to have a life they couldn't provide."

They spoke for almost an hour, with Meghan asking hard questions and Bonnie responding without pretending there were easy answers. Yet every statement concluded with a message of hope. Not an empty promise or callous platitude but a firm and fair call to trust that everyone involved would do their best for her child. Meghan finally reached a tipping point of information overload.

"You do realize you could be talking me out of choosing adoption, right? Isn't it your job to keep me on board so your clients get their baby?"

"Rachel, my job is to support *your* choice for *your* baby. If our conversation has helped you do that, then I have done my job."

Meghan ended the call. She fully knew what it felt like to be unwanted. At the same time, though, she knew her baby wasn't unwanted. She loved her child. She wanted her child. In fact, she wanted what was best for her child. Even if *best* meant giving the baby a life she couldn't be part of.

With a sigh, Meghan slid the furry teddy bear she'd been holding back into a tall gift bag and struggled to her feet. She didn't have to decide this minute. Certainly not after such a tidal wave of emotions. For now, she would leave everything in their packages and wrappers. Just in case.

CHAPTER 33

Week 38

Once again, Yasmine paged through Meghan's folder. "I think we are right on track with everything. Your adoption plan is complete. Your birth plan looks good but"—she pulled out a yellow sheet of paper—"I still need you to complete this form."

Meghan took the paper titled "My Birth Plan." The information was mostly filled in.

> Birth Mother's name: Meghan Lea McPherson
> Birth Father's name:
> Hospital preference: Saint Matthews Birth Center
> Expected due date: February 7
> Primary Doctor's name: Dr. Caygen, OB/GYN
> Names of people attending birth: Andrea Thomson, Laura Garrick
> Names of others invited to see the baby after birth: Peter McPherson, Teresa Sanchez, Maria Rodriguez, Matt and Suzanne Thomson, Glenn and Lucinda Maxwell, Pastor Nate and Beth DeVries, Tony and Patrice Carlson.

Meghan made no changes and handed the paper to Yasmine. "Looks fine to me."

"There's still one line to fill in." Yasmine set the paper down in front of Meghan.

With the end of her pen, Meghan pushed it back to Yasmine. "Zac turned in the paperwork. He signed away his right to be called the birth father."

"Are you certain you want to leave that blank? I am wondering if it would be wise to add his name. If for no other reason than peace of mind."

"I don't think Zac would like me giving out his information. Plus, it would leave a paper trail back to him, and he's set on denying his part in this."

"That is a common assumption among single birth mothers. But this piece of paper can't assign parentage. It is not a legal document and would never hold up in court. It's simply for our records until delivery and is shredded after you have the baby."

It sounded simple enough, in theory. "If that's the case, why do you need it?"

Yasmine placed the paper halfway between them. "Because things can get crazy once labor starts. Sometimes there's no time to talk. Sometimes, in the heat of the moment, a birth mother forgets decisions made during quieter, less-painful moments." Yasmine slid the yellow paper a little closer. "Sometimes the caseworker on call is unfamiliar with the situation. In all of these instances, having as much information as possible makes things easier for everyone."

All good points. "Okay, okay. You've changed my mind. If it will help everyone else, I will fill it in." Meghan hastily wrote Zac's name in the blank space.

Yasmine filed the now-completed yellow form and took out a blue sheet. "This is for the adoptive parents. Are you still thinking you want a semi-open adoption?"

"Yes."

"Do you want to go over the scenarios again?"

"No. I would want to receive updates and pictures, but I think I want to keep my personal information private."

"Okay. That's great. Our office will continue to facilitate correspondence for you." Yasmine slid the blue paper back into the folder. "And are Jackie and Jack the couple you would want to adopt your baby?"

"Yes. I'm sure." A lump formed in her throat. "Well, as sure as I can be." She remembered the shock of seeing TJ in the picture. "But I do have a question."

Yasmine took notes as Meghan explained her confusion about the sibling. "I don't know offhand. Let me check the office records. Sometimes they include more information than the profiles."

While Yasmine did some digging, Meghan stepped out for a break. She passed the reception area, and the office assistant chuckled.

"I recognize that walk. You're doing the pregnancy waddle. Congratulations. That means you're in the homestretch." She motioned Meghan over. "Here, I have something for you."

When Meghan returned, she was wearing a bracelet with a tiny penguin charm attached.

Yasmine noticed. "Welcome to the Penguin Club."

"Who knew there was such a thing?"

"It's just something we do to commemorate another pregnancy milestone." She turned her screen toward Meghan. "Mystery solved. Read this over, and then we'll talk."

It didn't take long to figure out she and Andi had missed the most obvious possibility of all. TJ was Jack and Jackie's biological child, an unexpected blessing who'd arrived after they'd begun the process of becoming adoptive parents.

Meghan looked over the top of the screen. "Before this, I didn't even realize how many misconceptions I had about adoption. I always assumed people adopted because they couldn't have kids of their own. And I guess I assumed babies were placed for adoption because the moms were unstable or trying to hide the fact they were pregnant."

Yasmine rotated the screen back to face her desk. "And what do you think now?"

"It's way more complex and complicated than I ever imagined."

"Well," Yasmine leaned in toward Meghan. "For whatever it's worth, I think you're doing a brave and admirable job navigating through all of the complexities."

Meghan exhaled loudly and smiled weakly. "What's next?"

Yasmine continued to peruse the file. Finally, she stacked the pages and placed them neatly back in the folder. "Everything is in order. Now you can focus on getting through the next few weeks and delivering your baby. We will be with you each step of the way and, before you leave the hospital, we will talk about your recovery plan."

"What recovery plan?"

"After your baby is born, there is a forty-eight-hour window before custody is legally transferred. Then your recovery plan begins." Yasmine pulled another brochure from the file. "It simply involves your care and support after the baby is placed with the adoptive family. We want to be sure you heal both physically and emotionally afterward."

Meghan hadn't given much thought to what life would be like if she left the hospital with empty arms. Her shoulders tensed as Yasmine continued.

"Unfortunately, people get so excited for the adoptive family, they often forget about the loss endured by the birth mother. There is actually a term for it. It's referred to as 'birth mother grief.'"

More grief? She wished she hadn't asked.

Yasmine rose and opened the door. Meghan, way past the point of slinging her usual cross-body purses, shouldered a small tote bag and walked into the sunny lobby. A volunteer greeted her with a bouquet of flowers. Pink and yellow roses.

"What are these for?" Meghan asked.

"For you." The volunteer gave her a hug. "A little reminder you are valued. You are loved." The grandmotherly woman had no idea how much she needed a hug at that moment.

Meghan steadied the roses on the passenger seat, then remained in the parking lot as the heated cushion behind her soothed her aching back. It had been an emotional morning. But it was the last step in this part of the journey. The final appointment at the adoption office. All future meetings would take place at either the doctor's office or Meghan's apartment. One small way to make her life easier as the baby's due date closed in.

She saw Dr. Caygen once a week now and always took someone with her. Andi had gone with her last time and was still posting pictures from the appointment. Meghan couldn't get over how huge she looked carrying an almost-full-term baby. The nurse said the baby would grow one-half inch and gain one-half pound per week. No wonder it was getting harder to be comfortable. As the baby's space got more crowded, Meghan experienced a persistent backache as well as relentless heartburn. Both the doctor and nurse assured her this was a normal part of third-trimester pregnancy.

She took their advice and completely cut spicy and greasy foods from her diet. Except for french fries. That craving was too strong to resist. Before that last appointment, Meghan had treated Andi to lunch at their favorite burger chain. Maybe it was the hormones, but no matter how much Andi objected, fries tasted even better when dipped in a chocolate milkshake.

"Eww," Andi said with a shudder. "That is absolutely the most disgusting thing I have ever seen someone eat."

"How many brothers do you have?" Meghan challenged.

"Fair enough."

Each day it got harder to find foods that agreed with her changing body. Even plain white bread and the blandest oatmeal caused stomach acid. She was physically ready to not be pregnant anymore. Emotionally, on the other hand, Meghan dreaded the finality.

CHAPTER 34

Week 39

*Y*asmine had left the apartment only a few minutes earlier when the doorbell rang again. Meghan assumed she had forgotten something and scanned the room for the missing item. Upstairs, Lucinda answered the door. Only it wasn't Yasmine's voice this time.

Beth descended the steps carrying a small white bag emblazoned with a red logo. "I come bearing gifts."

Meghan peeked inside the bag. "Waffle fries? You remembered."

"I thought they might tame a midweek craving."

"You were so right."

Meghan attempted to get herself off the cushioned sofa, but Beth stopped her. "What do you need? Let me get it for you."

Meghan pointed to a rectangular container on the kitchen counter. "I need some antacids before I eat anything made with potatoes. Otherwise, I will be up all night, swallowing stomach acid."

"I'm so sorry." Beth grabbed the bottle. "I should have brought something healthier."

"No," Meghan declared. "This is perfect. Would you pass me two chewies, please?"

Meghan was halfway through the fries before she realized Beth had come alone. "What's Nate up to today?"

"He'll be in shortly." Beth glanced nervously up the staircase. "He's in the driveway talking with Yasmine."

Meghan dug back into the bag. *They're talking about me. I just know it.*

"Don't worry," Beth added. "They aren't talking about you. They're talking about us."

"What do you mean, us?"

"Me and Nate." Beth chewed on her bottom lip. "Yasmine is our adoption caseworker."

It took Meghan a moment to put the pieces together. "You and Nate are trying to adopt?"

Beth nodded.

"How did I not know this?"

Tears filled Beth's eyes. "We haven't told anyone, especially you. It just didn't seem right. But now . . ."

Nate finally came in, and for the next hour, Meghan peppered them with questions. By the time they left, Meghan had a brand-new option to consider. Another decision to figure out. She tried to pray, but instead of answers, she had only an overwhelming sense of uneasiness. It was more than she could handle on her own. She needed to bring in a professional. She picked up her phone.

Forty-five minutes later, Father Joshua called back. "Sorry I couldn't get back to you sooner. I was in confession."

"What did you do now?" Meghan teased.

"Wouldn't you love to know?" When it came to being feisty, he could give as well as he could take. "What's up? Your text said you needed professional advice? I couldn't think of one thing I am professional at doing."

"You are a professional man of God, and I need divine wisdom to make an important decision."

"I'll do my best," he promised. "Hit me."

Meghan, with permission from Pastor Nate and Beth, summarized the main points of their adoption journey. "So today, two weeks before my due date, I coincidentally find out they've been waiting two years for a baby? That's too random to be an accident, isn't it? Don't you think it must be God's will for me to choose them? But then, why didn't He just show me from the beginning?"

"You weren't exaggerating when you said you needed divine wisdom." It sounded like Father Joshua put the call on speakerphone. "I do agree, the timing is interesting. The scenario seems too important to be random or coincidental." Two out of three. "Now as to the matter of God's will."

He paused, and Meghan filled the empty space in the airwaves. "I want to do whatever God wants me to do, but I don't know what that is. I've prayed as hard as I could, but I don't know how to figure out His will. That's why I need your help."

"I'm glad you prayed, because that would be my first suggestion."

"But God didn't give me an answer. I waited. I paged through my Bible. I concentrated really hard trying to hear His voice. Nothing." Meghan paced the perimeter of the room. "Can you please try? You will hear Him. He will tell you. He has to."

Meghan heard only silence. She remained quiet in case Father Joshua was praying. She didn't want to interrupt God's answer.

When he spoke again, he didn't give Meghan the words she hoped to hear. "Meghan, it is admirable for you to want to do God's will. Your faith and trust in God have grown so much these past few months. But—"

"No," Meghan interjected, "don't give me the 'but.'"

Father Joshua chuckled. "Hang with me. God doesn't always specifically tell us every single step to take. Sometimes His purpose in the journey is greater than the object of the destination. Does that make sense?"

Meghan gave up pacing and sank into an oversized papasan chair. "No. It makes zero sense."

"Hmm. Let's try another angle. Sometimes God clearly reveals His will. Other times He wants us to work through the process of making a decision ourselves instead of relieving us from the responsibility of making it." He paused so Meghan could consider his words. "How are we doing with that?"

"I think I understand, but I don't like it. That's a lot of pressure. If God wants us to do His will, why would He hide it from us?"

Father Joshua chuckled again. "Where were you when I was in school? These would be great questions for seminarians to wrestle with."

"Well, it's true," Meghan maintained. "Why does He make it so hard?"

Over the next half hour, Father Joshua talked to Meghan about God's character as shown through the biblical examples of people like Mary, the Israelites, and Joseph. Meghan came out on the other side understanding that God doesn't want robot followers. He wants relationship. He wants His followers to trust Him.

"I still wish He would just tell me. Send a text, a skywriting plane, something."

"That would certainly be easier," Father Joshua agreed. "I just don't think free will can coexist with that kind of control."

"So where does that leave me?" Meghan once again felt the weight of her decision pressing in.

"I think there are some foundational principles we can walk through. This is exactly where I go when I am having trouble making a decision."

If it was good enough for Father Joshua, it was good enough for Meghan. With that, a tennis match of questions and answers began. Father Joshua served first.

"What are your options?"

"Jack and Jackie or Pastor Nate and Beth."

"Choose one of the two and let's move forward."

"Pastor Nate and Beth."

"Would choosing them be aligned with God's truth?"

"I don't see why not. Sure."

"Is it within the realm of possibility?"

"Yes." Meghan's patience was running low. "How many questions are in this strategy of yours?"

"Hold on—we're getting there," Father Joshua said. "Is there a reason *not* to choose them?"

Meghan was silent.

"Meghan? Are you still there?"

Meghan remembered the peace she felt the night Andi was there. The night she saw the picture. "Yes," she whispered. "I'm here." *I hope Pastor Nate and Beth won't hate me.*

CHAPTER 35

Week 40

Meghan was used to not sleeping through the night, but nothing she tried relieved the pain gripping her lower back. If anything, it had increased and spread around to her lower abdomen.

She tried watching TV, but lying on the couch was uncomfortable. She tried doing homework, but sitting at the table was unbearable. She tried reading, pacing, and taking a hot shower. Nothing helped.

By early morning, Lucinda called down from the top of the stairs. "Are you okay?"

Meghan didn't answer. Her eyes were closed and her breathing rapid as Lucinda hurried down the steps.

"Glenn! Get the car! We need to go to the hospital right now!"

As soon as the contraction passed, Lucinda and Glenn helped Meghan upstairs and eased her into the back seat of their sedan. Glenn began the tense journey across town, while Lucinda sat with Meghan, guiding her breathing and making phone calls. Thankfully, traffic was not an issue at four o'clock on a Sunday morning.

Meghan was immediately admitted and settled into a birthing suite. This was definitely not a false alarm. This was the real thing.

Yasmine was first to arrive at the hospital. While a nurse helped Meghan through a particularly strong contraction, Lucinda filled her in on Meghan's progress and then asked, "Are you here to stay?"

Yasmine pointed to an overnight bag on a chair. "For as long as necessary."

After the contraction eased, Lucinda laid her hand on Meghan's swollen abdomen. "Glenn and I are going to run home and change out of these pajamas. We'll bring your suitcase back and then stick around in case you need anything."

Meghan nodded feebly. She was too tired to respond with words.

"Close your eyes and rest while you can," Yasmine advised. "I have a few questions, but you can answer with nods instead of trying to talk."

Meghan liked the sound of that. She had only a short respite before another contraction took hold. As soon as she entered recovery time, Yasmine began going through her list.

"Are there any changes you want to make to your birth plan?"

Meghan shook her head no.

"Any changes to your adoption plan?"

Again, no.

"Jack and Jackie are currently six hours away. It's about four o'clock where they are. Should I call them?"

Meghan glanced at the clock: 4:54 a.m. That meant Jack and Jackie were somewhere in the Central Time Zone. She pictured a map of the United States and began calculating the range of a six-hour drive from Grand Rapids. Yasmine interrupted her geographical analysis.

"That doesn't mean they *live* six hours away. It means at this moment they *are* six hours away. Even if you hadn't gone into labor, they still would be arriving in Grand Rapids today."

The coincidence, if it was a coincidence, wasn't lost on Meghan. She felt another contraction begin. "Call them," she whispered.

Laura arrived next, and Andi shortly after. The contractions increased in both frequency and duration.

Andi's eyes darted back and forth between the monitors and Meghan. "You're a rockstar, Megs. I couldn't do it."

"I didn't have another choice," Meghan reminded her.

Laura wiped Meghan's forehead with a cool washcloth as the nurse scrolled through the data on the monitor. "Andi's right. You're doing great."

"Do you have any idea how much longer it will be?" Laura asked.

"From all indications, not long." The nurse studied the information on the white board behind Meghan's head. "My best guess is this baby will be here before nine."

The nurse was correct. Not long after Meghan asked for an epidural, Dr. Caygen arrived.

"Are you ready to meet your baby?"

Meghan felt much better after the numbing took hold. "I'm ready." She held out her hands to her friends. Laura on one side, Andi on the other. "Let's do this."

15 Hours

In less than twenty-four hours, everything had changed. Labor. Delivery. Hearing her daughter's first cry. Holding her daughter for the first time. Feeling her daughter's first touch. Everything Meghan had feared had proven to be a lie. God had demonstrated His faithfulness. She'd seen His hand at work in the ways He'd cared for her deepest needs and longings.

Meghan was exhausted, yet at peace. Peter, Teresa, and Abuela Maria had arrived shortly after the baby was born. She'd sent a photo to Netta and Steve, Ava and Dante, and Father Joshua. Even Meghan's mom had sent a text. "Cute kid." Dad must have told her the news.

Now, it was late, and Meghan was alone. She took a shower, then rang the nurse and asked for the baby to be brought to her room. She was finally ready to have some alone time with her daughter. She wanted to savor every moment she could. She wanted to memorize every detail. The baby's soft skin, silky hair, tiny fingers, and rosebud lips. She was so focused on her baby, she didn't notice someone enter the room.

"How's it going in here?"

Meghan lifted her eyes only for a second. *Another unfamiliar face. Just when you remember their names the shift changes.*

The new nurse leaned over and peeked into the woven pink blanket. "What a beautiful little girl. Look at that dark hair and those long eyelashes."

Meghan lifted her gaze to the woman's identification badge. Her name was Donna. "Thank you."

"Have you given her a name?"

Meghan had chosen a name but wasn't sure she wanted to share it.

Donna didn't press the issue. "I know it's hard. In my heart, I still carry a child I never even got to hold."

"Do you think she'll hate me if I give her up?" Meghan blurted. "Will she think I didn't love her?"

Donna didn't answer immediately. "Even if she struggles with that, one day she'll understand it was the most loving act in the world."

"My head believes that, but my heart is breaking." Meghan spoke so softly she wasn't sure if Donna could even hear her. But God could. "I wish I could give her the life I want for her. It would be different if Zac and I—" her voice broke. "If we could have raised her together. I know what it's like to not have a mom and a dad. I don't want that for her."

The shoes disappeared, but Meghan heard the sound of bedsheets rustling and medical machinery whirring. Finally, Donna spoke again.

"There's a new science studying what is called *microchimerism*. It's a fancy way of saying DNA is passed between a mother and child during pregnancy. Some scientists believe those particles of DNA are carried for as long as a lifetime."

The possibility fascinated Meghan. She braved making eye contact. "Do you think that's true?"

"Well, I'm not a research scientist, but I believe life is a miracle designed by a Creator. It wouldn't surprise me at all to discover the bond between mother and child is held at such an intimate level."

Meghan held her daughter closer. What if it was true? What if they would always share a connection? Maybe even at a molecular level.

Donna gathered up a wet diaper and an empty bottle. "No matter what science proves or disproves, she will always be part of you, and you will always be part of her."

39 Hours

Meghan was thankful Andi and Laura were taking shifts to stay around the clock with her. Somewhere in the hospital, Jack and Jackie were spending time with the baby. Her baby. No, their baby.

Meghan wished she could sleep, but it didn't come easily. She decided to go for a walk so she wouldn't disturb Laura. The halls were deserted. Everything was dim and quiet. When she passed the nurses' station, Donna greeted her.

"I was just getting ready to come to your room and check on you." She reached under the workstation and pulled out a green plastic bag. "This fell off the baby's cart earlier. I wasn't sure if you meant to keep it or send it with her."

Meghan hadn't seen the bag before. What could it be? She reached inside and pulled out a tiny yellow baseball hat with a small, embroidered *G*. Her mind raced. *Is this supposed to be a joke? If so, it wasn't funny.*

She couldn't drop it fast enough. "Where did this come from?"

Now Donna looked confused. "I'm sorry. I assumed you knew. The young man left it."

"What young man?"

"I didn't get a good look. I only saw him from the back. But he was wearing a cap just like that. I know because the cap was turned around and I saw the green and white letter *G*."

Zac!?

No. But who else could it have been? Zac had been here? Zac had come to see their baby? But who'd told him? Teresa, of course. But why had he come? When had he come? It didn't matter.

Zac did care! He had come to say goodbye.

She reached for the little cap and handed it back to Donna. "It's from her daddy and belongs with her." She turned to go, then stopped. "By the way, her name is Graciela. No matter what anyone else names her, she will always be Graciela to me."

48 Hours

The waiting period was over. Meghan dressed, packed, and prepared to leave the hospital. Tears streamed down her face, rivulets of anguish flowing from her heart. Every step closer to the nursery was one step closer to letting go. *God, I don't know if I can do this. It hurts too much.*

She held up her wrist and scanned the coded hospital bracelet. The keypad responded with a gentle vibration and soft-green light. Meghan's hand shook as she pressed down the cold handle of the security door. *No. I can't do this.* She released the handle and backed away. When she turned, she saw Laura standing against the far wall, arms open wide. Without a word, she walked directly into the embrace and emptied her sorrow as Laura rubbed her back and wiped away her tears. No words passed between them, but they both spoke the language of a mother's heart.

Finally, barely above a whisper, Meghan found her voice. "If this is what I am supposed to do, why is it so hard? Why does it hurt so much?"

"Sweet Meghan. I wish I had an answer that would take away your pain. But I don't. What I do know is this—it hurts because you love your baby. It hurts because you are choosing to do what you've decided is best for her. It hurts because you know she was God's idea from the start and has always been part of His plan. It hurts because she will always be part of you and today you are saying goodbye."

Meghan buried her head again.

Laura asked, "What do *you* need right now?"

Meghan took a deep breath and turned toward the nursery door. Staring through the glass, she exhaled loudly and said, "Would you please go find Yasmine? I need to talk to her."

Inside the warm room, Meghan pulled a chair next to the bassinet where her little pink bundle slept soundly. She reached in and stroked the palm of the tiny hand. The baby's reflex responded, and five fingers closed around her own. Such perfect little fingers. She wanted to always remember this moment and how it felt to be held by the hand of her daughter. Slowly moving her gaze, she again studied every detail of her daughter's face. Soft cheeks. Tiny, perfect ears just below the edge of a pink knitted cap. So beautiful in pink, with her fawn-colored skin and long, dark eyelashes.

With her free hand, Meghan reached into her pocket, then set a small box inside the bassinet. She reached into the pocket again and pulled out a folded piece of paper. Someday, her little girl would read this letter, but today Meghan wanted to speak the words.

"Dear Little One,

I don't know how or when you will find these words, but I want you to know I love you.

There may be times you wonder if you were unplanned or unwanted. Let me be the first to tell you this: You were always planned and always wanted. At first you were a surprise to me, but never to God. From before time began, you were known by Him. You were His idea, His gift to the world. And I am so thankful He allowed me to be part of that plan.

Today I am giving you something to help you remember. It is a necklace given to me by my father, your grandfather. It was made with a real butterfly wing and expresses the truth of God's grace for me, for you, for all of us who choose to trust . . ."

Meghan stopped. She couldn't finish the letter. The clock on the wall read 7:20. In ten minutes, she would be discharged from the hospital. She tucked the gift and note under the far corner of the blanket and whispered, "I choose to trust." After one more kiss on the soft, pink cheek, Meghan reluctantly released herself from her baby's grip and hurried out the door. Everything was suddenly clear. She knew what to do.

ƐPILOGUE

*My frame was not hidden from you when I was
made in the secret place, when I was woven together in the depths of the earth. Your eyes saw my
unformed body; all the days ordained for me were
written in your book before one of them came to be.*
Psalm 139:15–16

This is where Meghan's story is supposed to end. Where
Meghan makes the "right choice" and we close the book. But
adoption isn't right or wrong. Parenting isn't right or wrong. And
no matter what Meghan chooses, God's not done writing her story.
Read on for two possible endings . . .

OPTION 1

It was another glorious summer day on Mackinac Island. Meghan left the busy road and walked along Lake Huron's rocky shore. Something just past the water's edge caught her attention, and she reached into the cold water to pick it up. Another perfect heart for her new collection. This would be number five. One each year since the summer she was pregnant. Like the Old Testament wanderers, she was using stones to mark the time and remember the journey. She dried the rock with the hem of her shirt and studied the pattern running through the middle of the stone. Then she heard her name.

"Meghan Lee McPherson, what are you doing? You're going to be late." Andi parked a tandem bike and skidded down the sloping bank.

"Chill, girl. You're so uptight." Meghan sat down and patted the spot beside her. "You'd think it was your wedding day, not mine. Let's build one more cairn. For old time's sake."

They sifted through the rocks around them and gathered a small stockpile of flat-bottomed possibilities. Andi laid the foundation stone. "Do you remember the day at the end of that summer? When our families left the island? You told me that God was turning your mess into something good."

It took Meghan a moment. After all, it had been four years ago. Suddenly she remembered. "Yes . . . You said your dad had a word for that, but didn't know what it was."

"Yeah. Well better late than never. Right?" She gave Meghan a playful nudge with her shoulder. "The word is *redemption*. It means God exchanges our failures for something of value. Gives them a new purpose, a new definition. It might not change the facts, but it can change the future."

It might not change the facts, but it can change the future. Meghan needed a moment to let that sink in. It certainly described what God had done with her life. Their lives.

Andi spoke again. "So I guess that makes this your Redemption Day as well as your wedding day. Did you ever for a moment think this would happen?"

Meghan tilted her head and looked over the rim of her sunglasses. "Which part? The part about Zac and I ever even speaking again? The part about us getting married? The part about taking the job in Williamsburg? . . ."

"Okay, okay. Enough." Andi put her palm over Meghan's mouth.

The answer to Andi's question was definitely no. Not even for a moment. Meghan only had fuzzy memories of the days and weeks after leaving the hospital with empty arms. When the fog finally lifted, she somehow put one foot in front of the other and moved on with life.

Andi stood, interrupting Meghan's reflection. She reached for Andi's outstretched hands and let herself be pulled toward the road.

"No looking back," Andi prodded. "There's a long white wedding dress and nervous groom waiting for you at the inn."

Wrong again. Meghan would always look back. She would look

back and she would also wonder. Wonder what her child looked like. Wonder if she was happy. Wonder if she would one day understand. Wonder if she would have made a different decision had she known she and Zac would end up together.

Of course she hadn't known. She hadn't known a lot of things. Yet somehow, God had led her through the darkest hours. It took time. It took trust. It took hard work. And they wouldn't be here today without all the people who threw them lifelines of hope instead of stones of condemnation. Today was a celebration of that truth. A celebration of life, love, and the transforming power of God's redeeming grace. For everyone.

OPTION 2

It was another glorious summer day on Mackinac Island. Meghan left the busy road and walked along Lake Huron's rocky shore. Something just past the water's edge caught her attention, and she reached into the cold water to pick it up. Another perfect heart for her new collection. This would be number five. One each year since the summer she was pregnant. Like the Old Testament wanderers, she was using stones to mark the time and remember the journey. She dried the rock with the hem of her shirt and studied the pattern running through the middle of the stone. Then she heard her name.

"Mama, tum see."

Meghan turned to find three-year-old Gracie perched on Dad's shoulders. Papa Peter looked just as excited as his granddaughter. He gently lifted her down and helped steady her little feet on the uneven surface. Then he waved for Meghan to join them. This was an important day. Another first in a day of many firsts.

Gracie and Papa Peter eagerly unveiled the result of their first attempt to build a cairn together. Meghan clapped with enthusiastic approval, all the while hoping it wouldn't topple over. "It's beautiful, Gracie. Did you help Papa build it?"

Gracie stuck out her bottom lip, propped a pudgy hand on her hip, and declared, "No! Papa help Gracie."

Meghan sat down by the wobbly stack and reached for her daughter. Then she placed the heart rock into Gracie's open palm. "This is a very special rock. Will you hold it for Mama? Just for a minute?"

Brown-sugar eyes opened wide with wonder. Meghan directed her daughter's attention back to the stack of stones.

"Our lives are like this cairn. God makes the stones, and we get to stack them. Like Papa helped you, God helps us. If we let Him help us build our lives, we will stand strong."

She tapped on the heart rock and took Gracie's hand in her own. "Together, we'll put this rock on the top because God's love is the greatest gift of all."

There was so much more to explain. So much more to unravel and understand. Each time they visited the island, Meghan would teach her daughter about God's love. And one day, when the time was right, she would tell her more. She would tell her people make mistakes, but no one is a mistake. She would tell her she was a surprise but always part of God's plan. She would tell her God has purpose for her life.

Another voice called her name and interrupted her thoughts.

"Hey, you guys. Ready to go? We don't want to be late for the wedding."

Gracie pushed herself out of Meghan's lap and squealed. "Daddy!"

Zac bent down to Meghan's level. Memories, thoughts, and feelings collided as she gazed into his brown-sugar eyes. When she'd brought Gracie home from the hospital, Meghan hadn't known Zac would come back into their lives. She hadn't known he had destroyed the legal papers and canceled the court date. Hadn't known

God was already softening his heart. It took time. It took trust. It took hard work. None of this would have been possible without all the people who threw them lifelines of hope instead of stones of condemnation. Today was a celebration of that truth. A celebration of life, love, and the transforming power of God's redeeming grace. For everyone.

AUTHOR'S NOTE

bortion. Adoption. Parenting. No matter which road you walk, there is no guarantee of a fairy-tale ending. God offers redemption and grace for everyone whose fingerprints touch a story such as this.

Who is Meghan in your life? You? Your daughter? Your mother? Your sister? Your friend? What if Meghan is the woman reading your Instagram post or your Facebook rant? The woman in the next cubicle who has been hiding a secret for decades?

Where are *you* in Meghan's story? Would you throw the stone of shame or the lifeline of grace? Because the truth is, we all have stones to throw. We all have secrets and scars. Some are outwardly visible, and others are hidden deep.

The Bible is clear. The wages of sin is death, but this glorious truth remains: Forgiveness and grace are freely given if we will only bring it to the cross. Through the death and resurrection of Jesus Christ, we can be made new. Though our sins be as scarlet, Jesus cleanses us whiter than Michigan snow. We can be given the spiritual DNA of Jesus and, through the work of His Spirit, mature into the full expression of our redemption. God doesn't want you to become someone else. He wants to see you become exactly who He created you to be.

And, if your life began like the baby in this book, remember you were God's idea. You are here because He wanted you. In fact, He's crazy about you. He delights in you and promises to never leave you or abandon you (Joshua 1:5). You may have been a surprise to your parents, but not to God. And God never makes mistakes.

You were never "unplanned," but always part of God's plan. You were created for a purpose and destiny only you can fulfill. There is and will only ever be one of you, so give the world the wonderful gift of you.

As long as we live on this earth, we will continue to experience brokenness, do hurtful things, and speak ill-advised words. When we humble ourselves enough to lay down our self-righteousness and quit striving to earn God's acceptance, we can begin to live out of His grace. The more grace we are able to receive for ourselves, the more grace we will have to extend to others. This doesn't mean we bend God's truth or negate His directives. It simply means we choose to trust His goodness and His power to lead His children to the Light of the World.

No matter where you fit into this story, may these final words bring your heart unwavering hope:

My past does not define me;
I am not my mistakes.
I am loved. I am His child—
A child of God.

ORDER INFORMATION

REDEMPTION
PRESS

To order additional copies of this book, please visit
www.redemption-press.com.
Also available at Christian bookstores and Barnes and Noble.

CPSIA information can be obtained
at www.ICGtesting.com
Printed in the USA
BVHW052259290722
643344BV00003B/11